Cedar Woman

By

Debra Shiveley Welch

ISBN: 978-1-897512-37-1
Saga Books
Sagabooks.net

This Book is Dedicated to My Sister

Julie Spotted Eagle Horse Martineu

in gratitude for her help and guidance in the authenticity of this
story

and mostly with deep love.

Acknowledgements

First of all, I would like to thank my sister, Julie Spotted Eagle Horse Martineau for her help in guaranteeing the authenticity of Native Americans and their culture represented in this book. Arlene O'Neil, my talented writing partner, whose first book *Broken Spokes* is a great success, Machiel L Bain for making the corn and four winds graphic, great job, Mish! Beth Weinhardt of the Westerville Public Library for her help in the historical research needed for this novel. A grateful thanks to my faithful readers, Rita Corcoran, Phyllis Finley Rettman, Rita Fisher, Millie Peterson aka Mini2Shoes, my dear cousins, Vicki Gaffin Osborne and Cathy Dees, my second cousin Marlena Dees Little, Cheryl Oertli, Darlene Sharples, Debra Webb, Amanda James from Gloucester, England, Joanne Pons, Paris, France, Janet Huderski from Strangebrews, Louise Golden and Kim Mutch Emerson, my friend and publicist.

A huge thanks to Greg Ayotte, Director of Consumer Services for the Brain Injury Association of America for his help in my research of TBI (Traumatic Brain Injury) and Brent Blount for his advise on the choice of songs and his generous support.

Lila Pilamiyayelo – with many thanks.

Forward

Cedar Woman is a project that I have wanted to work on for several years. Written with the help of my adopted sister, faithful readers, it is the finished product which I have thoroughly enjoyed writing.

In *Cedar Woman,* you will find many words of the Lakota Language along with their pronunciation. For the sake of my readers' comfort, I have only given the pronunciation and following meaning the first time I introduce the word. I decided to use this method because of such words as "Ate." Pronounced "ah-tay," and meaning Father, I was concerned that my readers would mentally sound out the word we use in English for the past tense of eat, and be confused as to its meaning.

For your further convenience, there is a dictionary with the meaning and phonetics in the back of the book. There are three dialects in the Lakota language and no standardized spelling. I have chosen the spelling and pronunciation of these words in keeping with the dialect of my sister, Julie Spotted Eagle Horse Martineau, who is of the Lakota Plains Native Americans.

Also included, is a cookbook, with some of the recipes mentioned in the story. I hope you try them and find them as delicious as my family has.

My wish is that you enjoy the reading as much as I enjoyed the writing!

Toksa Ake Wakan Tanka Nici Un – Walk With God

Chapter One

Hear Me

Hear me, four quarters of the world – a relative I am! Give me the strength to walk the soft earth. Give me the eyes to see, and the strength to understand that I may be like you. With your power only can I face the winds. Great Spirit, all over the earth the faces of living things are all alike. With tenderness have these come up out of the ground. Look upon these faces of children without number, and with children in their arms, that they may face the winds, and walk the good road to the day of quiet. This is my prayer. Hear me!

Black Elk

Slowly, slowly, Grandfather Sun began his ascent. Gliding, floating, he moved above the horizon as blue and lavender and mauve filled the sky.

Birdsong married with fragrant air, as Wakan Tanka[1] stretched His fingers across the sky, pushing back the night, heralding the dawning of a new day.

$$\square$$

July 18, 2010
6:00 a.m.

Sonny Glass walked briskly along the slowly awakening street. He enjoyed the sound of the heels of his cowboy boots against the hard concrete of Uptown Westerville's sidewalks. Soon the area would be busy, as the small but vibrant Central-Ohio city came to life.

Home to just over 35,000 citizens and the birthplace of the Anti-Saloon League, Westerville was a charming family oriented town with several parks, the Inniswood Botanical Gardens and Nature Preserve, and Otterbein, the private liberal arts college founded in 1847.

Continuing his walk along State Street, Sonny admired the warm, historical feel of the main thoroughfare of Uptown Westerville. The storefronts were comprised mostly of the original structures built since the incorporation of the city in 1858. The pride of her citizens was apparent in the spanking clean look of the 19th Century, picturesque suburb of Columbus.

Sonny reached the corner of Main and State and gazed across the street at the new restaurant, the grand opening of which would be celebrated this evening. Three stories tall, the large, stately building

---

[1] Wah-kah Than-kah – Mysterious Creator

1

stood solid and imposing as new-morning sun kissed her ancient, red bricks.

A red canopy shaded the entrance, with its centered blue stripe and eight-sided star, each point formed by a tipi, and representing the flag of the Lakota Sioux. From its frame, hanging pots of Impatiens danced in a slight wind. Soon pedestrians, busy with their early morning errands, would walk briskly by, some going to Schneider's bakery, others to Talbot's Florists, some intent on visiting Heavenly Espresso, the coffee shop across the street.

Sonny leaned against the corner lamppost and gazed in admiration at Lena Young Bear's labor of love: Cedar Woman, the first upscale Native American restaurant in Central, Ohio.

Studying the restaurant from across the street, Sonny tried to imagine how it would look to someone who had never seen it before. Pretending to be a new patron, Sonny contemplated the impressive building. As guests approached the large, cedar, double doors leading into the small entrance foyer of the establishment, they would first notice the top of the doorframe. Hanging above the striking entrance were four corncobs: one of white, one of red, one of yellow and one of blue, an ancient symbol proclaiming that all who entered the dwelling would be fed. *Now where on earth did she manage to find blue corn?* Sonny mused as he straightened and prepared to cross the street. *I'll bet she had Grandmother Nancy send it to her from Colorado. She would do that, seeing how sacred corn is. And of course there would be four,* he continued to ponder. *Lena Young Bear **would** use the sacred number representing the four winds, four seasons, and four directions of the earth.*

Beneath the corncobs was a simple carving. Engraved upon a cedar plank, and painted in the same deep blue of the awning stripe and star, were the words Mitakuye Oyasin,[2] which translated from the Lakota Sioux language simply meant, "We Are All Related." *I cannot believe what she has accomplished,* he reflected, stepping down from the curb and crossing the still silent street.

Sonny recalled that Lena chose the building, which was later to bear her Native American name, partly because of the location of the doors. The main entrance faced west where lived the Thunder Beings. From here came rain and nourishment so all may live.

The second door faced the north where the Great White Giant lives. From here came the cleansing white snows and the power of healing.

---

[2] Me-tdah-coo-yey oh-yah-seen – We are all related

Sonny took a deep breath. He could still smell sage. The night before the grand opening, Lena performed a smudging ceremony to cleanse herself and the new restaurant.

Carrying a smoldering bowl filled with sacred grasses, Lena walked to the center of the first floor of the building.

The white ceramic bowl, which she had thrown herself, its rim painted with red ochre to symbolize the blood of The People, contained cedar needles, to cleanse the area, its sweet smell attracting the good spirits. In addition, there was wild sage, for purifying the soul and the air, enhancing balance within one's self and the spirit world. Wild sweet grass, to cleanse the mind and body and to attract good spirits and energies with its fragrance, along with tobacco, to carry her prayers to Creator was also included.

Lena "bathed" herself with the fragrant fumes. Cupping her hand, and capturing the floating ribbons of smoke, she passed them over her head, shoulders, torso, and under each foot.

Facing the west, she extended the smoking bowl and intoned: "Grandfather of the West, this is Cedar Woman, I ask that you keep my feet true and on the Good Red Road.[3] I ask that you guide me on this day, and all days, so that I may continue on this path. I ask that you help in my daily life. Mitakuye oyasin, we are all related. She next turned to the north and offered the same prayer to Grandfather of the North, Grandfather of the East and then of the South. Lifting the bowl to the heavens, she repeated her prayer to Father Sky.

Kneeling, the bowl in front of her, her hands on the floor on each side of her body, she sent her prayer to Mother Earth.

Finally, she again raised the still smoking bowl to the sky and added a personal plea: "Creator, this is Cedar Woman. I ask that you keep my feet true and on the Good Red Road. I ask that you guide me on this day and all days so that I may continue on this path. I ask that you help in my daily life. I ask you that I may feed all people and that my venture here will be successful." Lena placed the still smoldering bowl on a table and sat, slowly relaxing, her mind, body and spirit in harmony.

Sonny pressed upon the heavy doors and entered the foyer. Fairly small in size, it served as a buffer between the changeable Ohio weather and the dining room within. Five paces across the vestibule stood a single door, also made of cedar. Entering the restaurant, he let his eyes move slowly around the first floor dining room, It was on this level of the three story building where casual Contemporary Native American foods would be served.

---

[3] The Good Red Road – To walk in balance. To follow the rules of Creator.

3

Built in 1881 in the Italianate style by M.S. Wyant, the structure had known many incarnations. From bookstore to telephone company, from grocery store to clothing emporium, from gathering place to thriving gift shop, the uptown site had been a popular landmark for Westerville's citizens.

In 1886, during a performance of "Uncle Tom's Cabin," the opera house, located on the third floor of the building, experienced a tragic fire. An actor, swinging an umbrella, accidentally hit one of the gas foot lights. Panicking, fleeing patrons ran, and the exit was blocked. Trying to find a window to throw the gas light out onto the street, the actor accidentally ran into a small hallway, discovering a woman and two children seeking refuge. None of them died immediately, but lingered through an agonizing death.

Remembering the heartbreaking story, Sonny took a deep breath, glancing toward the stairs, which led to the spacious third floor, now allocated to teachers and students for the study of pottery, dance and music. There was no sign of the little girl and boy rumored to haunt the third floor, their laughter and running feet echoing throughout the three-story building, but Sonny was nervous nonetheless. Lena assured him that she had sent the children "home" the day she smudged the restaurant, but Sonny remained skeptical.

Sonny glanced away from the staircase. Relieved that no sounds echoed down the flight of stairs from the region above, he relaxed and allowed his mind's eye to take a mental tour of the beautiful restaurant. Tonight would be a special night, the middle floor, the fine dining area, filled to capacity with friends and relatives, eager to celebrate this special day, to celebrate the happiness of Lena Cedar Woman Young Bear.

Lena appeared in Sonny's mind's eye. He constantly experienced a queer shock when he first saw her, even after seventeen years. In his mind, when picturing her, she always seemed larger than life, towering above all with whom she came into contact. In reality, she was quite diminutive in stature, barely reaching 4'11" and maxing out, he would guess, at 90 pounds. It was as if Wakan Tanka, in His infinite wisdom, created her body as an afterthought, concentrating on the immenseness of her soul instead.

But, it was her eyes which startled the most. Almond in shape and slightly tip-tilted, they sparkled as if lit from within. Her left eye was a luminous, deep brown, so dark that the pupil at times appeared to be the same color. Her right eye was the same unfathomable brown, but only on the inside half of the iris. The outside half was vivid amber.

Wakan Tanka must have drawn the line Himself, Sonny mused. How else could her iris be so divided precisely in two, the outside half the exact same color of the eye of Wambli[4] the sacred golden eagle of the Lakota?

_____

[4] Wahn-blee

Chapter Two

Go Forward With Courage

When you are in doubt, be still, and wait.
When doubt no longer exists for you, then go forward with courage.
So long as mists envelop you, be still.
Be still until the sunlight pours through and dispels the mists,
as it surely will.
Then act with courage.

Ponca Chief White Eagle

1955

Peter Spotted Eagle Catcher, named after his great grandfather, Chief Spotted Eagle, met his wife Mary One Feather Fools Bull on their wedding day.

Anxious to leave reservation life behind, Peter, twenty-one, strong and a handy man by trade, wood-carver by inclination, answered an advertisement posted in the *Adams County News* for a "jack-of-all-trades." A friend passing through Ohio saw the ad, circled it with a red crayon, and sent it to Peter.

Joseph and Evalena Countryman owned a 300-acre farm in Southern Ohio, which included a Grade-A dairy with 20 cows, two bulls, two dozen pigs, a flock of chickens and turkeys, 30 acres in alfalfa, and twin 10 acre sections, which rotated winter wheat, soy beans, and peas. Approximately 120 acres allocated to pasture and woods, the rest contained various buildings, a large farmhouse with a sizable kitchen garden, and a small apple orchard.

The farmhouse sat high atop a hill overlooking RT 32 on the north side of the property, and beyond, Serpent Mound, the Hopewell Indian earthworks. The property contained a deep, prolific spring, and was bordered on the south by a rambling creek named Wolf Run.

Joseph loved his farm, which he had purchased in 1929, but the same condition, which kept him out of the Great War, now necessitated hiring a strong individual to mend fences, assist in the dairy and generally help run the farm. Joseph suffered from chronic temperature and exertion-induced asthma, worsened with advancing age.

Peter answered the ad immediately, and to his surprise, quickly received a notice of hiring with a check to cover the gas it would take to drive from South Dakota to Southern Ohio. An enclosed note stated, "We look forward to meeting you and your wife."

6

His wife. Peter sat at his mother's kitchen table, and looked at the note. He had not considered marriage at this point, but it made sense. He would need someone to help out, to cook, clean, wash and mend his clothes. Besides, this farmer thought he was married. Maybe he assumed that he was hiring a couple, and Peter's wife was supposed to help Mrs. Countryman. What if he showed up minus a helpmate and was fired on the spot! *I don't know anyone!* He thought to himself frantically. Peter dated, *of course I do*, he chuffed to himself, but there was no one that he knew who would fulfill this urgent need.

"Ina[5]!" he called. "Mother," I need a wife! If I show up without a wife, I lose the job, ennit[6]!"

Reva Two Strikes Catcher, so named because she had survived two lightning strikes, snatched the letter from her son's agitated hand. Nodding solemnly, she agreed that a wife was, without question, necessary.

"I cannot go in a wife's place. We do not know what accommodations this farmer is providing." She gazed lovingly at her son, and placed a care-worn hand on his shoulder. "Besides," she added, "it is time I became a grandmother. Cha[7]! I am 41! I must see my grandchildren before I die." Reva turned to stir a bubbling pot of rabbit stew, her wooden spoon banging against the sides of the cast-iron vessel.

Looking over her shoulder, she added, "I will send a letter to Tanksa[8] in Crow Creek. Perhaps Elder Sister will know a girl who is strong and reliable. We will see what Wakan Tanka has in store."

Reva's sister answered promptly:

"Ohan,[9] yes, Cuwayla,[10] I have a young girl here who will be a perfect choice. She is the daughter of a good friend of mine. She helps her mother with the younger children, she is a good cook, is neat and clean, and she doesn't bite her nails. After long meditation, her mother has told her that she wishes her to marry your son, and Mary has agreed. She is an obedient daughter. She will arrive on the bus on Monday at 3:00 in the afternoon. Tanksa."

Handing the brief missive to her son, Reva Two Strikes nodded. "Cha, now you see. You will have your helper, and I will have my grandchildren."

---

[5] Ee-nuh - Mother
[6] Used to request or give agreement
[7] Cha – Sha – a form of interjection
[8] Donk-shah – big sister
[9] Oh-hanj - Yes
[10] Chew-way-lah, Little Sister

Mary had been a timid, solemn, yet sweet child, who always stayed near her mother, causing the concerned parent to despair of her daughter ever becoming independent, until one day, as she was stringing beans, Mary as usual at her feet, Roma Brings the Corn Fools Bull observed the child staring up into the sky. As if by magic, a single eagle feather landed upon her tiny nose. The child laughed aloud, and lifting the single feather in one, chubby fist, waved it in the air as if to say, "Wopila,[11] thank you for the gift!"

"Wambli has chosen our child," Roma solemnly stated to her husband, "and we should have no fears for her future." Upon hearing of the incident, and after long meditation, Mary's grandmother gave the name of One Feather to the young girl.

Mary One Feather Fools Bull prepared for the journey with increasing trepidation. While washing and ironing the few pieces of clothing she possessed, she would find herself trembling. As she packed her clothes in an old cardboard suitcase, which had been her mother's, she gently placed wild sage within the folds of each garment. She loved the smell of the sage, which always calmed her when she was troubled or under stress.

Mary held up the last item to go into the small suitcase. It was her mother's ribbon dress. Made of plain, white cotton, the A-line garment fell to her ankles, the bell sleeves and a boat neckline cunningly trimmed in blue and red ribbons. Cut four-times longer than the circumference of the sleeve's hem, and crossing at the back, the ribbons were sewn to the fabric, the remaining two feet floating freely, giving the garment an airy, elegant feel. The center of the bodice was decorated with chevrons represented in the same satiny trim.

Beginning at the knee, four couplings of red and blue bands encircled the skirt to the hem. It was a beautiful dress, and Mary was moved when her mother insisted that she take it.

"A woman has to have a wedding dress, and there is no time to make one. It would make me proud if you wore this on your wedding day. I cannot go with you, yet I will be there just the same."

"Ina!" Mary wept, throwing her arms about her mother's frail frame. Roma, patting her daughter's heaving shoulders, and gently breaking the embrace, left the room to begin the evening meal. There were other children to care for, and her duties must not be neglected.

---

[11] Woe-pee-lah – Thank you

Mary reverently placed the lovely garment into the suitcase. She started to close the lid, hesitated, and returned to the small chest of drawers where she kept her clothes.

"I can't believe that I almost forgot you," she whispered reverently. Stroking the eagle feather, caught in her infant hand years before, which her mother had been careful to save, she reverently placed it in among her clothes, and snapped the metal catches closed. Turning, and walking slowly, Mary left the small, sparsely furnished room to help her mother in the preparation of the foods for the evening supper, her farewell feast, the last meal she would take with her family.

The bus ride was interminable, swift, endless. Gazing at the passing landscape, her pleas to Creator flying out of the open, smudged window, Mary fought off a feeling of panic, a desire to flee. Clutching her dilapidated luggage, its battered form resting upon her knees, she found herself mesmerized by the sound of the vehicle's motor, the rhythm of the *bump, bump, bump* of the wheels on ill-repaired roads. She felt as if she were leaving her body, perhaps leaving her present predicament behind.

Without warning, Mary found herself leaping from her seat, her small, cardboard receptacle hitting the sticky, dirty floor of the bus with a muted thud. Racing to the driver, and clutching the steering wheel in her two, small hands, she began screaming, "Let me off! Stop the bus! I can't *do* this!"

Waking with a start, and gazing around the bus with confusion, Mary soon realized that she had been dreaming.

The bus was late. Scuffing the dirt on the dusty wooden porch of the bus depot, Peter tried to quiet his jangling nerves. *What will she look like? Will she at least be presentable? Will she be of a sweet nature, or will she be deceitful like Spider Woman?*[12] he wondered, thinking of the Lakota legend of Spider and his devious, conniving wife.

Dressed in a denim jacket, white tee shirt and jeans, Peter was a handsome man of the Lakota Sioux tribe. Approximately 5'10", slender, with deep brown eyes and flowing, dark hair, he epitomized the romantic figure of a handsome, young, Native American male.

Anxious, excited, filled with trepidation, Peter continually glanced down the dusty road as if the intensity of his longing would cause the bus to materialize.

---

[12] Lakota legend of Spider Woman and Coyote

Removing his black cowboy hat, pulling his red bandana out of his right hip pocket, and mopping his brow, Peter heaved a heavy sigh filled with impatience. It was June 15, 1955, and at least to Peter, getting warmer by the minute. Startled by the sound of a loud engine, he glanced down the road, and spotted the dust-covered bus. Fists clenched in nervous anticipation, he instinctively stepped back a few paces from the edge of the splintered porch, and took a deep breath.

Brakes squealing, the bus slowed to a stop, and the metal door screeched open. Silhouetted in a rectangle of dim light was a small, winsome figure. Peter felt his heart skip a beat as his soul recognized its mate.

Mary One Feather Fools Bull stood exactly 4'10" in height and weighed 80 pounds. Large, luminous eyes, gazing just above his head, filled a face, which appeared to be too small to hold the twin, shimmering orbs.

Pointed of chin, snub of nose, Mary appeared to Peter to resemble Theda Bara, the raven-haired silent star of the "silver screen" from 1914 to 1926. Peter remembered Theda's picture from the cover of several copies of old movie magazines, purchased by his mother when she was still a child. Mary was 16-years-old.

Taking a deep breath and attempting a trembling smile, suitcase in hand, Mary descended the metal stairs to the wooden porch upon which her groom stood.

Cha! he thought to himself, *she doesn't look like she could lift a spoon – somehow, I don't care. I will do all of the work if she will just have me.*

Mary, on her part, could not bring herself to meet his eyes. She was terrified! *What have I gotten myself into?* She panicked. *What have I done? I don't know this man! Have I lost my mind? Ina was so sure that I should do this – could she have been wrong?* Trembling, Mary stared at her groom's dusty boots. She was prepared to move back for each step he took forward. Overwhelming fear pressed upon her. Swaying slightly, she felt Peter's protective hand upon her arm. Somehow, this calmed her instead of making her more afraid.

Peter sensed her distress. He felt in tune with her emotions, almost as if he were feeling them himself. His heart ached for her, and yet, he was determined that she would be his wife.

"Come," Peter begged, "let us go now to my mother's house. Everyone is there, and there will be fry bread and corn, rabbit pie, berry pudding, and...." Peter's voice faltered. Afraid of scaring her off, he bit his tongue. *Be quiet!* he admonished himself.

Peter bent to take her suitcase from her tiny hand. As he did so, he caught the slight, evocative scent of wild sage. Straightening, he again tried to catch her eye, but Mary kept her shining head bent.

"Come," he repeated, and again taking her elbow in his hand, lead her to his 1939 Ford pickup, inherited from his father, and now badly rusted and dented.

Helping her into the truck, its upholstery torn and smelling of dust, and running around to the driver's side, Peter hopped in and started the engine. Very soon, this woman would be his. His body gave an involuntary shudder as he placed the truck in gear and drove away from the station. Peter Spotted Eagle Catcher was already deeply in love.

Reva walked to the truck as it came to a creaking stop, dust billowing around the cab and bed as the tires dug into the loose dirt of the reservation. She smiled at Mary, gazing deeply into her soon-to-be daughter-in-law's glistening, brown eyes. Opening the car door, Reva offered to help Mary out of the truck.

Mary accepted the older woman's hand and grasped it firmly. *She is as frightened as a bird who sees the shadow of the hawk*, Reva thought to herself.

"Come, Cuwitku,[13] I have a place for you to change, and then you will be wed." Reva nodded, as if to reaffirm to herself the verity of what she was about to say, and smiled.

"Come. It will be all right."

Face freshly scrubbed, her dark, shining hair newly brushed and hanging loose to her waist, a sage wreath, wrapped with red trade cloth, graced her shapely head. Her mother's ribbon dress replaced the skirt and cotton shirt she had worn on the bus, and hung gracefully to her ankles. Beaded moccasins, a gift from her mother for her sixteenth birthday, encased her small, graceful feet.

Standing in Reva's tiny bedroom and clutching the footboard of the rusted, tin, bed frame, Mary resolved to run if she had to. She would walk up to her groom. She would finally look into his eyes, and if she didn't like what she saw, she would run. She would run and run and run as fast as she could. *I don't care if I have to wash dishes and sleep in the back room of a diner. If I don't like him, I'm going to run!* Mary thought frantically to herself. She had barely completed her thought when the door squeaked open, causing her heart to give a frantic jump. Spinning

---

[13] Chew-weed-koo – Daughter

toward the sound, her beautiful hair fanning out around her slight body, Mary discovered Reva, arms once again held out to her for comfort.

"Come, Mary. It is time," Reva announced, enfolding Mary in a warm embrace, and placing a small bundle of wild flowers in her trembling hands.

Slowly, slowly, Mary walked to where a tight knot of people were grouped together in what would be the living room, but, in fact, was merely part of one room which served as kitchen, dining room and parlor.

She felt as if in a dream – as if she were walking in slow motion, or wading through deep water. Her heart was pounding against her rib cage as she slowly advanced toward a single man standing apart from the others, a wild flower tucked in the button-hole of his plaid shirt, his pony tail neat and freshly groomed, and a sage wreath, identical to hers, adorning his head as well.

She did not hear the words spoken, or her own replies. The Medicine Man/Justice of the Peace performing the ceremony, raised the Pipe and murmured some words. Peter turned and tied an eagle plume to Mary's hair, and still avoiding his eyes, Mary tied one to his. The medicine man picked up a star quilt, and wrapped it about the couple. Slowly, the newly weds turned to face their guests, and the reality of what had just occurred hit Mary with full force. She had obeyed her mother and married. Now was the time, now she must look into the face of her husband.

Hesitantly, oh so hesitantly, she turned toward him, and at last gazed into his eyes.

$$\Box$$

Time froze. All sound, all movement ceased. Within her ears was the single sound of her heart's beat, and as her hands touched his, the sound of his beating heart as well. As heartbeat fused with heartbeat, as soul merged with soul, and recognized its eternal partner, time seemed to stand still. Time no longer held any relevance; time was subjective; time held no meaning.

$$\Box$$

The wedding of Peter Spotted Eagle Catcher and Mary One Feather Fools Bull would reach legendary proportions in the minds of those who witnessed it, and later in those to whom the story was told.

Witnesses would report a shock of electricity, a wave of emotion flooding the room, as Mary's small bouquet fell, tumbling as if in slow motion, slowly, slowly to the floor. Mary reaching for Peter's hands, her hair seeming to float upon the air, Peter appearing to expand, to shimmer,

12

a silver light enveloping the couple, the bride looking deeply into the eyes of her groom, and he, wonderingly, into hers.

The small group was mesmerized. Somehow, they knew that an amazing thing was happening, and that they would remember this day for the rest of their lives.

Something had indeed happened to Mary. She had fallen irrevocably in love with Peter. She felt a new strength surge throughout her body, her very being, and realized, deep within her soul, that he was her destiny, her cuwihpiya okise,[14] her half side, her soul mate.

Mary, the timid, was now filled with courage. She knew that she had made the right choice, and that she could go forward without fear.

---

[14] Choo-weeh-pee-yah oh-kee-shay – one who makes you whole

Chapter Three

When you were born, you cried,
and the world rejoiced.
Live your life
so that when you die,
the world cries, and you rejoice.

White Elk

Born in Southern Ohio in Adams County, in a small village called May Hill, Evalena "Lena" Mary Catcher, soon named Long Awaited by her grandmother, finally arrived on December 2, 1975. Married in 1955, her parents despaired of ever having a child until their daughter's birth twenty years later.

Evalena was barely seven-years-old when she electrified friends, family and neighbors with a single act so poignant, it soon became legend within the entire county. Walking home from the small general store, where she had gone to fetch a sack of cornmeal for her mother, the corner of her eye was caught by a splash of vivid color within the shadows of the single, white, steeple church situated in the center of the small village. There, in a crevice where the portico of the church joined with the main building, a hummingbird lay struggling within a spider's web, its bill pressed to its crop, and its wings glued to its body, imprisoned by the tough fibers of the web. Floundering, fighting for its life, its frantic heartbeat visible beneath its jeweled breast, the tiny animal's struggle became evident to the young child. Bending over, she gently released the small creature from its death trap, ripping the web from the foundation of the church. Imprisoned still within the deadly embrace of the web, the bird thrashed, panic-stricken, within her tiny palm.

Cupping the small bird gently within the protective shelter of her hands, Evalena, called Lena for short, walked to a large boulder, which lay close by. Squatting upon the ground, and leaning against the stone for support, she slowly ripped away the gooey strands that held the hummingbird captive. Working quickly, she gently removed the sticky threads until he was free. Opening her hands to release him, she rejoiced as he soared into the air, wings beating in a blur of motion, fascinating the child who remained crouched beside the massive rock.

This, in and of itself, would have stirred the imagination of the villagers, but what impressed them further was the continued presence of the tiny bird. Whenever Lena ventured along the dusty streets of the village, a brilliant jeweled flash of color would be seen, darting about her head, her shoulders, and occasionally, lighting in the palm of her hand, as if to say, "Here is my protector; here is my mother."

Reading an account of this spectacular event in a letter sent to her by her devoted daughter-in-law, Reva Two Strikes decided that a new name be given to Lena, to signify the importance of what had just happened. After long meditation, and consultation with the medicine man on the Rosebud reservation, a new name was selected. Henceforth, Lena Long Awaited would be Lena Cedar Woman, the nurturer, the quintessential mother, her soul strong, rising from bedrock, its roots firmly planted into Mother Earth, embracing its core in reverence and wisdom. Instinctively she knew Lena was close to The Mother. She was a turtle woman, or medicine woman, and as such, her name should be a reflection of her spirit. And so, her feet were set upon her path of destiny as a holy woman.

The incident with the hummingbird was merely a revelation to the community, for no one could have guessed that, within this seven-year-old child's breast, dwelt a love for Creator and Mother Earth way beyond her years. With every endeavor, she would ask The Grandfathers to guide her feet, as she believed no incident, no task, no duty, which she performed, was trivial or mundane. Constant in her mind was a parable her father had told her upon the occasion of one of her infrequent transgressions.

"Within each of us, Little Bird, are two wolves fighting," he said, using her infant nickname.

Eyes stretched in amazement, she looked down at her own diminutive chest, as if she would see the two canines struggling within its cage. "There are?" she gasped.

"Yes. One wolf is filled with those things which are evil within humankind: jealousy, hate, greed, lies, fear, anger. In the other are those qualities which are pure: trust, love, generosity, truth, courage, forgiveness."

Mesmerized, Lena sat gazing into her father's eyes, struggling to comprehend the lesson. Moments passed. She could hear the crackle of the fire, and her mother's humming from across the single room, which made up the main living area of their small home. She swallowed and asked,

"Father, which one will win?"

"The one we feed," he answered, and rising slowly, he ruffled her hair fondly, and strode to the rocking chair he occupied near the fire, the better to enjoy his wife's nearness during the long Southern Ohio evenings.

15

It was just after the freeing of the hummingbird that a change in Lena's eyes became apparent. Standing at the table in the kitchen area of the small home, Lena watched her mother preparing fry bread. Mary playfully flicked some flour at Lena. Looking up at her mother and laughing, Lena caused her mother to gasp in surprise. The iris of Lena's right eye, heretofore the deep, unfathomable brown of her left, was clearly divided in two. The inside part of the iris was the same deep brown, while the outside was a golden amber. The condition, known as sectoral heterochromia iridis, could cause a difference in coloring in one eye from the other, or sometimes within the color scheme of one eye. Often genetic, and at times due to injury or disease, this striking anomaly would sometimes occur. In the case of Lena Cedar Woman Catcher, the belief was that, like her mother, she was chosen, and her right eye reflected the eye of Wambli, the sacred golden eagle of the Lakota.

On Lena's eighth birthday, her mother decided to begin her instruction in the preparation of the family meals. Most of their food was provided by The Mother, either in the crops they grew, or the various game her father hunted, and the vegetables and chickens with which the Countrymans often gifted the small family. Lena felt a reverence for the preparation of the food. Living plants and animals gave up their lives so others may live. There was nobility inherent within the concept, which filled her with respect for the living beings that filled the earth. Consequently, she learned quickly, and she learned well, becoming an accomplished cook. It was here that Lena began to realize her passion for food and its preparation. Through the making of a simple dish, she could say, "I love you" to anyone who partook of her offerings, no matter their color, creed or ethnic origin. In addition, to Lena Cedar Woman, the ruining of a dish was the negation of the death of the beings, whether plant or animal, that provided the ingredients. This she could not abide.

"Lena, here, let me show you," Mary said as she gently lifted her daughter's hands from the gooey bread dough.

"That is not how you knead bread. Look, you sprinkle some flour, like this," Mary sprinkled some white flour over the top of the sticky mound Lena was ineptly pushing around on the porcelain-top kitchen table.

"And you take the heel of your hand, and push the dough away from you. Then, turn it like this, and do it again. Now, you try." Lena did as her mother instructed, and after a few turns, gazed up in wonder.

"Ina! It feels so soft and smooth!"

"Ohan, it does. This is what is so much fun about making bread," Mary laughed tapping her daughter's diminutive nose in play.

"Now, we will let it rise. Here, spin it with your hands until it is round and then we will put a damp dishtowel over it. In about an hour, we will punch it down again, knead it a little more, and then put it on a baking sheet. When it rises one more time, we will bake it." Lena carefully spun the dough between her tiny hands, her pink tongue sticking out of the left corner of her mouth in concentration.

"Ina," she sighed, "I love the smell!"

"Ohan, that is the yeast," her mother instructed, smiling at her very willing pupil.

Lena loved these times with her mother. She enjoyed cooking, and enjoyed learning how to make the foods she and her family enjoyed. It made her feel important to be part of this aspect of the family's day-to-day life.

"Ina," Lena queried, again glancing up at her mother, "When can I learn how to roast a chicken? I love roasted chicken the way you do it. When will you teach me?"

"Cha!" Mary chided fondly, "You want to learn it all now. Child, you are but eight-years-old. There is time for all of this.

Lena didn't know how to express her urgency in learning all she could. She just knew she wanted to learn as much as she could as quickly as possible.

"I'll tell you what," Mary decided, "I am going to help Nellie in the garden tomorrow. She likes to see you, so you can go with me, and we will ask her for a nice hen. Would it please you, Little Bird?" her mother asked, smiling down upon her endearing daughter.

"Ohan! But I don't have to kill it, do I?" Lena queried. She loved to cook, and she respected the animals and plants who gave up their lives for her nourishment, but she was not prepared yet to do the deed.

"No, of course not! I will take care of it while you help Nellie with her vegetables. You know how she loves a visit from you. While you string beans or shuck corn together, I'll take care of what needs to be done."

Evalena and Joseph Countryman retired to a house on Fifth Avenue in the nearby town of Peebles shortly after Lena's birth. Their youngest child, Dean Countryman, and his wife Nellie, took over the farm. Mary was referring to Nellie Countryman. Sweet of nature, lovely of face, Mary often wondered why Nellie chose to become a farmer's wife. In any event, she was glad of it, as Dean and Nellie were as kind and

17

appreciative as Joseph and Evalena had been, and they and the Catchers ultimately formed a strong and loving, family-like relationship.

Dusting off her hands, Mary bent a kiss upon her daughter's smooth forehead and walked to the stove. Picking up the metal coffee pot, she walked over to where her husband Peter sat reading the newspaper, while also observing the activity at the kitchen table.

Bending and pouring him his favorite, "Reservation Coffee," as he called it, she returned the pot to the stove. Turning to her husband, she questioned:

"How can you drink this stuff? It's so strong!" Peter laughed, threw back a long, satisfying gulp, and smiled up at his wife.

"It's like mother's milk to me, ennit? This is how my mother made coffee," he laughed, referring to the very strong, almost thickened brew.

"She always said, if you throw a horseshoe in it, with the horse still attached, and they float, that's Rez[15] Coffee!" Peter guffawed.

"Well," returned Mary, "it may be Mother's Milk to you, but it reminds me of what you shovel out of the outhouse!" she quipped, laughing, turning once again to the stove.

Roaring with laughter, and slamming down his favorite, jadeite coffee mug, Peter leapt from the rocker he usually occupied when home. Grabbing his wife around the waist, he began to nuzzle her neck, spinning her around as she laughed, half-heartedly struggling to get away.

"It makes me want to eat you up!" he chortled.

"Oh, you hot mama, come to me now!" Peter laughed, again spinning Mary around and into his arms.

Standing beside the kitchen table, slowly wiping the flour from her hands, Lena smiled. She loved these moments. She could tell her parents were deeply in love. Somehow, this made her feel safe and loved as well.

"Cha!" her mother giggled, "I'll burn the jelly!" she exclaimed. Peter chuckled, giving her a smack on her still shapely bottom. Turning his head to gaze at Lena, he gave her a wink, threw a kiss, and with a great sigh of satisfaction, returned to his newspaper.

---

[15] Short for Reservation

Chapter Four

What is life?
It is the flash of a firefly in the night.
It is the breath of a buffalo in the wintertime.
It is the little shadow which runs across
the grass, and loses itself in the sunset.

Crowfoot, Blackfoot warrior and orator 1830 – 1890

Lena loved the mornings, and she treasured the evenings. The time in between was a waiting time, a holding of the breath, a longing for her parents to re-unite.

She waited for their meeting. If her father went to the Countryman farm alone, Mary joyously greeted him upon his return to their small house in May Hill. If they went to the farm together, they left and returned holding hands. Indeed, they were almost legendary in the community for their devotion.

For several years, a neighbor watched Lena from the time her parents left to go to the farm, until her school bus arrived at 7:30 a.m., and would watch her from the time the bus dropped her off, until her parents' return at dusk. Now twelve, Lena would knock on the neighbor's door to let her know she had arrived, and walk the few steps to her own house where she would begin the preparations for the evening meal. Lena would wait in anticipation of the sight of her parents, hand in hand, laughing, sometimes stopping to kiss. Her mother's hair appearing to float upon the air and both seemingly surrounded in a white, shimmering light. As if in slow motion, they would approach their small home. Lena was sure she heard twin hearts beating in unison.

"Cha, Cuwitku, watch how it is done," Mary instructed as she took the ball of dough from her daughter's hands.

"Not like the yeast bread we make. This is fry bread, very good, the best bread. We fry it, not bake it. Look, sometimes we want the fry bread to be fairly big – sometimes we want it to be smaller. It depends on what you are serving it with and what you want to do with it.

"Tonight we want them kind of small for dipping into our stew, so let's use this size," Mary demonstrated, using a sharp knife to slice away a piece of dough about the size of a small egg.

"Now, roll it out a little with the rolling-pin and then we flatten it in our hands. Ohan, that is right. Now we slip it into the skillet with the lard and fry until it is golden on one side. That's right, now flip it over.

See! It's fun, ennit?" Mary laughed as she watched Lena turn a piece of fry bread over in the shortening with deliberate care.

"Cha! Good job! Turn it away from you so the oil will not splatter you. You are becoming a good cook, Little Bird!"

Lena smiled into her mother's eyes, happy to spend these times with her ina, learning how to cook, working together in the preparation of the family meals, anticipating when they would sit down together as a family and enjoy the foods she and her mother had prepared.

Lena could not wait to see her father's face when he finally tasted her creation. Closing her eyes, she saw her father pick up a piece of the golden bread. Dipping it into his stew, his eyes widening with astonishment, he would exclaim,

"Who made this delicious bread? Cha! It is the best I've ever tasted!"

"I made it!" she would cry with pride and excitement. Her father would look surprised and say,

"Cha! The child didn't do this, ennit?" and her mother would laugh and assure Peter that, in fact, their daughter had prepared the scrumptious fry bread.

Lena used a slotted spoon to lift a finished portion from the simmering oil. It looked perfect! She placed it on a towel-covered plate and inspected it critically. It was golden brown all over. She smiled at herself in self-congratulation. *I did not burn it! Waste!*[16] she thought to herself.

Smiling into her mother's eyes, Lena's heart filled with pride. At twelve, she was old enough to appreciate her mother on many levels. She found her patient, kind, loving and, Lena thought, still beautiful, although she was old. Cha! She was 48!

Mary gave her daughter a swift hug.

"Now, Lena, we must clean up our mess. If you clean as you go, you will have more time to rest in the evening," Mary admonished with a smile. She turned to wipe down the kitchen table, when Nellie Countryman literally burst through the door.

"Mary! Peter has been in an accident!"

What did he say? What did the doctor say? Lena's brain could not seem to latch on to the information issuing from the mouth of the scrub-clad man standing before her stricken mother. Ina was nodding dumbly, signing some papers, her eyes blank with shock.

---

[16] Wash-tday – Good

Lena swayed, her mind in chaos, as seemingly foreign words poured over her…words she couldn't grasp…words which changed her world forever:

Traumatic brain injury, coma, condition critical, Glasgow Coma Scale, prognosis uncertain, CT scan, craniotomy.

Lena looked at her mother with astonishment. She seemed diminished, smaller than Lena remembered ever seeing her. *She looks like the baby bird I found that fell out of its nest,* Lena thought, thinking of the small, frightened being that had peeped futilely, hurt, frightened and abandoned. Her thought just completed, Lena turned to see Nellie Countryman rushing to her silent mother, giving a small cry and pulling her into a protective embrace.

"Mary, it's going to be okay," Nellie affirmed. Dean has given the hospital all the insurance information. You know they got insurance together? No? Well, it doesn't matter, because it's okay. I'm going to stay here with you, and Dean is going to take Lena to our house for the night."

"No!" Lena cried, causing Nellie to spin toward her in astonishment. Simultaneously, a small flicker of light appeared in Mary's eyes.

"I won't leave Ate![17]

Kneeling to reach Lena's level, and embracing the trembling girl, Nellie drew the child to her ample bosom. Rocking her slowly for a few seconds, Nellie crooned, "It's all right, Sweetheart. You can stay. Dean will stay too, and if you become too tired, he'll take you to the farm."

Reassured, Lena leaned into Nellie's hug. Gently breaking the embrace, and walking to a plastic molded chair, she sat, placing her hands beneath her thighs.

Was it hours or days that passed? Footsteps clicked through the waiting room. Jerking her now nodding head upright and turning it toward the sound, she observed the doctor taking her mother by the arm and escorting her to one of the hard, plastic chairs.

"Mrs. Catcher," he began, "Hi, I'm Doctor Gaffin," reaching for Mary's hand, and gently lowering her into the chair, the doctor continued.

"Your husband is resting from the surgery and remains in critical condition." Dr. Gaffin paused for a moment, carefully watching Mary's reaction. It was clear she was in deep distress, understandable, but he wanted her as calm as possible.

"We're certain your husband's head struck some object several times, possibly the seat of the tractor since, according to the paramedics,

---

[17] Ah-tay – Father

21

no large stones were present at the site, and because of the multiple contusions on his head.

I ordered a CT scan, which revealed swelling and hematoma, or bleeding, and took him straight into surgery where we performed a craniotomy to relieve the pressure on his brain. That is, we have opened up a small portion of his skull to remove any accumulated blood. We've put him on anti-seizure medication, just in case, as there is a risk of seizure after brain surgery." Mary gave a small cry. Gently placing his hand on her arm, Dr. Gaffin continued.

"Your husband is in a coma. He shows no reaction to stimulus around him. It means, his eyes don't open, he doesn't move, he doesn't seem to respond to anything." The doctor sighed, moving his hand to Mary's sagging shoulder, and squeezing it gently.

We can't tell right now how extensive the damage will be. We will keep a close eye on him. He is on a ventilator, and is lightly sedated. This is to slow the operations of his brain. It keeps the pressure down, and hopefully helps the brain to begin healing. Right now, we have him on an IV, and a nasogastric tube inserted through his nose and down to his stomach. It's a safety measure to keep him from vomiting. Later, we will use it for supplemental feeding. As soon as he is stable, Mrs. Catcher, I want to move your husband to the medical center at Ohio State University in Columbus. They are better equipped to help your husband recover as much of his former brain function as possible, so you will want to make any arrangements necessary if you plan to be with him.

I am sorry, but that's all I can tell you now. Why don't you go home and get some rest?" Mary nodded, eyes wide with disbelief and sorrow. Dr. Gaffin hesitated for a moment. He was a young doctor, and new at giving bad news. It was at times like this that he was at a loss as to how to give comfort. No one involved could predict how well Mr. Catcher would inevitably recover from his devastating injuries. Dr. Gaffin began to rise, resumed his seat, and again took Mary's small hand in his.

"Mrs. Catcher," he said softly. Mary slowly returned her gaze to his. "Mrs. Catcher, please try to remember, this is a marathon, not a sprint. It will take time, but during that time, everything that can be done for your husband, will be done." Dr. Gaffin reluctantly released Mary's hand, and rising slowly, a look of regret and grief upon his young, tired face, quietly left the room.

Lena awoke with her head in Dean's lap. Dean's head lay back, his mouth open, a light snoring issuing from his throat. Lena straightened and looked around the Intensive Care waiting room. Where was Ina?

Alarmed, Lena jumped up and looked around. She saw a door with Intensive Care printed on it, and moving slowly, pressed the door open. A group of nurses sat at desks with monitors, and what appeared to be TVs, scattered around the room. Individual glass-enclosed booths, or cells, lined two sides of the room. Walking slowly, Lena peered into each enclosure until she spotted her mother's shining head.

Leaning over her husband's still form, clutching his hand in her's, Mary's hair appeared to float upon the air. Surrounding her was a nimbus of white light, but Peter's form was dark. Lena heard only one heartbeat...or was it two now fused together as one?

Chapter Five

May the stars carry your sadness away,
May the flowers fill your heart with beauty,
May hope forever wipe away your tears,
And, above all, may silence make you strong.

Chief Dan George

Dean Countryman groaned and straightened, stretching his spine and rubbing the back of his neck. Lowering his shovel to the stone-strewn ground, and slowly hunkering to a sitting position on a large rock near the creek bed, he allowed himself a few moments of rest.

He had been working at the south end of the pasture most of the day, building a sweat lodge and fire pit for Mary Catcher.

Dean left the hospital in the early morning hours, bringing Lena home to the big, white farmhouse overlooking the Appalachian Highway where he and Nellie lived. Mary refused to leave Peter, but turning to Dean, her beautiful eyes luminous with unshed tears, asked if she could build a sweat lodge down near the creek.

"It's rocky there, and there will be no danger of fire. I need to pray and find guidance. Would you mind, Dean?" He looked at her in surprise. *What is a sweat lodge?* he wondered to himself, and then dismissed it as unimportant. If that is what she needed, then that is what she would have. She had explained:

"The Lodge is where you can be kind of born again. It's a chance to make a fresh start in life, and learn from your mistakes. You learn from what comes to you in the Lodge, and use it in a good way. It's kind of a 'do over.' We leave all the bad things behind, and take only the good. We Lakotas consider the Lodge to be like a womb, and to leave the Lodge is to be born again, in a good way. So, when we go into the lodge tonight to pray for Peter, not only will we be reborn, but hopefully he will be as well."

Dean nodded slowly. He understood what she meant. It was a way of praying for a new start, a new beginning, a way to make Peter whole.

"Mary," he pleaded, "let me do it. You can stay here with Peter and get preparations underway for moving to Columbus. Tell me what to do. I need to *do* something!"

At first, he was worried she would refuse, but always a practical woman, Mary acquiesced readily. She gave him the instructions, and said she would like to have the lodge ready by sundown. In the meantime, she would talk with Peter's doctors, and arrange for his transportation to the medical center in Columbus.

Dean was grateful to Mary. *My God*, Dean thought, *I've known Peter and Mary since I was a teenager. They're like my brother and sister!* Placing his sweating face in his work-worn hands, he allowed himself a brief mourning. He *loved* Peter, loved Peter's family. *Hell, Lena calls me Uncle Dean*, he grieved. Now he was losing them.

Next to his wife Nellie, Dean admired Mary more than any woman he knew. He remembered the first time he saw her – a bride, arriving at the farm, she and Peter still freshly in love. Mary had glowed like a candle flame in a cozy room, warm, loving and comforting.

What is the word she used? It was in her first language, the Lakota language. Wouanihan,[18] to respect, to honor. That's how he felt about her, and Peter and Lena as well. He honored them. They were family, and now he was losing them.

Dipping his red bandana into the cold water of Wolf Run, and bathing his face, neck and chest, Dean stood at the north bank of the meandering creek, admiring its clear water, blue clay walls, and bending willows. A crawdad darted by just below the surface of the bubbling stream. A hawk circled above, and the distant lowing of cattle, the twitter of birds, the smell of sun-warmed earth and clover, surrounded him in a display of life that moved him deeply.

He felt as if God, or Creator as Peter, Mary and Lena called Him, were touching his shoulder, giving it a small pat of approval and saying, "Good work, my son. You have done well."

And he had. Dean knew that the work was good, and that Lena would be pleased with what he had accomplished.

The snap of a twig caused him to turn. Nellie, a basket on her arm, walked up to her husband. Touching his face lovingly, she placed her cheek against his, still cold from the sparkling waters of Wolf Run.

"Sweetheart," she whispered, "I brought us a little something. Mary said that she is fasting, but that we should eat. She has no idea how long the ceremony will take tonight." Walking to the large, flat rock, which Dean had rested upon moments earlier, she laid a small cloth and placed the basket in the center of if it.

"I wasn't sure what we should have for supper," Nellie explained. "This is a solemn night," she continued, "even if we don't fully understand it. Still, as Mary and Peter are always saying, 'we are all related' and I don't want us to do anything to desecrate what is to be done here tonight. So," Nellie explained, "I hope you don't mind. You've been working so hard, but I've brought us a simple dinner of

---

[18] Woah-oo-ah-njee-hahnj (nj is a French J sound)

some beans, cornbread and spring onions with water from the spring."

Dean smiled:

"Only two of 'the three sisters[19]?" he chortled quietly, referring to the combination of beans, corn and squash which Mary had introduced them to.

"I remembered!" Nellie smiled, pulling a small dish of fried zucchini from the depths of the woven basket.

Leaning over in silent gratitude for this dear woman, who reached out to those she loved, always in the best way she knew how, Dean placed a reverent kiss upon her smooth, slightly plump cheek.

"You're a good woman, Nellie," he crooned, giving her a swift hug, and almost absent-mindedly, helping himself to the plain yet satisfying meal.

Yes, the work was good. Early in the morning, Dean dug the fire pit where 16 rocks, each about the size of a cantalope, lay heating for most of the day. He had not thought to ask how many he should prepare, and didn't know how important the numbers were, so he decided to play it safe.

Dean remembered that four was a sacred number, representing the four seasons, four winds, and four directions of the earth, and he knew that Mary would need enough rocks to produce the sauna-like effect she needed for her ceremony. Keeping this in mind, he gathered 16 large stones, resulting from multiplying the sacred number by itself, or 4 x 4. Should she need that many, at least they were available. A good thirty feet from the pit was the sweat lodge.

Facing west, where the great Thunderbird lives and sends rain, and where all things end, the igloo-shaped lodge stood complete. Cutting willow saplings about the thickness of his thumb, Dean lashed them together with baling twine after embedding them in the ground.

Covering the frame with first tarp and then burlap, the sweat lodge, large enough to seat four people comfortably, appeared to be tightly insulated and draft free.

Stepping into the structure, Dean sat down and assured himself that the centralized pit, where the heated stones would be placed, would be far enough from the legs and knees of the participants who would be involved in tonight's ceremony. Dean crawled out of the sweat lodge again surveying his work.

---

[19] The three sisters of corn, beans and squash, were grown together by Native American farmers, who asserted that they only grow and thrive together. This belief was very sophisticated in its foundation, as each plant replaces to the soil what another one takes.

Yes, the work was good and true, built, not only with the sweat of his brow, but from the love within his breast, and the crying out of his spirit to help his friends – his adopted family, taken to his heart not long after they arrived in Southern Ohio these many years ago.

He walked around the lodge one more time, tugging here, securing loose ends, anticipating the event which would take place this night.

Dean had invited himself and Nellie to the ceremony. He wasn't sure if it was appropriate, but he didn't care. He wanted to be here for Mary and Lena, and mostly for Peter. He was sure that his Christian-based prayers would evoke no feelings of disrespect, as he was here to honor his friends – his family, and not to dishonor them.

It was ready. Mary and Lena would soon arrive with Nellie, who was picking them up from the hospital. Dean was proud of his work, and happy to have been of help to people whom he loved with all of his heart.

He nodded and murmured to himself, "Not bad for a wasicu,[20]"

"Waste! Lila[21] waste," Mary exclaimed as she and Lena approached the sweat lodge constructed for her with such devotion.

"I could not have done better, Chia,"[22] Mary whispered, overcome with gratitude for this dear, strong man who stood beside her in anticipation of her approval.

"We can begin."

Picking up a pitchfork and walking to the fire pit, Dean scooped up four of the stones, and brought them to the sweat lodge. Placing them in the cavity in the middle of the lodge, he turned and exited, returning with four more stones. This he repeated until all 16 were in the circular depression.

Lena sat upon the large, flat rock which played so much in the day's events. Some crumbs lay upon the stone. She picked them up and scattered them on the ground, where a small sparrow eagerly bounced forward to devour them. Her mother was preparing to smudge the area, to cleanse it, and prepare it for the important event about to take place.

She watched solemnly as her mother performed a rite Lena would perform twenty-two years later when she cleansed her new restaurant.

Lena smelled the cedar needles, wild sage, wild sweet grass, and tobacco. She watched as Mary "bathed" herself with the fragrant fumes,

---

[20] Wah-see-chew – White person
[21] Lee-luh – Very or much
[22] Chee-aah – Older brother

27

as she cupped her hand and captured the floating ribbons of smoke, passed them over her head, shoulders, torso, and under each foot. Observed as she prayed to the Grandfathers of the West, the North, the East, and then the South, and then to Father Sky. Kneeling, she sent her prayer to Mother Earth.

Finally she again raised the still smoking bowl to the sky and added a personal plea:

"Creator, this is One Feather, I ask that you keep my feet true and on the Good Red Road. I ask that you guide me on this day, and all days, so that I may continue on the path of wisdom. I ask that you send to me the signs to heal my husband, Spotted Eagle. I ask this with all humility."

"Tunkasila Wakan Tanka,[23] please hear me. This is One Feather. I ask that you have pity on us, as we are pitiful and small and weak."

The heat in the sweat lodge was building. Mary poured water, collected in a bucket which sat to her right, onto the heated stones, causing a burst of steam. Next, she sprinkled lavender to help the occupants relax. Mary then instructed everyone to send a personal appeal.

Nellie bowed her head and breathed a fervent plea for Peter's healing. As she prayed, scenes flew through her mind like a nostalgic slide show. Peter, coming up the gravel road to their front gate, his face lit with a smile. *He's always smiling* she thought to herself.

Mary and Peter walking in from the fields, happy, gazing into each other's eyes. Lena, running up to her father and leaping into his arms. Nellie supressed a sob and continued her prayers.

Dean's mind was a whirlwind of thought: Peter, like a brother, working in the fields along side his employer/friend. Mary and Nellie at the sink, laughing, washing dishes after they'd shared a meal in the summer kitchen of the old farm-house. Lena, climbing into his lap and wrapping her childish arms around his neck. "I love you, Uncle Dean."

Lena rocked upon her buttocks, her prayer repeating over and over: "Please save Ate. Please save Ate."

Memories of his sparkling eyes, his lifting her into his arms and swinging her into the air, laughing,

"You are a bird, my little one."

Pictures flew through her mind – Ate teaching her how to fish, walking down the long dirt roads surrounding May Hill, lifting her to the counter of the general store and handing her an orange pop.

"Ate!"

---

[23]Tdoon-ka-she-la Wah-kah Than-kah – the Grandfathers or spirits

Mary leaned toward the smoke and prayed fervently for the life of her husband. In her left hand, the one closest to her heart, she held the eagle feather her mother had saved for her.

"Your prayer feather," her mother had advised.

Surprisingly, her mind was blank except for the vision of a blue heron against a dark, turbulent sky.

Mary stared into the pit where the super-heated rocks seemed to pulse. Beating, beating, like a human heart, the stones began to glow with a new intensity. A mist began to form in the lodge, and the other three participants began to fade. Slowly, slowly, the intensity of the heat built, and the pulsations of the rocks increased.

"Come, One Feather," a trumpet-like voice intoned.

Mary raised her eyes to the roof of the sweat lodge. There, floating above her, was Zitka Mine.[24]

"Follow," he commanded, and Mary felt herself rise through the roof of the lodge, and out into the cool air of the night.

"Where are we going?" she queried.

"To the edge of Wanagi Canku."[25]

"Wait!" Mary turned in answer to a pleading voice. Lena was following her, soaring toward her, one small arm outstretched. Zitka Mine gave his silent assent, and the three of them flew until they arrived at the fifth step from the edge of the world.

"There," Zitka Mine said, "is Spotted Eagle." Mary turned slowly and beheld a flickering light, not unlike a small star.

"Take him," Zitka Mine commanded. One Feather drifted to the flickering light of her husband's soul, and cupping it in her left hand, lovingly held it to her breast.

"One Feather," Zitka Mine intoned, "You are entrusted with the spirit of Spotted Eagle for the passing of four seasons. You will place it in a medicine bundle and guard the spirit within it. Cedar Woman," Zitka Mine instructed, turning toward the small soul drifting silently behind her mother, "must make the bundle."

Soaring upward, Zitka Mine gave his final instruction.

"Spotted Eagle must dwell within silence. He will remain silent for the total of four seasons. He will awaken, and he will teach."

---

[24] Zhee-tdkah min-eh. Also called Hokagica To – Hoh-kha - (glottal G) - ee chi-ah Td-oh – the Water Bird or Blue Heron. A healer who also symbolizes self-reflection.

[25] Wah-nah-ghee Chan-koo – the place five steps away from the edge of the world. On the fourth step a spirit steps into the spirit world.

There was the loud whoosh of sound, as if mighty wings were pulling the evening air beneath them to mount to the highest parts of the heavens. Then, silence.

Lena came to awareness with a start. She shook her head and gazed about her. Dean and Nellie appeared to be deep in prayer. Her mother was bathed in a nimbus of light, her hair floating, floating on the super-heated air of the sweat lodge.

Chapter Six

Earth, Teach Me

Earth teach me quiet – as the grasses are still with new light.
Earth teach me suffering – as old stones suffer with memory.
Earth teach me humility – as blossoms are humble with beginning.
Earth teach me caring – as mothers nurture their young.
Earth teach me courage – as the tree that stands alone.
Earth teach me limitation – as the ant that crawls on the ground.
Earth teach me freedom – as the eagle that soars in the sky.
Earth teach me acceptance – as the leaves that die each fall.
Earth teach me renewal – as the seed that rises in the spring.
Earth teach me to forget myself – as melted snow forgets its life.
Earth teach me to remember kindness – as dry fields weep with rain.

A Ute Prayer

Lena stood before the restaurant and tried to screw up the courage to enter. The sign in the window, "Help Wanted," seemed to draw her to the entrance while pushing her back at the same time. At age 14, she wasn't sure if she could convince the owner that she was qualified, but she was determined to do so.

The advancement of an older woman, a look of purpose upon her face, propelled Lena through the doors. If there was to be competition, she needed to plead her case first.

She saw the woman pass the entrance, and felt a little foolish, until she realized that she was finally in the restaurant, and was the only person there. She relaxed for a minute, walked to a small table, and sat down. Taking a deep breath, she looked around, calming her nerves as she prepared to convince the owner that she was just the right person for the job.

Lena first noticed the establishment when she decided to go on a small adventure. She quickly coaxed her friend Nickie Greene to walk to the downtown area with her as a way to spend a sunny Saturday. Nickie's one objection was the two-plus mile walk from the south end of Columbus, but Lena won out, and Nickie admitted that she had actually enjoyed their walk.

Lena wanted to see the City Center, which opened recently. Stories of the many stores and restaurants, the glass elevator, which transported patrons from the first, the second and third floors, intrigued the young girl.

Lena particularly enjoyed walking through the restaurants, which populated the gargantuan complex. Quietly asking permission, she strolled through each space, taking note of fabrics, layout, seating and ambiance. There was a quickening within her young breast, a feeling of excitement. How exhilarating it would be to own such a place, prepare good food, and present it to the public.

It was upon leaving the center, and beginning their walk back to the south end, that Lena noticed the sign in the window of Vicki's, a small eatery on the west side of High Street and just south of Town Street. Lena suggested that they enter, and Nickie, always ready for a snack, readily agreed.

The room was narrow with an eight-stool counter running along the north wall. Cracked linoleum lined the floor in a black and white checked pattern. Tables for four were scattered throughout the space, their varnished wooden tops scarred from many years of use.

A four-burner stove butted against a griddle, which sizzled beneath a large black board upon which, scratched in chalk, the specials for the day were presented, the standard foods offered each week, and the prices. The restaurant was old, but it was spotless.

Lena studied the menu. The blackboard listed several drinks – the usual: Coke, Sprite, Iced Tea and coffee. A chalked line down the middle separated the beverages from the foods available for that day.

Hot dogs and hamburgers, egg sandwiches and various soups were available. Lena sniffed the air and made the quick assumption that the soups were canned and not freshly prepared. Her interest peaked.

She decided that she would return on Monday and apply for the job.

Vicki Compton moved to Columbus upon her marriage to her husband, T.J. Theirs was a happy union until his death a few years back. She decided to keep the restaurant. The house was too empty without her husband, and the extended hours, from providing just lunch, to lunch and dinner, gave her something to do.

Standing at 5'4", and weighing 120 pounds, the dark-haired, childless widow made the restaurant her child. It was her baby, and she loved it immensely. Here she worked side-by-side with her husband until the afternoon he collapsed upon its cracked, linoleum floor.

Vicki's earned a small profit, enough to keep the business going and her personal bills paid. She was content.

Preparing for the lunch crowd, and prepping the griddle for the first rush, Vicki did not notice Lena's arrival at first. Turning to wipe down the counter, she was startled to see the young girl waiting patiently at one of her tables.

"I'm sorry, Sweetheart. I didn't see you. What would you like?"

"I'd like a job, please."

Lena placed her key into the front door lock, and slowly entered the living room of the first story apartment where she, her father, mother and grandmother lived. She entered the small, three room dwelling, and gently closed the door. Seeing that her father was not in the living area, she assumed that he was taking a nap, and did not want to wake him.

It had been a grueling two years since his tractor accident. The hospital in Peebles transferred Peter to the medical center at OSU in Columbus. Mary accompanied him with only a small bag, in which was packed only the barest necessities. Lena stayed with the Countrymans until her unci,[26] Reva, arrived at the Columbus Greyhound Bus Station on Town Street, and proceeded to the small apartment, located on Front Street, which Dean and Nellie rented for them.

Uncle Dean, as Lena called the devoted farmer, drove her to the apartment, arriving just as her grandmother stepped out of the Yellow Cab she had rented at the station. Dean entered the apartment and was satisfied. He and his brother worked together, and made sure that the refrigerator was stocked, the few pieces of furniture from the May Hill home were delivered and arranged, and all of the basics such as towels, sheets, soaps, dishes and pots and pans were in place.

Dean's brother Gary owned the apartment building, and moved by the story of the little family, and swayed by his brother's love for the Catchers, cut the rent to the bare minimum, including utilities and a phone. It was a gift of love from complete strangers that captivated Lena's heart with its generosity.

Placing her purse on the counter, which separated the living room from the kitchenette, Lena opened the refrigerator door and pulled out the ingredients for the evening meal. Tonight it would be Three Sisters Soup.

Ate! Lena ran to the huddled form of her father as he emerged from the largest bedroom, shared by him and Mary. Partially paralyzed on his left side, Peter sometimes struggled to remain upright in his wheelchair when tired or newly awakened.

"Ate!" Lena repeated, and leaned forward to kiss her father on his cheek. Straightening, she smiled at her grandmother.

"Unci, I've started our supper. Why don't you and Ate come into tho kitchon area and talk while I cook?"

Reva smiled at her fourteen-year-old granddaughter. *Wambli is definitely her totem*, she thought. *She is strong. Also, the turtle, which*

---

[26] Unchee - grandmother

urges her to nurture. A fine, young woman, Reva Two Strikes assured herself.

It had been a difficult time for Reva. Her only child, her strong son, had been cut down in an horrific accident. It hurt to see him reduced to a wheelchair for most of the day. Hurt her to see his left hand curled into a claw, caused by spasticity, a common symptom of a brain injury. Hurt her to see him stumble for words. Peter Spotted Eagle, once so strong and handsome, was now reduced to being cared for by his women, a deep blow to a man of his cultural upbringing, or any upbringing for that matter.

Reva nodded, and wheeled Peter to the doorway of the kitchenette. Hiking herself upon a stool, and leaning her elbows on the counter, she said,

"So, what have you been up to today?"

The opening of the door interrupted Lena's rehearsed reply. Mary, just home from her job at a nearby German bakery, entered slowly. She looked tired, worn out in fact.

Mary One Feather was a tireless advocate for her beloved. She seldom left his side, and was indefatigable in his physical therapy exercises. Returning from work, tired and stressed, she would walk directly to Peter, kiss him, and only after she knew that he had eaten a good meal, would she allow herself the sole luxury of a hot bath. That finished, Peter's exercises would begin and continue for an hour at least.

It didn't matter that Peter's mother had given Peter his therapy a few times during the day. Mary was his wife, and it was her duty to make sure that all of his needs were taken care of.

More in love with her husband than ever, Mary was deeply grateful to Wakan Tanka for Peter's return, and was determined to bring him back as close to his former self as possible.

Walking slowly into the room, Mary placed her purse upon the coffee table and walked to her husband. "Mihinga[27]," she murmured lovingly, placing a lingering kiss upon his forehead. Peter attempted a smile, and with his right hand, touched her still unlined cheek. "Mitawin,"[28] he murmured in return, forming the word slowly.

Mary was still a beautiful woman. At 50, she retained her youthful, willowy figure. The only change was the look of fatigue in her still glowing eyes, and the numerous strands of silver, which wove their way through her shimmering, dark locks.

---

[27] Mee-heen-gha – Husband
[28] Mee-tah-ween – Wife

Lena gazed in wonder. Was she the only one who saw the phenomenon whenever her parents' hearts seemed to fill with love for each other? Was she the only one who saw the floating hair, the nimbus of light, which encircled her parents? Was she the only one who heard two hearts beating in unison?

Lena did not have the chance to share her news. Actually, she was glad, because she needed to formulate a plan in which she could make her announcement in such a way as to guarantee permission to take the job.

She cleaned the kitchen after supper, and claiming homework, went to the smaller bedroom which she and Reva shared. Lying down upon the double bed, she closed her eyes and reviewed the past two years of her young life...

Lena filled the hours until she was reunited with her family with prayers and frenzied preparations. Uncle Dean looked puzzled when she asked if he had a piece of rawhide he could spare. Luckily, he remembered a good-sized piece stored in the barn, and handed it to his spiritually adopted niece. His heart constricted at the site of her childish face – so purposeful, her lips pressed together in determination. She accepted the gift of the rawhide with her left hand, the hand closest to her heart, and murmured,

"Wopila, Uncle Dean."

Dean drove her to May Hill, and entered the small house with Lena. She didn't waste time. Walking purposefully to the kitchen, she picked up her father's jadeite coffee cup, and placed it in a basket she'd brought with her to the house. Entering the bedroom, she located the eagle plume Mary tied to Peter's hair during their wedding ceremony. A pipe, given him on Christmas by the Countryman's (one of his favorite possessions), and a whittling knife she gave to him for his birthday, went into the basket as well.

Finally, she selected a picture of herself, her mother, and the three of them together, and added them to the collection. These items, so plain and seemingly of little value, would go into the medicine bundle that Zitka Mine commanded she make.

Later that evening, Lena went to the upstairs bedroom of the Countryman's house. She called it "the red room" because everything was red. Papered in red roses, the room boasted an airy atmosphere, not unlike you would feel in a rose garden. A dresser, painted in indian red, upon which sat a pitcher cradled within a matching bowl, an iron bed and a wardrobe painted in the same rich shade, were the only furnishings.

Pictures of ancestors graced the walls, and Lena was positive that one of them was a woman of the Cheyenne.

Lena loved this room, and enjoyed playing in it on the occasions when the Countrymans offered to babysit, but she was not up here to play today. Today she had important work to do.

Lena cut the rawhide to the size she needed, leaving enough to act as a tie. Placing the objects she'd selected into the middle, she wrapped it carefully, and tied it with the reserved rawhide. The medicine bundle was ready. Lena sat upon the floor, the bundle in her lap, and prayed to Creator:

"Creator, this is Cedar Woman. I ask that you have pity on me, as I am pitiful and small and weak," she intoned, remembering her mother's prayer in the sweat lodge.

"I come to you in humility, and ask for the life of my father."

The ride to Columbus was interminable. She was leaving her beloved May Hill, her loving Uncle Dean and Aunt Nellie, and the friends she'd made in her twelve years on this earth. But, she was anxious to be reunited with her family, and to find out how her ate was. She prayed most of the way, silent, gazing out the windows, as farm land and standing corn soon turned to rows of houses, industrious towns, and finally, the tall buildings of downtown Columbus, Ohio.

Dean exited off of US 23, and drove the short distance to the Front Street apartment, breathing a prayer of gratitude at the sight of Reva Catcher stepping out of a brightly painted Yellow Cab.

Dean walked up to Reva Two Strikes Catcher, hand extended in welcome.

"Mrs. Catcher," he murmured. "I wish we could have met under better circumstances, but I am still glad to finally make your acquaintance."

Reva gazed at the sun-bronzed farmer and smiled gently.

"Creator has decided that we meet, and so we have. Thank you for taking such good care of my son and his family."

As Reva spoke, she reached out to Lena, smoothing her glossy hair gently, finally placing her left hand upon her only grandchild's shoulder.

"Wakan Tanka has chosen a great friend for my son. I am grateful."

Dean blushed, not an easy accomplishment under his permanent farmer's sun-bronzed tan, and thanked her.

"Now," he offered, clearing his throat from the emotion-inspired tears which filled it, "let's get your bags into the apartment, and I will take you to Peter.

Lena sat in the corner of her father's small room in the medical center. The door was closed, and Mary had requested that they be undisturbed until the door was opened. The nurse to whom she'd spoken looked a bit concerned, but she trusted Mary's judgment, even though she'd only known her for a week, and decided to give her some time. She knew that Mary was performing something called a healing ceremony, and held deep respect, as well as a certain awe, and a lot of curiosity, for Native American practices. She wished she could be included so that she could see what a healing ceremony was all about. She hoped that Mary would give her an Indian name, so she acquiesced, and looked longingly toward the door the entire time.

Beside Mary was Tell Wolf Catcher, Peter's cousin, who drove from Iowa to help with the healing ceremony which Mary was about to begin.

Mary first smudged the room, bringing all spirits into harmony. They had not been able to perform a sweat lodge ceremony, so Tell Wolf requested the use of the sweat lodge of his brother, Joe Red Bear, before leaving Iowa.

Mary placed the medicine bundle Lena made in the bed beside her husband. Waving her prayer feather above him, she prayed to Tankasilus[29] to make her husband whole, and to make her whole again. She prayed that Peter's taku skan skan[30] be returned to its shell. Tell Wolf held the canumpa[31] above Peter and prayed as well, as Mary continued to wave her prayer feather above her husband's body, waving, waving, entreating his taku skan skan to return to its shell.

Lena observed her mother solemnly. Again she was enthralled with her mother's floating hair, which began to turn gray the day of the accident. It floated upon the air like a wisp of smoke, not unlike the transparent ribbons that rose from the bowl when her mother smudged. A shimmering light surrounded her, but her father's form remained dark.

An half hour passed, and then another. Still her mother and Tell Wolf prayed, sometimes chanting, sometimes silent, their mouths moving with their entreaties. Slowly, slowly, her father's body began to glow. Their heart beats separated, but continued to beat in unison. Lena leapt to her feet! Her father was alive!

---

[29] Tdun-khash-ee-lahs – The Spirit Helpers
[30] Tda-koo-skhahn-skhan – soul
[31] Cha-noom-pah – pipe or sacred breath

As Zitka Mine prophesied, Peter remained in coma for a full four seasons. On the anniversary of his accident, his eyes fluttered open and he murmured one word:

"Mary."

Lena lay on the bed she shared with her grandmother, and remembered. She remembered that Zitka Mine prophesied that her father would teach. Her brow wrinkled as she considered this extraordinary statement. She continued to remember: her father struggling to learn to walk again, talk again. Struggling to eat on his own, to read, but never struggling to love again.

He was as entwined with the heart of his wife as before the accident. Daily Lena watched the nimbus grow brighter and stronger. Stronger too were the heart beats of her parents, beating in unison. Day by day she watched him struggle, and she was in awe of her father's ability to endure.

She watched him patiently learn to talk again, to communicate, to voice his feelings and dreams. She witnessed his pain as therapists worked with his weakened limbs, teaching him to walk again, to perform tasks as simple as holding a spoon. She observed his courage as strangers bathed him, emptied his bed pan. His love for his wife, daughter and mother, and for Dean and Nellie when they came to Columbus to see him, was evident in the glow of his eyes and his patience in re-learning everything he had done before without thinking, was a lesson the young Lena would never forget.

His soul was encased in a body that would not respond, yet his soul was free, and his acceptance of his condition, and faith that he would be restored to his former self, never flagged.

His concern was for his family and not himself, so he worked even harder to regain his strength, to walk, to talk, to be the husband and father he had been before the accident. Finally, his gratitude for Dean and Nellie Countryman, Dean's brother Gary, and the friends who came together to help his small family, filled his heart in every waking moment.

Lena stood back mentally and contemplated her father, and she was filled with wonder.

Chapter Seven

Lakota Instructions for Living

Friend do it this way - that is,
whatever you do in life,
do the very best you can
with both your heart and mind.

And if you do it that way,
the Power of The Universe
will come to your assistance,
if your heart and mind are in Unity.

When one sits in the Hoop Of The People,
one must be responsible, because
all of Creation is related,
and the hurt of one is the hurt of all,
and the honor of one is the honor of all,
and whatever we do effects everything in the universe.

If you do it that way - that is,
if you truly join your heart and mind
as one - whatever you ask for,
that's the way it's going to be.

Passed down from White Buffalo Calf Woman

"This injun is gonna kill me!" Vicki cried exploding through the front door, hands waving above her head. Proceeding into the restaurant, she playfully bumped her hip against Lena's as she passed the counter and continued her way to the back of the establishment.

Nickie questioned with a raised eyebrow as Lena laughingly explained,

"I guess last month's figures were good."

Nickie allowed herself a twirl on the swivel stool on which she sat and queried:

"Good?"

Lena smiled. "Yeah," she affirmed, "real good."

In the three years since Lena began working at Vicki's, many changes had taken place. Vicki managed to obtain a lease on the store on the north side of her restaurant at a very economical rate. A new, large doorway between the two units created, the entire space expanded and completely renovated, the restaurant, under Lena's direction, opened to rave revues in record time.

Vicki made her way to her office, a feeling of gratitude overwhelming her as she walked through the newly refurbished restaurant. *That girl is such a blessing to me!* She thought to herself. *Blessing?* she chuffed inwardly, *hell, she's a bloody miracle! Look at this place, I'm a goddamn entrepreneur!* Vicki smiled to herself at her infrequent swearing. It made her feel good, like she had grown up all of a sudden – finally.

Too restless to stay in her office, Vicki slowly walked around the restaurant, soaking it in – gloating, actually – to herself.

Shining hardwood flooring replaced the cracked and worn linoleum. Reflected in its shining expanse were new maple tables and chairs. The walls, painted a soft, creamy white, mellowed the room, and simple, pendant lights replaced the old, yellowed globes of before.

The counter remained – a nostalgic gesture on the owner's part, highly polished maple replacing the worn Formica. The old chalkboard was gone, and freshly printed menus lay waiting at a small hostess station. A new kitchen, built behind the wall against which the griddle stood, boasted all new equipment.

Vicki's was not a fine-dining establishment, but it was up-scale from most of the restaurants surrounding it, excepting those located in the various hotels within the downtown Columbus area.

Comfortable and warm, Vicki's was a nice alternative to the fast food chains and high-end restaurants available to office workers, shoppers and tourists, but its main attraction was the food.

Vicki returned to her office. Putting her feet up, and resting them on the top of her desk, she nested the back of her head in her cupped hands, leaning back in the comfortable, leather chair which Lena insisted upon for her employer's office.

She loved going back over the past three years. She enjoyed the remembering, savored the memories, like a child carrying her Christmas stocking around until she went to bed on Christmas night, cradling it in her arms until she slept.

She saw herself turning from wiping down the counter, saw Lena sitting stiffly at a table, hands clasped, an intent look upon her elfin face. She heard herself ask if there was anything she would like, heard Lena answer,

"I'd like a job, please."

She remembered her reaction: surprise, confusion, incredulity. She heard her mind say:

"I'm sorry, you're too young. I need someone for more hours than you can work. I don't have time to train you," and instead heard herself say,

"When can you start."

It wasn't a question. It was a statement.

Were there really guardian angels? Vicki could have sworn that she felt a hand press her shoulder, a body lean into hers and whisper into her ear:

"Take this opportunity!"

Was it T.J.? Was he still here watching over her?

She remained frozen, still in the position of wiping the counter, bar rag in her hand, pressed upon the old, scratched Formica surface. She saw Lena rise, smile, and answer,

"As soon as you'll have me."

Vicki swung her feet from her desk and crossed her legs, and then her arms. She treasured the remembering – prized the reflections.

She gave Lena a key to Vicki's six months after she began working at the restaurant. Arriving one summer morning, she was surprised to find Lena already there, a delicious aroma wafting through the narrow room. Sniffing with enjoyment, Vicki exclaimed,

"What is THAT?"

"Three Sisters Soup," Lena explained, turning from the four-burner stove adjoining the griddle.

"Three Sisters Soup?"

"Yes," Lena returned.

"I walked to the fresh vegetable and fruit stand down by State Street. I talked to the owner, and he let me have these vegetables for nothing. I told him, that if this worked, we'd be ordering from him daily."

Taken aback, Vicki queried,

"You promised him that I would order from him every day?" shock and dismay sending shivers down her spine.

"It's okay," Lena reassured, "I didn't say for sure. I told him what I was trying, and he said it sounded like a good idea. If it works, he'll sell us fresh vegetables and fruits at a nice discount.

"You see, you're selling that restaurant-issue, canned soup, which is okay, but so is everyone else. So, I thought I'd make fresh. It's cheaper, tastes better, and no one else is selling this. I promise, people will be coming here for THIS soup!" Lena averred, gazing solemnly into Vicki's worried eyes.

Vicki looked her doubt. Lena grabbed a ladle, and gently prepared a portion of the fragrant, delicious soup.

"Here," she said, "try it and see!"

The restaurateur in Vicki noted that the serving was very attractive. Something orange...

"What's this?" Vicki asked.

"Squash," Lena replied. Vicki looked closer at the steaming bowl. The vivid orange of the squash, glowing white of potatoes, verdant green of string beans and bright yellow of whole kernel corn presented to the eyes a vibrant, enticing dish. The aroma of the homemade turkey broth, coupled with the squash and vegetables, was unbelievable. Vicki picked up a spoon and tasted the soup.

There was no going back.

A rapid knock, and the opening of the door, interrupted Vicki's musings. Lena entered, carrying a fragrant mug of herbal tea.

"Here you go oh, Great One!" she intoned laughingly, setting the mug on a coaster at the corner of the desk.

Smiling, Vicki retrieved the mug, and blowing gently upon the surface of the aromatic liquid, took a timid sip. It was just right.

"This is good," she thanked. Lena smiled, and plopped into a leather side chair beside the desk.

"I want to go over today's menu with you. I know it will be fine, but you know that I like to double-check."

Vicki smiled her agreement, and settled back in her comfortable chair, the warm mug cupped within her hands.

"Okay, Three Sisters Soup, of course," Lena began.

"Can't open without that," Vicki affirmed.

"Right," Lena smiled. "Chili, for the meat eaters."

Vicki nodded agreement.

"Now, main courses: hamburgers, of course. Gotta have those. French fries....listen, this time let's try the sweet potato fries, okay?" Lena entreated.

Vicki thought for a moment and nodded.

"Okay, but let's offer both." Lena smiled her agreement.

"Of course. Let's see, baked salmon with tomatoes and shallots..."

Lena continued until the entire menu was gone through. Satisfied, Vicki stood up, and walking around her desk, encircled Lena in her arms.

"Good job as usual," she beamed.

Chapter Eight

Humankind has not woven the web of life.
We are but one thread within it.
Whatever we do to the web, we do to ourselves.
All things are bound together.
All things connect.

Chief Seattle, 1854

Vicki created a special place for Peter in her now popular restaurant. At the entrance of the doorway separating the two rooms, and within four steps of the counter, was the Spotted Eagle table, as Vicki liked to call it. Here, Peter could sit as long as he liked, chain-smoking, and drinking the endless cups of rez coffee provided.

He was content. Mary and Reva both worked part-time in the restaurant, Reva less than the others. Now 78, she was still spry, and capable of a full days work, but Vicki and Lena were careful not to overtax the elderly, yet still vibrant, senior citizen. Wife and mother kept a careful eye on husband and son, and were thankful for the opportunity to earn more money for the family while caring for their loved one.

As with all serious brain injuries, Peter had not fully recovered from his accident. His personality was still sweet and loving, but he seemed incapable of putting a string of new thoughts together. His days were filled with old Indian jokes, proverbs, stories, and long, relaxed silences.

He'd become a mascot as it were. Regulars would walk by, raise a hand in greeting, and proceed to their tables. Occasionally, Peter would stop them, look up and smiling ask, for instance:

"How many Oglalas does it take to change a light bulb? Seven! One to change the bulb and six to sing the 'changing of the light bulb song.'"

They would laugh politely, wave and move on, sometimes confused, and sometimes genuinely entertained by Peter's jokes and stories.

Vicki would often take her break at Peter's table, bringing him a treat – a muffin or fry bread to munch on. Vicki would solicit his advice, drawing him in to the running of the restaurant so as to make him feel as though he were contributing.

This did not go unnoticed by Mary and Reva, and on one particular occasion, when Vicki asked Peter's advice on how to improve the rez coffee, Mary turned to Reva and said,

"I think you're absolutely right."

Lena leaned back on the old sofa in the three-room apartment in which she now lived by herself. Her mother, father and grandmother, now owned a small house on City Park Avenue in German Village. Equipped with handrails and ramps for Peter, it made life easier for the physically and mentally challenged patriarch of the family. With the help of intensive physical therapy, Peter learned to walk again, but he tired quickly, and experienced frequent bouts of vertigo. As a result, he would often revert to his wheelchair. Mary felt that the little house would be more comfortable for her husband, and so the move was made.

It was Lena's day off, and she was spending her time going over new menu ideas, and sketching endless scenes of restaurant designs and seating arrangements. There was a rapid knock on the door. Lena called, "come in," and Reva entered. Approaching tentatively, Reva sat down beside Lena, gingerly placing her left hand upon her granddaughter's shoulder.

"Cedar Woman," she said. Lena looked up with surprise. Seldom did her grandmother use her NdN[32] name. This must be important.

"Cedar Woman," she repeated, "I have spoken to the grandfathers, and we are to go to Keokuk this summer for the Annual Gathering of the People. There we will meet with Tell Wolf and Ina Mahto Luta[33], and Mahto Luta.[34] I have asked Vicki to become my daughter. She has agreed.

Lena was surprised, to say the least!

"Your *daughter*?"

"Ohan," affirmed Reva. She is family here," Reva stated, patting her bony chest.

"She has been good to us. She has given us work. She has given you opportunity. Yes," Reva continued, nodding, "It is good. She will become my daughter. We will go to Keokuk and we will have the Hunkapi.[35]

The air smelled of rain. Gusts of wind passed over sweat-soaked brows, bringing temporary relief. It was eleven a.m., and temperatures rose to above 100 degrees.

---

[32] Indian – preferred spelling used in written materials
[33] Ee-nuh Mah-to Loo-tah – Mother Red Bear
[34] Mah-to Loo-tah – Red Bear
[35] Hoon-kah-pee – Adoption Ceremony

44

The aroma of food drifted upon a moisture-rich breeze, making mouths water with thoughts of food: Indian tacos, corn and fry bread, washed down with lemonade, sodas and cool, cool water.

Eight men entered the encircled enclosure, taking their places around the large can cega[36]. They began to beat the drum and sing in unison, their voices, soaring to the vaulted dome of heaven.

The Grand Entrance began, and people of the Lakota and Dakota, of the Cheyenne and other tribes, entered in full ceremonial dress. They stepped around the arena, *toe, heel, toe, heel.* Lena marveled at the beauty of the regalia. Here was a woman in a silky dress with a gorgeous shawl with long fringe. Another dancer, a woman again, her tube-like dress covered in metal cones that tinkled as she walked. A man danced by in a magnificent headdress. It was then that she saw *him.* His regalia was white and black, with multi-colored beading in a striped design. He wore a kind of cape, fringed with what appeared to be airy feathers or ribbons, Lena couldn't tell for sure. A beaded headband encircled his head and matched the beaded moccasins he wore upon his feet. He wore a headdress, called a Roach, of what Lena later found out was porcupine guard hair and deer hair, dyed to the dancer's specifications. His dark hair was braided, and his regalia seemed to sway as he spun and danced in time to the powwow drum.

Who is he? Lena breathed to herself, as she watched him dance along with the other participants.

Nickie grabbed her hand and pulled.

"Come on," she said, "We can at least be one of the heartbeat dancers.

Lena followed, and took her place beside Nickie along the edge of the arena. Bending her knees in time to the beat of the powwow drum, she mimicked a heartbeat.

"Women are the heartbeat of the tribe, and demonstrate this by supporting the dancers in the center of the arena," a friendly woman explained earlier to Nickie and Lena.

Gazing at the male dancer, mesmerized by his movements and artistry, she leaned toward Nickie and whispered,

"Do you know who that is?"

"I haven't a clue," Nickie replied.

"I wonder what kind of dancer he is," Lena questioned.

"I have absolutely no idea," Nickie retorted, a bit impatient with Lena's constant inquiries about the young man.

"He's a Grass Dancer," offered a voice to Lena's left.

---

[36] chahn-chay-ghah - drum

"Hi, I'm Julie Spotted Eagle Horse, originally from Pine Ridge rez,

of the Pesla[37] Oyate[38]. Just call me 'Julie' or 'Spot,' everyone else does ennit. Anyway, he's a Grass Dancer, you can tell by his regalia and the way he moves. See how he bends and sways like a blade of grass in the wind? He is one of the old style Grass Dancers, the ones that try to become one with the spirit of the Grass, so that they can better control it."

Lena watched the young man, mesmerized by his dance.

"The Grass Dancer," Julie continued, "lays the grass down in the arena for the other dancers. To do that, he must become the grass," she finished.

Lena smiled at the friendly woman who stood before her in magnificent regalia. She noticed that Julie had a slight accent, one that was hard to place. Wait! Now she had it. It was exactly like the accent of Elaine Miles, who played Marilyn Whirlwind in *Northern Exposure. Yes, that's it!* Lena was intrigued.

When Unci announced that they were going to a powwow, Lena was excited. She wanted to know more about her people. When Lena told Nickie about the trip, she begged to come along. Comanche by birth, Nickie too had not been given the opportunity to be around other Native Americans, living as they did in the Greater Columbus Area, which showed a census of less than 1 percent.

Lena's father's tragedy consumed the small family, and what teachings might have occurred, did not. Instead, Lena continued to learn how to cook, so that her mother could care for her father.

Lena gave herself a mental shake, and turned again to the impressive woman who stood beside her.

"Your dress is beautiful," Lena admired.

"Wopila, thanks! It was my grandmother's originally. I've added to it, of course, but essentially it's her dress. I am a Northern Plains Traditional Buckskin Dancer, that is, Sioux Style Traditional."

"Do you go to many powwows?" Nickie asked with a questioning look.

"Yeah, I try to get to as many powwows as I can, depending on how 'Protector,' my war pony/rez rocket, is feeling ennit!" replied Julie with a laugh, referring to her second-hand truck.

Chuckling, Lena queried:

"So, do you mind telling me about your dress, and what everything means?" Lena asked with an admiring look.

---

[37] Pesh-lah – The Bald Heads, the Green Berets of the Sioux
[38] Oh-yah-tay - People

Julie smiled at the eager young woman, happy to comply. She liked Lena, and her friend Nickie, and appreciated their respect.

There was something about Lena. Julie wasn't sure yet, but she had a feeling that this would be an encounter she would never forget: there was something about the young woman, something that spoke to her own woman's heart.

"Well, first of all," Julie continued, "the style of the dress itself is a hold over from the early rez period when we first got our hands on white man's cloth.[39] Many of the women started to create a fusion of trade wool, or trade cloth, with the more traditional leather. The shells on my dress represent Elk teeth, used originally to decorate our dresses.

"Back then, your choices were either Elk teeth or quill work, and since Unci got her clinic teeth, she doesn't do quill work anymore," Julie joked, referring to her grandmother's false teeth.

"Elk teeth are expensive, and hard to get, so Unci used these Ring Top Cowrie shells instead," Julie offered, referring to the small, creamy shells ringed in gold.

"The braid wraps are made from a single otter skin that I had to split in half, and then I actually had to behead the poor thing in order to be able to use it! Otherwise, they would be dragging the ground. And, these ties here are for decoration, I think my auntie made them for me, but I can't remember. The pattern is an old sunburst design, and has been in our family for generations. The satin kerchief is sort of a holdover from earlier times as well, and it is good for hiding some minor flaws on the back of the dress.

"This long black, white, and red ribbon thing, with all the decorations hanging from the back of the kerchief, is a 'dragger' and it has a lot of meaning for me. The red ribbons are to honor the warriors and veterans in my family, to let them know that I remember them and honor them. The black and white are my personal colors, I had to earn the right to wear them by being struck by lightning twice. The pins and such show part of my medicine. The little lightning Kachina[40] was given to me by a good friend named Mike, who is also a lightning survivor. He lives in Tucson, and I think he got it from one of the Dine[41] artisans down there. Anyway, the spotted Eagle feather and the horse represent my name," Julie continued.

"The breastplate and choker are supposed to represent the armor that our boys wore back before the whites came, and they were effective at stopping arrows and bullets to an extent. The leggings and moccasins

[39] Much of dialog contributed by Julie Spotted Eagle Horse
[40] Meaning "Life Bringer" now seen in Native American forms of art as in dolls, pottery and jewelry.
[41] Navajo Artists

are traditionally done in an old family pattern, and you will notice that I am covered from the neck down, ya? That's because Sioux women are very modest, especially the Traditionals, so as a Traditional Dancer, I try to remember that. When I am in regalia, I need to be modest and ladylike, although a lot of times that is hard for me!" Julie chortled.

"Let's see... my shawl was hand-made by me, and I can't remember how many hours it took me to hand tie the fringe. The shawls are also a hold over from the early to mid-rez period when the whites started introducing us to the idea of social dances.

"Many of the women wore shawls back then, and we try to carry on that tradition by carrying one as part of our regalia. They are treated with the same sort of respect as the American flag, and are never supposed to touch the ground if you can help it.

"Okay, my beaded bag here is sort of like a purse, I can carry a lot of stuff in here, but mostly just money and maybe some tobacco in case I need it for whatever reason. Since tobacco is sacred, gifting a person with tobacco is a sign of respect, and keeping it on hand is always a good idea.

"I won the crown in a Senior Ladies' contest last year, and I have also won several championships as well. This year I am defending my title as Ladies Traditional Buckskin Champion and Champion Potato Dancer[42] at this event!

"Let's see...oh yeah! My feathers! Cha! They are the real things. The plumes on the back of my head here are from an immature Bald Eagle, and have been mounted on an African Porcupine quill. Can you imagine the size of critter that produced this! I think that it is pretty close to six inches long ennit! Anyway, one of my cousins, Jerry from Ancient Visions, did the mounting and beadwork for me. This little cluster of fluffs here on the side are from a Red Tailed Hawk's tail, and plumes like these and the Eagle are highly prized by NdNz[43].

"The plumes represent femininity and grace, so the women like to wear them! My fan here is worth about $65,000 if it were to belong to a non-NdN, because it is made from an immature Golden Eagle wing. It's illegal for non-NdN people to have raptor feathers, because they are protected. You need a CDIB card, or special permits, to have them. I think that the fine is something like $5,000 and prison time if you are caught with them without the right papers."

"What's a CDIB?" Nickie asked, with a quizzical look.

"A CDIB is part of my tribal enrollment paperwork. It's basically a tribal census number, and CDIB means 'Certificate of Degree of Indian

---

[42] A potato is placed between the foreheads of two dancers. The last two dancers to keep the potato in place are the winners.
[43] Indians – plural for NdN

Blood'. It documents, not only your family lineage and tribal membership, but also shows your blood quantum. I'm a quarter blood myself, but I still qualified for enrollment. It's kind of a touchy subject for most of us, as we are the ONLY race that has to prove our blood quantum to the government in order to establish our identity. Cha! Maybe we ought to start making the other races prove their blood quantum ennit, although somehow I doubt that would work.[44]"

"So you are a Sioux? From Pine Ridge?" Questioned Lena. She was intrigued. She couldn't help but notice the use of 'ennit,' a term used by her parents. It made her feel close to this kind woman whom she'd just met.

"Yep, Pine Ridge born and bred! I'm from the Pesla Oyate, or familial group. My ex says that I have more relatives than trees have leaves! We jokingly call it 'skinship'[45] in the NdN world...you know how it is when you get two NdNz together ya? Within five minutes we will have figured out how we are related to each other, even if we are from two different nations ennit!" Julie grinned. Lena laughed, and again noted a similarity. Her father loved to tell NdN jokes.

"You look like a Lakota yourself, what Tiyospiya[46] are you?"

"Well," offered Lena, "my mother was born on the Crow Creek reservation, and is of the Pehan[47] Oyate. My father was born on Rosebud, and is of the Wiacca Ska[48] Oyate. They left Rosebud the day they were married, and traveled to Southern Ohio where I was born."

Julie nodded, as if reaffirming a conclusion she had come to, and then continued with the "lesson."

"See that guy over there, the one with the big ball of feathers on his head and the old style outfit?" asked Julie, pointing with her fan.

"He's my cousin Bill Thunderhawk. He's a Traditional dancer. One of the best! The guy over there with the huge black and white bustles is my cousin Chris War Bonnet, and he's a Men's Fancy Dancer. He's a Dakota, but that's ok, we try to overlook his speech impediment! Them Dakota's, they don't talk right!" Julie chuckled.

Lena took advantage of the stately woman's reference and asked, "Your accent, it's like the actress on *Northern Exposure*."

"Ya," replied Julie, "that's a Northern Plains accent and most NdNz have something similar, ennit. I thought your parents are Lakota. They don't speak like me?"

---

[44] End dialog by Spotted Eagle Horse
[45] NdN term for common ancestors
[46] Tdee-yosh-pee-yah – Family
[47] Peh-hahn – Crane
[48] Wee-ah-kah-shkah – White Plume

"Ate and Ina lived in Southern Ohio for many years before I was born, mostly around farmers and such. I guess they must have lost their accents. It's lovely, Julie," Lena averred, smiling.

"Wopila," Julie replied, returning her smile.

Julie gazed at Lena for a long minute, as if making a decision.

"Just a minute," Julie said, and hurried away. Turning around, she waved and said, "Be right back!"

"Wow!" Lena breathed. "There is so much to learn. You know, Ate and Ina taught me a lot of the language and basic beliefs, especially after Ate's accident, but I guess they wanted to blend in. You know, we were the only Native Americans in May Hill, at least that I know of, so I can't really blame them. Julie is so nice to tell us all of this," Lena exclaimed.

"She likes you," Nickie offered.

"Well, she likes you too!" laughed Lena.

"Not like she does you," Nickie added.

Julie returned with two shawls draped over her arm. "Here," she said. Handing Nickie a white shawl with black fringe, she turned and offered a teal shawl with mauve fringe to Lena. "Wear these," she instructed, "whenever you go into the arena. It's a sign of respect."

"Thank you," exclaimed Lena and Nickie in unison.

"We'll take good care of them and return them when the powwow is over.

"Sni,[49] they are a gift."

Turning to Lena again, she pointed to a tipi at the perimeter of the powwow grounds.

"Hey, see that blue and white lodge at the end of the row? Why don't you both come by after we dance the Drum out[50] and hang out, ya? My chia, Joe, might come by for some Forty-Niners.[51] I can make some wakalapi.[52] Now, I must go. The women dancers are getting ready to start." Toksa."[53]

---

[49] Shnee – No
[50] Dance to the Powwow Drum until it ends for the night
[51] Less formally structured NdN love songs which include English
[52] Wah-kahl-lah-pee – Coffee
[53] Doh-k-sha – Good bye or see you later

50

Chapter Nine

The True Peace

The first peace, which is the most important,
is that which comes within the souls of people
when they realize their relationship,
their oneness with the universe and all its powers,
and when they realize that at the center
of the universe dwells Wakan Tanka, the Great Spirit,
and that this center is really everywhere, it is within each of us.
This is the real peace, and the others are but reflections of this.
The second peace is that which is made between two individuals,
and the third is that which is made between two nations.
But above all, you should understand that there can never
be peace between nations until there is known that true peace
which, as I have often said, is within the souls of men.

Black Elk, Oglala Sioux & Spiritual Leader (1863 - 1950)

"Hau Kolas![54] So what did you think of your first day at your first powwow? Pretty cool ennit! Have a seat!" grinned Julie, gesturing to the camp chairs scattered in front of the tipi, as Lena, Nickie, Vicki and Reva approached her lodge.

"Watch out for those ropes there, tied to the spear. Those are holding my smoke flaps where I want them." Julie warned.

"Are you hungry? How about something to drink. I have some wakalapi, or water, or soda in that cooler there! Are you sure you are not hungry? I have some fry bread in that bowl over there," Julie offered, pointing with her lips.

Again, Lena was struck by the similarity between her parents, grandmother, and Julie. It had never struck her as unusual that her parents would use their lips, instead of a finger or thumb, to indicate which direction they would like for you to look, until she saw Julie do it. It made her warm toward the generous woman even more. She felt relaxed and at home.

"Have you ever seen the inside of a tipi? No? Well then go ahead and have a peek inside! I think that my husband Matthew is done changing. He had better be by now!

Did you see the Traditional Dancer with the white, blue and red regalia and HUGE roach earlier? That's him. I keep telling him that I will make an NdN out of him yet! I keep teasing him that he is my 'token

---

[54] Hoe Colas – Hello friends

51

white guy,' and the running joke in my family is that a lot of my male relatives have blonde or red-headed white women hangin' around lookin' for NdN names, and now I can go one better 'cause I have my own cowboy! Well, I think he's a keeper anyway!" Julie joked with a smile, as her guests looked inside the tipi with awed expressions.

"It's an eighteen footer, and we have tried to furnish it as authentically as possible over the years. Anyway, I think there is some wojape[55] left, unless Jaws, I mean my nephew Jacob, got to it first! I usually have to give him his own bowl of wojape so that the rest of us can get some! Cha, that boy can eat!

"Jacob! Hecusniyela![56] We have company! You save some for the rest of us!" Julie commanded as said nephew abruptly entered the camp and started to pick up the bowl of pudding. "Jaws" grinned and said:

"Sorry, Ina, I didn't realize we had company!" he apologized, giving his aunt the traditional name of Mother. Winking, he turned and left to find some friends.

"Sorry about that, that was 'Jaws' in the flesh. He's our Head Singer, and he thinks he's the 'Powwow Romeo', ennit!" Julie exclaimed with a fond smile and a sigh for her nephew's antics.

"I think he's snaggin', ya. I keep telling him that he doesn't always have to be the powwow Romeo, he CAN share the title with others!" Julie laughed.

Amenities taken care of, and the wojape saved, Julie, Lena, Nickie, Vicki and Reva sat upon the camp chairs scattered in front of the lodge. Julie passed out beverages and a bowl of fry bread. As she passed the bowl to Lena, her eyes met those of the young woman.

"Ista Wambli-win!"[57] Julie whispered to herself.

She had not noticed Lena's eyes earlier, as she had been busy instructing Lena and Nickie on the various dancers and her regalia, but she noticed them now, and was astounded. Julie was never rude, and her reaction was barely noticeable, but Lena caught the surprise in her generous hostess' own eyes. Lena wondered how to broach the subject, when her thoughts were interrupted, as Reva began the important tradition of announcing her clan ties.

"I'm Reva Two Strikes, from the Rosebud rez, of the Wiacca Ska Oyate. Wopila," Reva offered, "and this is our friend, Vicki, who is to become my daughter tomorrow night.

---

[55] woah-jza-pay – Berry pudding in which fry bread is dipped
[56] Hey choo schnee yeh lah – Don't do that
[57] Eeesh-tdah wahmblee ween – Woman with the eyes of an Eagle

As an elder, Reva traditionally held the privilege of being the first to speak. Julie would not address her directly until Reva gave her permission by speaking to her first.

In the Native American culture, respect and privileges are extended to the elders for their accumulated knowledge and experiences. In addition to respectfully waiting for tacit permission to speak, Julie was careful not to look Reva in the face. Not only was Reva an elder, but a full blood Lakota. As a quarter blood, out of respect, Julie would not look her in the face until given permission, albeit unspoken, to do so.

"Hau Kola," Reva offered.

"Hau Kola," Julie returned, nodding to Vicki and the other guests. Turning to Reva, she continued,

"Unci, I'm Julie Spotted Eagle Horse, originally from Pine Ridge of the Pesla Oyate" Julie responded, giving Reva the honorary name of Grandmother, giving her clan ties, and acknowledging Vicki and her guests all at the same time.

Julie turned to Lena and smiled.

"I am happy that you accepted my invitation, and have brought your friends and your grandmother. I am honored to welcome you to my camp."

Guests and hostess settled down to light conversation. The wojape was sweet and delicious, the fry bread light and satisfying. Lena was just taking a bite, when she almost choked with laughter. Upon entering Julie's lodge, her eyes focused on the tipi itself, its construction and furnishings. She had not noticed that Julie had changed out of her regalia. Now, sitting across from her, she became aware that Julie was wearing a tee shirt: "Body by Fry Bread" emblazoned across the front.

Julie was an impressive figure, statuesque, in fact, standing at 5'7", with waist length, medium, brown hair, a gray streak spilling from her widow's peak, and brown/green eyes. Her figure was what one could only call Rubenesque. The lettering of the tee shirt stretched across her ample bosom, causing the letters to elongate.

Julie noticed the direction of Lena's surprised gaze, and laughingly explained, "It's kind of a running joke that I'm a fry bread babe: round, brown and delicious, ya!" Lena choked, laughed, and the rest joined in.

Reva put her hand over her mouth and actually snorted, causing Lena to turn and look at her grandmother in surprise. Lena could not remember when her grandmother had laughed like this! Lena reached over and put her arm around Reva, giving her an affectionate squeeze, laying her head upon her grandmother's shoulder for a brief moment, wondering at the changes in her normally stoic grandmother. The conversation stayed light, as Lena and Nickie, and sometimes Vicki, asked various questions about the powwow.

"Julie," Vicki ventured, "you mentioned Forty-Niners. What are they?" she questioned, eager to know the answer.

"Heyyyyy, they're sort of non-traditional songs. Forty-Niners contain a combination of NdN and English words and are usually love songs. They almost always have four push-ups, or verses, and are usually used for Rabbit, Two Steps, and Round Dances, which are social dances, and they are also popular at the informal jams that often happen after the powwow. We sometimes call them 'snaggin' songs' because a lot of the time they are all about snaggin'!"

"You used that word a minute ago. What is 'snaggin'?" Vicki wondered.

"Snaggin' is when a man or a woman begins to flirt with someone – 'hitting' on them," Julie explained.

"Forty-Niners differ from the competition songs in that, comp songs are usually either vocables, or sung in NdN rather than English, and are either old songs, or old style songs. When we are dancing in competitions, we try to stop on the last beat of the fourth push-up. That's called "pinning the tail on the song. You can be disqualified for not stopping on the beat in competitions. A good dancer, who knows how to listen to the song, can hear it coming. You also have to be able to hit the Honor Beats,[58] especially if you are a Fancy Shawl or Jingle dancer.

"Then there are the specialty songs like sneak-ups. A sneak up is exactly that, a sneak up song. The Drum will try to trick a dancer into false stops, or not being able to stop on the beat, and they have special songs just for that. Each one has an unpredictable stopping point somewhere in each push-up, and a good dancer will be able to anticipate them.

Also, the beat for a sneak-up gets faster as the song progresses, and the dancers have to be able to keep time with the beat. Usually only Grass and Men's Fancy dancers get sneak-ups, although sometimes the Men's Traditionals get them too. Sometimes for fun, they will also throw one at the women for switch dances, so you really have to know the style and how to hear a song."

"What's a switch dance?" asked Lena.

"Ah, those are where the ladies will pick out a man from the crowd, and give them their shawl to dance with. If the man refuses, he has to pay her twenty bucks or give her an article of clothing, and if he accepts, he has to dance her style. Then it is the women's turn! They are a lot of fun to watch! A lot of the dancers have been on the circuit long enough to know most of the dance styles, and some of them are pretty good! And then, some are really bad like my Matthew. You would think that as long

---

[58] Three accented beats that occur in between the choruses

54

as we have been together, he would have learned my style by now!" Julie giggled.

"That bad huh," Nickie commented with a grin as Julie nodded, suppressing her laughter.

"Can you give us an example of a Forty-Niner?" asked Vicki.

"Sure!" Julie smiled. Let me see. This is called, 'When I'm Far Away,'" Julie informed, and clearing her throat began:

Wey hey ya,
Wey hey ya hey hi ya
Wey hey ya,
Wey hey ya he hi ya,
Weyao hey yo hey hey heyo,
Wey heya heh ha,
Wey yeh ha,
Hiyowaeyey.
When I'm far away,
When I'm far away,
When I close my eyes,
There you are.
There you are,
So beautiful to me,
He wey hiya he ha
Wey hiya
Hiyowayey.

She sang the haunting melody four times, ending abruptly on the last syllable of the last word.

Reva leaned forward, hands clasped around her waist, her eyes glowing,

"That's from Rosebud! My husband used to sing that when he was courting me!" Reva exclaimed.

Collecting herself, she leaned back into a straightened position, and placing her hand over her mouth, giggled like a young girl.

Reva seldom referred to her husband. Logan Eagle Brings Him Catcher died at Pearl Harbor when Peter was seven. He was a solemn man, who seldom laughed, but he loved to sing, and had a remarkable voice.

Reva would often hear him singing as she was drifting off to sleep. He was still with her in this life, whispering to her in the voice of the wind, and in the murmur of the stones beneath her feet, offering protection and guidance, as he did in life. Reva knew that he was with her, patiently waiting for her to finish her work here, so that they could ride the wings of the Thunderbird to the edge of the universe together, and walk those five steps to the Spirit Path and into the Spirit World.

Using a simple gesture with her chin, Reva pointed to a silver Kachina figure on Julie's Dragger, which was a long piece of red ribbon framed with black and white ribbons, and decorated with various pieces of jewelry, attached to a black satin kerchief, where it lay draped over the back of a chair.

"I recognize that figure! That's a Lightning Kachina ennit! Tell me, is that part of your medicine?"

Julie focused on the bridge of the elderly woman's nose, careful to avoid looking directly into her eyes.

"Hahn,[59] Yes. Unci," she ventured, "you are called Ape Numpa,[60] ya? Am I wrong in thinking that, like me, you too have survived the touch of the Wakinyan Zitka[61] ya?"

"Ohan," Reva affirmed.

"Oh, cha, it hurts like hell, ennit," Julie commiserated."

"Hahn!" Reva smiled, nodding, remembering the pain of the strikings.

"Would you please tell me what happened, Unci?" Julie requested.

"I was very young," Reva explained. "I was in boarding school. That was the first time I was struck. I was riding my bicycle when a storm came in. It didn't seem like it would be anything more than a quick shower. I was hurrying to get back to school, when I felt myself surrounded by the Thunderbirds. I pedaled faster, but it was no use. Wakinyan Zitka entered my left shoulder and exited through my left thumb," Reva recounted, holding up her left hand, thumb upward. The end digit, which would have contained the thumbnail, was missing.

"It burned and I heard this eerie sound. I finally realized that it was me, keening. I was still pedaling my bike, and my left hand was fused to the handle. I finally made it to school where I was given help. I slept through the rest of the day.

"The second time, I was walking across the street to get our mail. It had started to drizzle, and I was afraid that our mail would get wet. I was married to Logan then," Reva offered. "I was just a few feet away from our mailbox, when a tree just a few feet from me was struck, and I fell to the ground. When I awoke, I was in my bed, and I couldn't use my left arm for a long time."

Reva sat for a moment, studying Julie. She liked her, and had already reached the conclusion that they possibly shared skinship. She was curious, but wanted to hear Julie's accounts first.

---

[59] Hanj – an informal form of Ohan or yes
[60] Ah-pay Noompah – Two Strikes
[61] Wah-keen-yahn-zheet-kah – The Thunderbird

"It isn't often that I meet another person who has been touched by the Thunderbirds. What happened to you?" Reva queried, leaning forward with anticipation.

"Wait, Unci, I have something for you." Julie said as she offered a small bag of tobacco to Reva.

Reva accepted the bag with a small, but satisfied smile. *This one knows how to do things right!* she thought to herself, while waiting for Julie's reply, settling herself more comfortably in her camp chair.

With a deep sigh, Julie began.

"Well, Unci, do you want the long or short version of how it happened?" Julie queried.

"Long!" all cried in unison, their excitement at hearing a new story clearly evident in their faces.

"Okay...well, it happened in late July of 1989, the same year that the village of Oglala was hit with that tornado. I had been back home to the rez for a week-long powwow at Brotherhood, and to visit my Tiyospiya about a week before my strike, and right after the tornado."

Reva interrupted,

"Yes, I remember that powwow! My daughter-in-law urged me to go and see my relatives. Was sure a good one, ennit! Them 'Ridger[62] boys from around the Porcupine area are pretty easy on the eyes, huh!" she chortled, as Lena looked at her grandmother in amazement.

I've never seen her like this, Lena whispered to herself, amazed.

"I'm old, not dead" retorted Reva seeing the stunned look in her granddaughters' eyes.

"Ya, I know ennit!" Julie continued with a coy grin. "Anyway, my ex-husband and I lived in a mobile home at the time, with our 2 kids, and out the back door was a HUGE old Oak tree and an empty lot between my trailer and the next one.[63] My poor neighbor had a great view of my living room window and back door, which I thought was kind of funny!

I was workin' on the laundry, a whole week's worth. I think it breeds once it reaches critical mass, cha! While we were at Brotherhood, I ran into my sister Karin Eagle, and her fiancée and their kids on the second day of the powwow. I had heard that she was living with some Arikira[64] guy somewhere in Wyoming, and had not talked to her in a few years, so you can imagine my surprise when she shows up with some Latino guy and a couple of kids in tow!

[62] A slang term for someone from Pine Ridge, or who has ancestors from Pine Ridge
[63] Begin dialog of Julie's lightning strikes provided by Julie Spotted Eagle Horse Two Strikes Martineau
[64] Ar-ih-kih-rah – an allied nation of the Sioux

"So long story short, Karin and Efram moved into my Lodge for the rest of the week. It was a stormy week, and them Heyokas[65] and Wicaca Wakankis[66] had their hands full just keeping the weather good enough to hold the powwow!

"I was camped by Tanikawin Blo,[67] and about ten yards away from the Dance Arbor. We had just gotten back from chasing a tornado to Gordon, Nebraska, and Efram decided to climb the ridge to check out the damage to the arbor and powwow grounds. There was still a lot of lightning happening, along with a rainbow that ended in a Choke Cherry bush, which all the NdNz thought was hilarious!" she chortled. "Of course, the wasicu get a pot of gold at the end of theirs, and us NdNz get a scraggly ole Choke Cherry bush!" Julie guffawed.

"Anyway, we got to talkin' about lightning, and the old-time Heyokas, and what they went through," Julie continued, referring to the fact that anyone who dreamed of the Thunder Beings while on their Vision Quest had to act in a contrary manner for a proscribed period of time. Their actions were dictated by the vision that they had and what the Holy Man interpreted from the Thunder beings.

"I had a funny feeling that something was important about our conversation and the Heyokas, but could not put my finger on what it was. I got home the following Monday after the powwow, and was doing my laundry a couple of days later. I was just getting ready to take the laundry out of the dryer so that I could dry another load.

"I heard a loud crash, and I can remember a bright, white light, like someone had lit the place up with a thousand halogen lamps. I had my right hand on the door of the dryer, and my left on top of it, when it happened. I could feel the power of the strike, and it was as if time had stopped. I counted the moments in the beating of my heart, and then it was over. I could smell ozone, and something like an electrical wire overheating. I knew that something was very wrong, You ever grab hold of a live one-ten wire?" Julie asked, looking at Lena. "Imagine that multiplied by a million, and that will give you some idea of the pain I felt in that instant!

"I called my ex at work, and told him that I thought that the trailer had been hit, and I had no idea of how to handle it. I then realized that my hands hurt like they had been burned, and my arms felt as if they were on fire. He asked if we were okay. I was so dazed that I told him that I thought that we were all right, but I wasn't sure. He asked if I

---

[65] Hey-oh-Ka – Laughs on the outside and cries in the inside. Chosen not self-appointed, they are considered holy people.

[66] Wee-chah-sha wah-kahn – Holy men

[67] Tdah-nee-kah-ween – Old Woman Hill or Old Woman Ridge

wanted him to come home, or if I needed to go to the hospital, and again I told him no.

"The next day, the neighbor came over and asked me if I knew anything about the weird lights that had surrounded the back door, outdoor power outlet, porch light and dryer vent the night before. I told her no, that I didn't know anything about it, but that I thought that the trailer had been hit by lightning, so we walked around back to see if there was any damage. There were what resembled scorch marks around the light fixture, outlet, door and dryer vent. I realized that there had been something like St. Elmo's fire or a ball lightning. I called my insurance agent, and he came right over to see for himself what happened.

"He told me that I had to go to the doctor to have my burns treated, and he would deal with the trailer. I refused to go, and insisted on treating my burns myself, although none of us had ever seen anything like them before. They resembled something like a fern pattern, and traced up both my forearms. After suffering with the burns and migraine for almost a week, I finally broke down and called the doctor. She insisted that I come in to be seen, so my ex got a neighbor to stay with the kids while I was at the clinic.

"It turns out that no one in the clinic had ever treated a lightning strike victim, and had no idea as to how to treat me, so they basically 'band-aided' my wounds and sent me to a neurologist. He had never treated a lightning victim either, but he was willing to listen to me and take my symptoms seriously.

"I had a whole battery of tests and blood work. Other than the burns and a few other minor things, I looked fine on paper, but his instincts told him that something was wrong, so he ordered a CT, MRI and EEG test done on me. They found minor burns in my brain, and I had some digestive problems, but nothing too serious there. Then they realized that I had burned off the myelin sheaths for my nerves in both forearms and the palms of my hands.

"I'll spare you the rest of the gory details, but I was given some antidepressants, a migraine medication, and something to help me sleep, since I could not sleep, no matter how tired I was.

"We later realized that the lightning had missed the metal siding on the trailer and the oak tree, and had entered the trailer through the metal roof, traveled down the wiring and plumbing for the washer and dryer, and somehow I completed the circuit, which caused me to get hit by lightning.

"About a year later in early October, we had bought a house, and I was sleeping in our water bed. A storm came up, and a bolt of lightning came in through the window of the bedroom and flashed over the water bed mattress, getting me in the process. I woke up, realized what was happening, and could only lie there, waiting for it to be over. I then rolled over and went back to sleep after taking stock of my body, realizing that I was not burned and would be ok.

"I called my sisters Sharon and Bekki, who were living in Des Moines at the time. They told me that I needed to go to Lodge and pray about it, so I made arrangements to go stay with them so that I could go to Lodge.

"Our Lodge Keeper lived in the Ames, Iowa area, so we had to leave almost as soon as I dropped off my clothes at Sharon's, since it was roughly an hour to get there. It turns out that I had several cousins there, and two of them were Sun Dancers.

"My cousin Paul had invited another cousin, Lester, to pour water for us, so I made my offering of tobacco to both of them, asking them if I could sweat. They both accepted, and very soon, my sisters and I were tying our prayer ties[68] in preparation for the ceremony to come.

"While we were getting ready to sweat, a storm moved in, and I knew I was in deep poo, as I was terrified of lightning. I was told that if I prayed and offered my pipe as I made my way from the house to the Lodge, I would be ok. It took a bit to convince me to walk out there, but I finally gave in. And ya know, I will never forget the sky that night. All around us, in each of the four directions, were sheets of lightning, but right above the Lodge the sky was clear!

"I was joking around with my friends about how I was NOT going to get the 'hot seat', you know," Julie said, nodding to Reva, "the seat directly across the pit, and cracking all kinds of bad jokes, then suddenly it was time to go into the Lodge. We were stacked in, two deep, and of course I was in the 'hot seat'," Julie said wryly, grimacing at the irony.

"As I settled into my seat, I realized that there was a prayer staff in front of me and on it was an owl feather.[69] I groaned and asked if anyone would be willing to trade places with me, with no takers, cha!" she chuckled. "Anyway, the ceremony started, and as we reached the Third Door,[70] our Water Pourer suddenly announced:

'There are two people here who have a connection to the storm outside of this Lodge. One of them claims to be Heyoka but they are not, while the other refuses to acknowledge the path before them.'

He then turned to our friend Mark and said:

---

[68] Small squares of cloth, about 1" square, usually made as a group: pinches of tobacco are placed in them while praying. Different colors have different meanings, and the color used depends on what is being prayed for. Participants also tie in the Altar colors of the Water Pourer. The number that you tie depends on what the Water Pourer tells you to tie.

[69] The owl is the messenger often used by hayokas.

[70] The third of the four doors or rounds of a sweat lodge ceremony

'Mark, you have a fascination with the Wakinyan, but you are not a Heyoka. That is not the path that you are meant to follow. Spot, YOU are the one who the Wangi are speaking of when they say that there is one here who is refusing the path before them. You need to stop and look at your actions today, in this sacred place, and tell me that you are not a Contrary.'

"Well, you can imagine my reaction to THAT!

"However, it was made clear to me that this was my path, and that I had no choice but to follow it, however unorthodox it may have been. Normally to become one of us, you must dream of the Wakinyan while on your Vision Quest, but I was never given that option.

"After the sweat, it was decided that there would be a naming ceremony, and three people would receive names. The first two were called out, and an Eagle plume was tied in their hair as they were given their new names, then my name was called. Lester told me that I was going to be given a Heyoka name that night.

"As my new name, Two Strikes, was announced, I realized that there would be no Eagle plume to tie into my hair. None was offered, and then I understood what it truly meant to be Heyoka. We are the ones who laugh while crying, the sacred fools who are both above and below the rules."

"Do you still have problems with injuries from the strike?" questioned Nickie.

"Ohan, yes, I do!" replied Julie. "I still can't sleep, and my memory is really bad! I also go through light bulbs, computer parts, TVs, and anything else electronic because of the strike!

"I still have pain issues, but have learned to compensate for my memory and pain over the years. I stopped taking all the meds, and now just take B vitamins for pain management and an over-the-counter pain reliever with a sleep aid to help me sleep at night. Oh, and I have post-it notes and notepads everywhere at home so that I can remember important things more easily!

"It's funny though," she continued, "my symptoms seem to change over time, new ones can appear, old ones disappear and some never quite seem to go away. My neurologist says that I am doing remarkably well, and he is astounded at how well I have learned to adapt to my limitations. I am one of the lucky ones, I had two indirect strikes, and I have relatively minor problems compared to some of my friends that belong to the Lightning Strike support group I belong to! Every day I thank Tunkasila for the new day, and I try to own my symptoms, rather than them owning me." she concluded with a sigh.[71]

---

[71] End dialog by Julie Spotted Eagle Horse Martineau

Lena realized that she had been sitting with her mouth open. Closing it abruptly, she attempted to digest all that she had seen and heard. Unci, giggling like a young girl, and then voicing appreciation of handsome, young men, the description of her lightning strikes and the easy manner which she had slipped into with Julie.

Lena was also in awe of what both women had endured. She had never thought about her unci's lightning strikes before. They were a part of everyday life, nothing unusual, just there, like the color of her hair and the remarkable color of her eyes. Her reverie was interrupted at the sound of her unci's voice.

"I too carry with me the marks of the Wakinyan Zitka," Reva continued.

"My left ear no longer receives the sounds of Creator's birds and my right ear rings like the old test pattern they used to have. You know, with the old Indian head on the TV screen," Reva chuffed. "My left arm often has spasms and my left hand is weak." Reva contemplated her left thumb, bereft of its last digit.

"There are nights when sleep evades me, and there is often a weakness on my left side," Reva continued, almost to herself. Lena was astounded. Never had she heard her unci voice these symptoms, and her admiration for the matriarch increased tremendously.

"But enough of that," Reva announced. Leaning forward, she playfully tapped Julie's knee with a bony finger.

"I wonder if we are related. What Oyate are you from?"

"Pesla, from over around Brotherhood. I'm one of the Young Bear cousins." Julie replied.

"Hey, some of your Tiyospiye are from Rosebud ya? Most of mine are too, and I have some family over on Pine Ridge, although we try to over look that, ennit! Not all of us can be Sicangus,"[72] Reva grinned as Julie rolled her eyes.

"My mother passed on the name of Wambli Gleska[73] to my son," she continued. "He was named in honor of his great grandfather, Nathaniel Spotted Eagle. Are you one of his Oyate?"

Julie nodded and smiled. "Yes Unci, he is my great-Uncle."

"Ohan! Lila Waste!" exclaimed Reva, clasping her hands together. "I knew we were related" she crowed. "You have a strong resemblance to that family!"

"Ya, I know" Julie replied, shaking her head and making a wry face. "I get that a lot!"

---

[72] Shee-kahn-gjoo – the name of the dominant group or "camp" that inhabits Rosebud. One of the Seven Camps of the Sioux Nation.
[73] Wahmblee Glay-shkah – Spotted Eagle

Once skinship was established, Julie felt comfortable with looking Reva directly in the eye, and felt free to offer her home for the Hunkapi.

"Unci," she offered, "I live about an hour north of here, and I have an inipi[74] set up at home. You are welcome to use both the Lodge and my home for the ceremonies."

Reva gazed at Julie with gratitude. She had planned to ask Joe Red Bear for the use of his lodge, but he was called away suddenly to help a relative in South Dakota. This would solve her problem nicely and allow her to get to know this fascinating young kinswoman better.

"Ohan," Reva nodded. "I will be grateful and honored."

The air was ripe with moisture and sat heavy upon the sweat lodge, located in the middle of the long backyard behind the small house of Julie Spotted Eagle Horse. Her husband, Matthew, whom she jokingly referred to as her "token cowboy," was acting as the Door Keeper for the Lodge, and was getting ready to transfer the large stones, which had been heating all day, into the central pit of the sweat lodge. As it was a woman's lodge, no men would be entering it with them, but they were permitted to act as Door Keepers and Helpers.

Julie was overseeing the feast that would follow, and greeting the guests who were arriving for this most solemn occasion.

As relatives, Julie and Reva held mutual status, and Julie was therefore free to invite various relatives and friends for the occasion. Lena was in awe as she was introduced to one relative after another. Julie, ever gracious, tried not to overwhelm the girl, but felt that she needed as much exposure to her culture as possible.

Earlier that afternoon, Julie invited Lena to her bedroom.

"Cha!" she exclaimed, "I have some things I would like for you to see," Julie said, as she started toward the back of the four-room house.

Smiling, Lena acquiesced and followed Julie to her small, but neat, sleeping chamber.

As they entered, Lena touched Julie's shoulder and offered, "I guess you're interested in my unusual eye color."

"Ohan, yes." Julie affirmed. "Your eyes are quite beautiful and remarkable."

Lena explained to Julie the condition, called sectoral heterochromia iridis.

"I remember the first time my mother noticed," she remembered, "She actually gasped!" Lena laughed.

"I can only imagine that your mother was quite surprised." Julie responded.

---

[74] Inipi – Ee-nee-pee - Sweat lodge

Lena nodded and offered,

"So, you wanted to show me something?" ending the conversation graciously. Smiling, Julie linked her arm in Lena's, and drew her to a chest of drawers which stood near a window. The subject was finished, but Julie's thoughts continued her contemplation of the amazing gift Creator had bestowed upon the lovely girl.

Mentally shrugging, Julie pulled out a jewel box, and began to show Lena different belts and purses executed in exquisite beadwork. There were knife sheaths and chokers, roaches and earrings, all done with the same superb artistry.

Lena examined each article with awe, exclaiming over their design, colors, and the mastery of workmanship.

"Most of what you see has either been handed down over the generations through my family, or has been made by myself or Matthew," Julie explained.

Lena nodded, a look of admiration in her exquisite eyes.

Julie watched Lena carefully, and clearing her throat, posed the question,

"Lena, how much about The People do you know?"

Lena gazed into Julie's eyes for a few seconds before answering:

"There aren't many of us in Ohio, so I don't know as much as I'd like to. My mother has taught me many things, but she left the reservation so young: she was only sixteen. My father works, or used to work, sixteen-hour days until his accident. Still," Lena continued, "my parents have made sure that I understand the ways of The People, our prayers and beliefs, and how to walk the Good Red Road. They have taught me to walk *with* the earth and not just upon it. But I want to learn more, you know? I've enjoyed being here and filling my soul with these experiences."

Julie smiled. She had guessed as much, and was pleased with Lena's honest answer.

"Watch tonight, wincincila,[75] and you will learn much. Now, to the kitchen! Where are Vicki and Nickie? We are gonna need help! This is a Lakota house, and no one must go unfed!"

It was late afternoon. Julie prepared to smudge herself and the surroundings, in order to prepare for the ceremonies about to take place. Carrying a smoldering bowl filled with sacred grasses, Julie walked to the center of the enclosure where the Naming Ceremony, Sweat Lodge Ceremony and Hunkapi were to be held.

---

[75] Ween-cheen-chee-lah – young woman or young lady, often applied as a term of endearment

Lena remembered her mother performing this exact cleansing before they entered the sweat lodge to pray for her father. The scent of cedar needles, wild sage, wild sweet grass and tobacco brought back vivid memories.

Julie "bathed" herself with the fragrant fumes, facing the west, north, east and then south, and then kneeling upon the ground, ending her prayer by raising the bowl to the sky. The area was now sanctified, and the next ceremony could proceed.

Reva and Vicki sat upon the ground facing each other, legs crossed comfortably. This was the Naming Ceremony where Vicki would receive her NdN name.

Reva's eyes closed as she prepared to announce her choice of name, inspired by The Grandfather's, after many hours of meditation.

Opening her eyes slowly, Reva gazed into Vicki's wide orbs.

"Vicki will be known as Ina Waste Otawin[76] Good Mother of Many. You have shown a great heart in taking my family in as your own, and have assured that we received the care we needed. I have seen you feed the homeless and the struggling students. You have shown special care for my son, and I have watched as you have taught my granddaughter, Lena. The Spirits call you Ina Waste Otawin, Good Mother of Many, and so will we from now on."

Vicki and Reva rose, and made their way to the sweat lodge, a dome shaped-tent, erected earlier that day above a deeply dug hole. Water was poured upon the heated rocks, which Julie's husband had placed within the sweat lodge in preparation of the ceremony.

Lavender was sprinkled upon them, so that its smoke would relax those within the lodge. Julie lead the Sweat Lodge Ceremony, explained its purpose and progression, and at intervals requested specific prayers be offered up to Creator. Holding a canumpa, or pipe, and passing it, Julie murmured a prayer. The heat increased within the dome-shaped lodge, and Lena began to feel light-headed.

"Now we must pray for someone other than ourselves," Julie commanded, and various prayers were offered up. Lena prayed for her father to continue to improve. Looking toward the top of the dome at the prayer ties attached to the framework of the inipi, she wondered if Zitka Mine would show up again and carry her up into the darkening sky.

The prayers finished, the ceremony ended, and everyone exited into a cooling night, thankful for a slight breeze upon their sweat-soaked brows.

Stepping out of the lodge, Reva took a star quilt, and wrapped it around Vicki's shoulders, then tied a hand dyed imitation eagle plume to her hair. Turning toward the relatives and guests, she announced,

---

[76] Ee-nuh Wash-tday oh-tdaween – Good Mother of Many

"I take this one as my daughter. We have a bond through Hantewin[77] and now she is my daughter. The spirits say that I am to make her my family. And so, Vicki, you are now my daughter who will be known as Ina Waste Otawin." Reva announced, as Julie prayed over them with the canumpa pipe.

Traditionally, she would have tied an eagle plume to her new daughter's hair, but since it is illegal for a non-Native individual, someone not listed on the tribal census of a Federally recognized Indian Tribe, to own one, an imitation feather was substituted. Reva then handed a lovely fan of macaw feathers to Vicki as part of the ritual. The Hunkapi Ceremony was now completed.

Julie stepped forward and motioned for Lena to stand before her. Surprising everyone, she tied an eagle plume in Lena's hair and announced,

"This is Ista Wambli-Win, Woman with the Eyes of an Eagle."

Lena gasped, pleased and awed by the sound of her newest NdN name.

Julie turned to the guests and proclaimed,

"This is Hantewin Ista Wambli-Win." She then handed Lena a fan of Hawk feathers, and placed a star quilt around her shoulders. Smiling into Lena's extraordinary eyes, Julie intoned, "Waste. Lila waste."

---

[77] Hahnz-tday ween – Cedar Woman

66

Chapter Ten

Half Side

Walking the path
of my ancestors,
I bow to tradition,
And become Sioux once more.

Seeking, but not knowing
What it is I seek,
I search within myself
And find only a longing.

A chance encounter
Reveals a destiny,
In the touch of a hand....
The flash of a smile.

Our eyes meet across the arena,
I duck my head...
Knowing but not seeing,
What lies before me.

Love at first sight,
Thought to be a myth,
I find myself confronted
With a glorious truth.

A sacred touch
From the Creator above,
Two souls become one
And Half Sides are found.

Julie Spotted Eagle Horse Martineau

Lena sat outside of Julie's tipi, a cup of Starbuck's coffee nestled within the palms of her hands. Dawn was just breaking, and a sky of china blue and tender pink was beginning to emerge.

Dreamily searching the heavens, her breath caught within her throat. A single, white cloud, edged in pink, contained a smudge of apricot, as if Creator had wet his thumb and smeared the upper layer of the cloud to reveal the tender pastel color beneath. The effect was that of stained glass: ethereal, tender, unworldly.

Was it an omen? What did today hold for her? Lena felt a sense of urgency, a feeling of expectancy. The very air was full of portent.

Her path is not just with The People, Julie thought to herself. *My path is here, learning the ways, living my life here among my own kind, but this wincincila will walk with all people.*

Julie stood at the opening of her tipi, watching Lena as she gazed into the tender dome of Heaven. An overwhelming feeling of change washed over the stately matron. Turning to enter her lodge, Julie paused and looked again toward Lena. She gave an inward gasp. Lena sat within a nimbus of light, her beautiful hair floating on the fragrant morning air.

Lena and Nickie placed their powwow shawls over their shoulders, being careful not to allow the fringe to touch the ground. The Wopila, or Thank You Ceremony, in which Vicki would express her thanks to her new family for her adoption, was about to begin.

Vicki was already in the arena with Reva. Reva wore a blue shawl with red trim, the scarf beaded with chevrons and thunderbirds, which she had made shortly after her first lightning strike, and Vickie was in a beautiful shawl of pink and yellow, with beaded butterflies, made for her by Reva in anticipation of the Wopila.

Lena and Nickie, along with Julie, took their places near the front of an ever-growing line of family members, who wished to dance in support of their new kinswoman. Soon The Drum would begin the beat and sing a song in celebration of a new relative. A young man ascended the podium and leaned into the microphone.

"Hello, everyone. I am Sonny Glass, your narrator for this joyous occasion. We are here to celebrate the Making of Relatives Ceremony, culminated here today in the Wopila, or Giving Thanks Celebration."

Standing at 5'11", with long, blue-black hair, Sonny was a striking figure in a white cotton shirt, turquoise bolo tie and jeans. Polished Western boots and a black cattleman cowboy hat caused many a young woman present to catch her breath in awe. His deep, brown eyes sparkled with humor and intelligence as he deftly held the crowd with his deep, resonant voice.

"For those of you here who are not NdN, I will explain what is happening here today," Sonny continued, his voice melodic, his manner regal.

"Since the first memories, it has always been such: if a loved one was lost through death, or moved away, it was not uncommon for an individual, or a family, to adopt someone to fill the empty place left by the departed family member. Similarly, if a person had no siblings, or family members, the situation could be remedied through the same means.

"The Making of Relatives Ceremony, or Hunkapi, was celebrated last night, and is a rite not entered into lightly and meant to last for life.

"Today we witness the celebration of the adoption of a daughter, and she is here today to show her thanks to her new family."

The crowd surrounding the showground applauded, and watched as the formed group began to proceed around the arena in time to the beat of the powwow drum, Vicki and Reva in the lead.

In slow procession, they progressed. Vicki held a straw hat into which those wishing to congratulate her, dropped money.

"Congratulations," they said. Vicki replied, "Wopila," in return.

Around the arena, they danced two, three, then four times. The Drum ceased and Vicki walked to the group of men surrounding it, offering them the collected money with her left hand, the hand closest to her heart. She and Reva, Lena, Nickie and Julie then strode to a blanket spread upon the arena floor where gifts were presented to anyone who wished to partake of Vicki's offerings.

There were Styrofoam gliders in the shape of birds, Frisbees and toy binoculars for the children, quilt squares of cloth in the four sacred colors, tied with raffia for those in the crowd who liked to sew, tobacco for the Head Man and Sonny and candy for The Drum to "ease their throats." A simple quilt, lovely in its lack of pretension, was presented to the Head Woman, and a special gift that Vicki brought, completely on a hunch: a stuffed-toy lamb, which she presented to a two-year-old child who had performed his first dance in the arena the day before.

Lena noticed that no one was greedy. Each chose one gift, then approached Reva and Vicki.

"Wopila," they each said, smiling, some adding, "Welcome to our family."

Lena hurried to Julie's lodge. Throwing herself into its dusky interior, she flung herself upon the ground. Hands pressed against her flaming cheeks, she fought for control.

Her mind went back to the arena, the Wopila, to the blanket where she stood with her family to welcome Vicki's new relatives.

Lena was enjoying herself tremendously. Vicki and Reva's happiness was apparent as they beamed at each other, and each person who approached them to offer their welcome. Lena was very fond of Vicki. No, she loved Vicki, and was happy and proud to welcome her into her family.

Vicki was good to Lena and her parents and grandmother. She made sure that the family earned a decent wage in order to be able to survive in comfort and to accord Peter the special care his condition required. She was like a second mother to Lena, so it was appropriate that she formally became just that. For, by becoming the sister of Mary, Lena's mother, Vicki also became Lena's mother, as the Lakota did not recognize aunts and uncles as such – at least not traditionally. A parent's siblings were also considered the parents of any children born within the family.

When Vicki learned of this, she wept with joy. Taking Lena's beautiful face within her hands, she kissed her forehead and both cheeks, whispering,

"I finally have a child." Lena was touched.

She knew that Vicki cared for her, but did not realize the depth of Vicki's affection until that moment.

A slight breeze kicked up, and the smell of rain rode upon the puff of air. Lena gazed into the sky. Cumulus clouds now filled the china blue expanse of Creator's heavens. The feeling of portent overwhelmed her for the second time that day, and she felt a shiver run down her spine.

She could tell that he was beside her before any of her earthly senses: sight, hearing, smell, taste or touch, told her so. She just *knew*. She found it difficult to breathe, and a trembling coursed throughout her body. Turning slowly, her head bowed in confusion, she found herself gazing at a pair of exquisitely beaded moccasins. Little by little, she allowed her gaze to move up and up, her heart beating with such tremendous force, that the pulsation of the fabric of her white, cotton blouse bore witness to its frantic pounding. Before her was the regalia admired just two days before. Up, up, a strong, tanned throat, dark, flowing hair. She saw the flash of a brilliant smile. It was *him*. It was the Grass Dancer!

She heard him say,

"Congratulations," heard Vicki's happy reply,

"Wopila,"

and he moved on.

There was a slight release of tension, but she could feel that he was still looking at her, his gaze focused upon her and her alone.

She couldn't breathe! As soon as the Wopila was over, Lena walked rapidly from the arena and made her way to cover, like a rabbit searching for a burrow in which to hide.

Lila Waste Winyan,[78] Michael Young Bear breathed to himself. She caught his eye two days before, and he looked for her the following day, his disappointment in being unable to locate her surprising him. Now, here she was again, and a feeling of protectiveness, possessiveness and, yes, passion, overwhelmed him.

The scene of only a few hours before played out before him: approaching her cautiously, stopping beside her, and being unsure of what to do, his nervous smile freezing as she looked up, meeting his gaze, giving him full view of her magnificent eyes.

Michael Spirit of the Grass Young Bear sat cross-legged on a patch of lawn in front of his cousin Sonny's tipi. To say that he was in a state of shock would be an understatement. In fact, Michael was shaken to the very core of his being.

He knew that she was in the tipi across from Sonny's. He had seen her fly into the entrance of the lodge like a rabbit running from a predator.

Did she feel the same thing I did there in the arena? he wondered to himself.

Upon approaching the family standing behind the gift-strewn blanket, with the mere intention of congratulating them on the adoption of a new relative, he saw what he thought was a small child standing at the far edge of the group. Stopping and waiting for her to notice him, he murmured,

"Congratulations."

As she turned, he realized that she was, in fact, the young woman who caught his attention the first day of the powwow. Surprised and intrigued, Michael waited patiently as she slowly raised her eyes. *Was she trembling?* he wondered? *How could I tell?* he answered himself, *for the moment her eyes touched mine, even for that brief second, I was lost.*

Michael had never been in love before. Oh, there were crushes and infatuations, and Michael dated his share of women, both NdN and wasicu, but these soul-shattering emotions were new to him. It was if she was already a part of him, his heart, his soul, his very breath.

Michael Young Bear was a tall, attractive man of the Lakota, his oyate of the Wiacca Sinte[79] or Tail Feather People.

---

[78] Lee-lah Washtay Ween-yan – Lovely young woman
[79] wee-ah-kah sheen-tay – Tail Feather People

Standing six feet, with long, glossy black hair and deep, dark, brown eyes, his chiseled features and muscular body reminded many of the iconic actor, Christopher Reeve. Michael was unaware of his outward beauty. His awareness of himself was inward, rather than wrapped up in his appearance. Carefully planned, his regalia represented his dancing and included designs and symbols which reflected, not only his chosen dance as a grass dancer, but his family as well. How he looked in it, as far as women were concerned, never entered his mind.

Albeit only twenty-two, Michael led a frequently examined life, reflecting on his relationships with family and friends, even to his most inward thoughts and emotions.

He gazed at the tipi into which Lena had fled. *She is but a little bird*, he reflected, unknowingly using her childhood name as a metaphor. *So small...so delicate...so beautiful.*

Michael sat and watched the doorway of Julie's lodge, waiting for *her* to appear again. Waiting...waiting.

Sonny stood within the opening of his lodge and contemplated Michael. He knew what was going on in his young cousin's mind. He had seen Michael's reaction when Lena turned and finally looked into his eyes. Michael gave a start, and although Sonny could not hear it as far away as the podium, he could sense the gasp emanating from his young cousin's throat.

Sonny fully understood. His reaction mirrored his cousin's the first time he beheld the exquisite eyes and tender, diminutive form of the beautiful young woman Michael now sat patiently waiting for.

Sonny Steals the Song Glass, son of Emma and Emmit Glass, and a descendant of the Red Leaf People, was nephew to Julie and cousin to Michael. Sons of two of Julie's sisters, they shared many characteristics, as well as childhood memories. In fact, they were as brothers and were devoted to each other.

Sonny was deeply disturbed. The moment he laid eyes upon Lena, he knew in his heart that she was the only love of his life. Then he witnessed the meeting of Michael and the incomparable young girl – and his heart broke.

Chapter Eleven

Men should look upon the Woman with a Sacred Eye.
She should be respected.
The Woman is a role model for love.
When the Woman talks, we should listen;
When she shares, we should be grateful.
We should all learn about each other.
Grandmother, teach me to love with the power of the woman.

Lakota Proverb

Reva entered the lodge shortly after the Wopila ended, only to find Lena hunkered down on the floor, rocking – her hands cradling her flaming cheeks.

"Cha!" she exclaimed. "What are you, a mere child who runs away the minute an adult enters a room? Get up. There, that is better," Reva affirmed upon Lena's slowly rising to stand in front of her grandmother.

"Why are you here huddled like a frightened animal, when there is the powwow to enjoy?" Reva queried.

Lena looked into her grandmother's eyes, her own exquisite orbs shimmering with unshed tears.

"Because of…him," she quivered, limply raising her right hand and pointing toward the opening of the tipi. The tears began to flow.

"Who him?" Reva asked.

"Him," Lena repeated weakly, again pointing toward the circular section of sunlight.

Reva walked to the opening and peered out toward Sonny's lodge.

"Sitting or standing?" Reva questioned.

"There are two of them?" Lena asked, rushing to her grandmother's side.

Looking toward Sonny's tipi, Lena could see Sonny standing in the doorway and Michael sitting in the grass. Both were staring toward Julie's lodge, and both gave a start as Lena's small, tear-stained face peered out. Lena jumped back and ran to the center of the tipi.

"Ah," Reva breathed with satisfaction, "my granddaughter has captured the hearts of two very attractive men.

"Sitting or standing?" Reva inquired again.

"Sitting," Lena whispered.

Reva peered across the lawn toward Michael and made little smacking sounds with her lips.

"I wouldn't tell him no, that's for sure," she affirmed. "Yes, he could get anyone excited under the blankets."

"Unci!" Lena cried with surprise.

73

Her grandmother continued to surprise her again and again, as she left the stoic façade she usually presented to the world behind, to continually shock her granddaughter.

"Do I look to you like I have ridden on the wing of Thunderbird?" Reva asked with consternation.

"I am still a living woman, and I can appreciate a nice piece of man flesh when I see it." Reva dropped the flap and walked over to her granddaughter.

"Lena," she whispered, "you can't run away from something such as this," Reva counseled, pointing with her lips toward the tipi opening.

Reva gazed with intense love upon her granddaughter. She understood what was going through Lena's heart. She was afraid to love.

Reva did not see the ever-growing love between her son and Mary after they left the reservation. Her reunion with her son was after his accident. But Dean and Nellie both bore witness to the love of Mary and Peter upon their frequent visits to Columbus to see how Peter was improving.

What a beautiful thing it must be to see such love between your parents, Reva mused. *Perhaps, however, this is what is causing my granddaughter's dilemma. She is an eyewitness of an incredible love between a man and a woman and the pain caused by her father's accident. Surely, she sees the strengthening of that love – the beauty of her parent's devotion to each other.*

Reva pulled her takoja[80] into her arms and held her close to her heart.

"Little Bird, it will be all right." Reva murmured tenderly.

"Wakan Tanka smiles upon the love of a man and woman. Do not fear love, Granddaughter. You are about to enter the most important phase of your life," Reva murmured gently. Pulling away from Lena, she squared her shoulders and nodded.

"Come, it is time for the broom dance. Let's have some fun. Maybe I'll find a nice, handsome man to dance with," she teased, then clucked at Lena's surprised expression. Shaking her head, Reva took Lena by the hand and led her out of the lodge.

Lena and Reva proceeded to the arena. Michael and Sonny shot into action, following the two women to the enclosed area where the broom dance was to take place. Sonny veered away from Michael, guilt filling his heart.

I'm acting like a fool, he thought to himself, and he felt shamed by his actions.

---

[80] Ki-dah-koh-zhah - Grandchild

Boy Ladd walked up to Sonny and threw a strong, sinewy arm around his friend's shoulders.

"We need an ugly man, ennit," he laughed, "and you're it tonight," Boy Ladd guffawed, handing Sonny a ragged broom.

Tradition has it that a young man of a less than attractive countenance invented the Broom Dance. Tired of sitting out dance after dance at the various powwows he attended, he fashioned a woman out of straw and began to dance with her. His appearance with his "young lady" caused quite a stir of hilarity, and soon the young men around him began to take his partner from him. Thus, the Broom Dance was born.

Sonny looked at the broom in his left hand. He wasn't in the mood for frivolity, but there he was, obviously chosen to be the ugly man. To leave the arena would cause embarrassment to all involved.

What the hell, he thought. *Perhaps it will get my mind off of a wincincila who has stolen the heart of me **and** my cousin,* Sonny thought with pain.

He walked to the center of the arena as couples began to form around him.

The Broom Dance, or Ugly Man Dance, was a variety of tag. Couples would form a circle around the central figure, the broom-wielding ugly man. Hands held and crossed in front of them, they would dance to the beat of The Drum around the arena. The object of this dance was for the woman to protect her man, and the ugly man to "tag" him with the broom. If he was successful, he would get to partner the woman, and the "tagged" dancer then became the ugly man.

Sonny waited patiently for the ring of couples to form. The sun was beginning its slow descent to the west and the day was a bit cooler than it had been at noon. He could smell Indian Tacos in the air, and realized suddenly that he was hungry.

Cha, he thought to himself, *I was so wrapped up in that beautiful girl, that I forgot to eat.* Sonny pulled a bandanna from his pocket and wiped his damp brow.

What is her name? I don't know her name!

Lena walked to the edge of the arena with her grandmother. She knew that *he* was behind her somewhere, but was afraid to turn around and look. Her grandmother's words, spoken moments earlier in Julie's lodge, had not reached her heart, residing still in her brain, tumbling over and over each other like so many peas in a boiling pot. Julie saw Lena and Reva approach, and walked to them, noticing as she did, the handsome young man who stopped just behind Lena.

75

Julie peered closely at the two beautiful, young people, and noticed something, which she had only seen once before in her life, as she had observed Lena that morning. Lena stood within a nimbus of light.

Boy Ladd stepped to the mike.

"As you see, I have replaced our illustrious emcee tonight to announce the Ugly Man Dance," he stated.

"Sonny, you will notice, is the ugly man: a role to which he is well suited."

Laughter filled the air as Sonny hugged the broom to his chest, kissing the fanned out bristles in mock romantic passion.

Julie's eyes began to twinkle, as an idea formed in her mind. Placing her right hand between Lena's shoulder blades, and grabbing Michael's hand with her left, she pushed the young girl into the arena, while pulling Michael to stand beside her.

"Defend your man!" she called as Michael, quick to understand her intention, grabbed Lena by the hands and began to dance around the arena.

Lena tried to control her trembling, but it was impossible. She couldn't breathe, and her thoughts whirled around in her head like a bird trapped in a cage which it couldn't escape.

He was holding her hands, and the searing touch of his skin against hers was more than she could bear.

She could feel his shoulder, his hip, his thigh against hers, as they processed around the arena in dosido fashion.

"Little Bird, you must protect me from the ugly man," Michael teased. He held his breath. He had yet to hear her voice. Somehow, he knew that she would sound like a songbird. Her voice would be beautiful to his ears.

I have waited for you all of my life, he thought to himself. *I did not know that I was waiting, but I was....for you.*

Strangely, his voice brought her some calm. Somehow, it's very timber reached into the depths of her being, filled her ears and her body, and her heart began to slow. She sucked in a deep breath, fully realizing Michael's own unique scent.

My God, she realized, *even his scent fills my soul.* Reva's words, residing still in Lena's brain, slipped into her heart, and she understood.

76

Chapter Twelve

Hold On

Hold on to what is good,
Even if it's a handful of earth.
Hold on to what you believe,
Even if it's a tree that stands by itself.
Hold on to what you must do,
Even if it's a long way from here.
Hold on to your life,
Even if it's easier to let go.
Hold on to my hand,
Even if someday I'll be gone away from you.

A Pueblo Indian Prayer

Sonny held the broom in his arms and continued his comedic display. Through deft slight-of-hand, he removed his bolo tie and used the leather cord to slap himself on the cheek, as if he'd made an inappropriate advance to his "lady," and she had reprimanded him. Sonny feigned shock, and then bowing to his partner, mimicked an apology.

The crowd laughed with pure enjoyment. Sonny was popular among the powwow organizers for his incredible presence, wit and spontaneity. Sonny was not afraid to make a fool of himself, and therefore, never did. He was pure entertainment.

Conversely, when the occasion called for solemnity, Sonny was your man. His dignity and sense of the appropriate was unsurpassed on the powwow circuit.

The circle of couples quickened their steps as they processed around the arena. There was a feeling of high humor as the dancers laughed at Sonny's antics. The general consensus was that this was going to be one of the best broom dances ever.

Sonny stepped into an exaggerated waltz, while still dancing to the beat of The Drum. It was an odd mixture, to say the least, and extremely entertaining. Swaying, circling, and gliding with his "woman," he executed an elegant dip, and surreptitiously glanced around the circle. Spotting an old friend, he began to work his way toward the amused couple.

Nick was a handsome, jovial man of Cherokee decent. A certified Emergency Medical Technician, or EMT, he would bring a Medic Unit to the powwows he attended, sitting patiently within the vehicle, explaining the use of the various pieces of equipment contained within to any child or adult who would inquire. He saw Sonny coming toward him, guffawed in delight, and swung his partner in front of him.

Sonny, in true Fred Astair fashion, placed the wooden end of the broom on the ground and gave it a spin. With his right foot, he kicked the end of the broom, close to the ground, flipped it upward, and caught it mid handle. He thrust it toward Nick, but his aim was blocked by the laughing dancer's partner. A jingle dancer, the bells on her costume gave out a merry tinkle as they swung by Sonny and on to safety.

Sonny turned to the right and spotted a middle-aged couple. The woman covered her mouth, an old habit to hide her bad teeth, and giggled. Sonny recognized her: her beadwork was beyond compare and highly sought after. Her husband, an accomplished auto-mechanic, chortled as he watched Sonny approach. He twirled his wife under his right arm and swung her into place.

Broom held at an angle, Sonny now strummed it as if it were a guitar. Making chicken neck movements with his head, he swooped toward the couple and lunged. Squealing with delight, the woman thrust her ample body in front of her husband's, thus saving him from being tagged.

Sonny dropped the broom and looked dejected.

"Cha, beautiful one, do you not wish to dance with me?" he begged, side skipping to keep up with the couple. The woman, once again covering her mouth and blushing, laughed with pleasure.

Sonny retrieved his broom and again began his search for his next victim. That's when he saw.... her.

All sound stopped. Birdsong, laughter, the rustle of trees – ceased. There was only...her.

Dressed in a simple, sleeveless, white cotton blouse tucked into stone-washed jeans, her small, exquisite form stood out among the other women in the arena. Long, silky, black hair, parted in the middle and falling to her hips, danced in the cooling, slight breeze which wafted over the arena. Her magnificent, tip-tiled eyes sparkled in the dying light of the day.

Her throat was a column, smooth and creamy, embraced by a turquoise necklace which ended in a pendant and nestled between small, perfect breasts.

Her full, shell-pink lips were slightly parted; she appeared to be breathing heavily, as if in the throes of love-making. Sonny was undone.

Michael moved into view, and as if claiming ownership, encircled her tiny waist with one strong, muscular arm. Sonny picked up the broom, hefted it as if in battle and charged.

78

He was aiming for Michael, but at the last-minute, Lena stepped in front of him to protect him from being tagged. By observing the other dancers, she knew that she was supposed to protect her partner.

In an instant, Sonny realized that he would, in fact, hit Lena and possibly injure her, but it was too late to stop. Michael realized that Sonny's advance was too aggressive; Lena could be hurt.

Michael lifted Lena from the floor of the arena and spun her around just in time. The broom flew by her and landed on the floor of the arena.

"Cha, Brother! What are you doing?" Michael exclaimed in a whisper, so that no one else could hear.

Sonny was mortified. He needed a quick excuse…something…no one could know of his passion for this delectable girl.

"Brother," he apologized, "my foot slipped on the dew-covered grass." Sonny looked at his cousin and gave a shame-faced, lopsided grin. Michael looked closely at Sonny, confused, but he was so captivated by his new love, that he did not possess the ability to look beyond the surface of his brother/cousin's actions. Smiling, Michael clapped Sonny on the back and laughed.

"You almost got me, ugly man, ennit!" Michael chortled, and walked off to join Lena.

Sonny picked up the broom and watched his cousin take her by the hand and walk into the deepening darkness. His heart again broke, as a single tear traced its way down his cheek. Sonny brusquely brushed it away, straightened his back, put on a smile, and turning, started to dance with the broom.

Julie watched as Michael and Lena walked toward her lodge, hand-in-hand. She noted that Lena still walked within a cloak of light – and wondered.

Michael drew Lena into his arms and bent to kiss her full, sensuous lips. She tilted her face toward his, all of her fears gone. Complete trust was implicit in her action.

Their lips touched. Michael drank from her sweet, moist mouth as from a cool, clear stream, a stream from which the water did not quench his thirst, but, in fact, increased it. Lena's wondrous hair floated on the cooling breeze and brushed Michael's cheek. He breathed her in, reveling in her unique scent, making it part of his heart, his very soul.

Reluctantly, he ended the kiss, but held the embrace. He cradled her in his arms, his heart full, his spirit soaring.

"We must be married, Little Bird," he whispered.

Lena stood within the circle of his arms, trusting, loving, happy. Her heart lifted at his words and she marveled at the fact that she could love this man so deeply, so quickly. A thought came to Lena, and she gave a start.

"What is it Winyan Mita?[81]" Michael asked with alarm.

"I don't even know your name, Wicasa Mita,[82]" she replied with a chuckle. Lena gazed into Michael's eyes with adoration and he into hers.

"Nor I yours," Michael replied, love filling his voice.

"I am Michael," he offered.

"Michael," Lena repeated.

"Say it again," Michael begged.

"Michael."

He smiled his love, worship in his eyes.

"And what is yours, Little Bird?"

Lena gazed at the tall, beautiful man in her arms, her love beaming from her exquisite eyes.

"That is my infant name," she offered. "My father called me that as a child. My name is Lena," she offered in a whisper.

"Lena," Michael repeated, looking toward the deep, velvet sky.

"Lena," he repeated, drawing the syllables out, as if tasting her name on his tongue and savoring its flavors.

"Lena."

Julie, Vicki and Reva approached the lodge slowly. Michael and Lena's silhouettes clearly seen in the moonlight, their bodies were as one, joined as they were in a tight embrace.

Reva gave a cough and the couple slowly disengaged, as if mesmerized and unaware of their surroundings. Michael whispered a question to Lena.

"Unci," she replied. Michael whispered again.

"Catcher, Reva Catcher," Lena answered.

Taking Lena's hand in his, Michael approached Reva.

"Mrs. Catcher," he began, "I will return shortly."

Michael turned, and kissing Lena on the tip of her nose, walked to Sonny's lodge and entered. He quickly exited and returned to where Reva was standing. Extending his left hand, the one closest to his heart, he offered an eagle feather and a pouch of tobacco.

"I would like to marry your granddaughter," he said softly, "tonight."

Lena and Michael stood outside of the lodge. Reva, Vicki and Julie were inside, and the murmur of conversation wafted through the circular

---

[81] Win-yan Meeta – My Woman
[82] Wee-cha-sha Meeta – My Man

opening of the tipi. Michael tried to hide his anxiety, but Lena could feel it. It amazed her that, within a space of but a few hours, she could feel and sense Michael's every mood. It was as if he were a part of her, like her arm, or leg, or...heart.

Julie stepped into the lantern-lit circle and signaled for them to enter.

Reva stood in the center of the lodge, her hands clasped in front of her. Lena peered into her grandmother's face with trepidation. It was important to receive the blessing of the family before a couple were joined – what if Unci refused to bless the union!

Lena walked closer, her eyes fixed anxiously on her grandmother's face. Unci was...why, she was smiling!

Reva approached the young couple, and taking Lena and Michael's left hands into hers, brought them together, placing Michael's hand on top of Lena's.

"Spotted Eagle Horse has convinced me that you are in love and should be wed," Reva intoned. "However, your father is not here to give his blessing.

"I, as his mother and elder, will speak in his behalf and give that blessing." She turned to Lena, "Your parents met on their wedding day, and their love is a beautiful thing to witness. It is a blessing when half sides meet and are joined, without family censure, as we join you today."

Reva stepped back and Julie forward.

"Lena," she began, "you are not yet 18, and must have a parent's permission to marry. In addition, there is no time for a license. You are leaving tomorrow, Ohan?"

Lena nodded, her heart sinking.

"However, I can join you tonight in the old way, and you can legalize your marriage after you have obtained a marriage license."

Lena and Michael looked at each other with joy. Julie approached them, and taking a strip of red trade cloth, joined their hands together. She walked to a chest situated at the perimeter of the tipi, opened the lid, and withdrew a star quilt. Returning to the couple, she wrapped the quilt around them. She returned to the chest and withdrew two eagle plumes and a pipe. Standing before the couple, she handed a plume to each. Michael tied his feather to Lena's hair and she, in turn to Michael's. Lena turned to Julie.

"Please, could we go outside? I would like to be married under the stars." She turned to Michael, who smiled his agreement.

The evening was soft and fragrant. Shimmering moonlight lent a majestic quality to the night. Julie took a deep breath, enjoying the fragrance of the dew-tipped grass.

It was a good choice to come outside, she thought to herself.

The small group re-assembled and the ceremony commenced.

Julie began to pray in the language of The People:

"Grandfather, Great Spirit, it is me, Two Strikes. Have pity on me. I am pitiful; I am small.

"This couple has come to me with good hearts, and with love for each other. They see each other as a half side and wish to walk their life roads together.

"Bless these two people. Grant them the wisdom to see that it takes two hearts to work together.

"Tunksila[83] Wakan Tanka, we offer smoke and we ask that the smoke carry the prayers skyward that they may be heard."

Julie turned to Michael:

"Spirit of the Grass," Julie began, "In the old way, I would ask you to show proof of being able to make meat for Lena. Since this is not practical in these times, I will ask that you pledge your life to Lena and that you will provide for her."

Michael turned and looked into Lena's incredible eyes.

"I promise that you will never want for the rest of your life," Michael vowed.

Julie now turned to Lena:

"Cedar Woman," she intoned, "will you pledge to always take care of your husband? Will you make sure that he is not shamed by his wife's negligence?" Lena looked into Michael's deep, brown eyes.

"I swear," she breathed.

Julie took the couple's bound hands and held them in hers.

"Your two lives are now one," she announced.

Michael and Lena turned toward each other. Embracing, they kissed. Vicki let out an audible sigh, Reva wiped a glistening tear with the sleeve of her dress, and Julie stood, beaming, at the newly joined couple.

Giving Reva a nudge, and Vicki a wink, she waited until the couple parted.

"This woman's life is now yours. Take her into my lodge, join with her and know her as your half side. Make her your own.

Cricket song filled the moonlit lodge. Lena lay, curled against Michael's side, her leg across his hips, her lips against his throat. Michael sighed. It had never been like this before. Lena, he knew, was a virgin, but he was not, or at least he didn't think he was. But if you judged this experience by the others he'd had, he *was*, for tonight he had *made love* for the first time.

---

[83] Toon-cash-eela - Grandfather

Michael ran his fingers through Lena's long, lustrous hair. He couldn't believe his luck in finding this beautiful woman. She smiled at him, a trusting smile, full of love and contentment.

"My sweet woman," he murmured, and kissed her deeply.

She clung to him, holding him to her in a tight embrace. Michael moaned. They made love again.

Ⅱ

Michael lay with his hands behind his head. The night had cooled and a light blanket covered the supine couple. Lena's head rested contentedly on Michael's chest. He needed to talk to her, so he took her chin in his hand and lifted her face toward him.

"Mitawin," he murmured, and kissed her lightly on the forehead.

"Yes, Mihinga," she answered, savoring the word as she spoke it.

"We have to be practical for a moment. There are things which we must discuss."

Lena sat up abruptly. She was beautiful. Her small breasts were high and firm, her lustrous hair fell about her like a silken veil, brushing against his chest – tantalizing his senses. Her skin glowed in the moonlight, shimmering and pale, like a spirit visiting a mere mortal. The turquoise pendant fell just to the beginning of her cleavage and seemed to nestle there contentedly. Michael lifted it from her warm, glowing skin and examined it.

"This is a beautiful stone," he offered, stalling for time.

"It's my birthstone – December," Lena smiled.

Michael processed the information, and realized that his bride was 17, as Julie had mentioned just before the ceremony. It had not registered with him then, but now he grasped the fact that Lena was not of an age to marry legally without parental consent. Reva, as an elder of the family, and Peter's mother, gave verbal consent for the traditional NdN wedding, but parental consent was necessary, or they would have to wait until Lena turned 18 in December to marry legally, if they wanted to do so without involving her parents. In addition, he thought to himself, it may take a few months before he could resettle, so they may as well wait until she turned 18.

Michael wrapped her in his arms and began.

"Lena, I have a life here in Keokuk. I have an apartment, a job and my family is here.

Michael tightened his embrace when he felt Lena attempt to sit up.

"Cha, listen now, Little Bird – excuse me, Cedar Woman," he laughed quietly, chucking her lightly under the chin.

"I will need to close up my apartment, give notice, and begin the search for a new job. When I have accomplished these things, I will meet you in Columbus. It's going to take me a few months, Mitawin, but

I will be there!

Lena lay quietly in his arms. A glistening tear fell from her eye, and dropped onto Michael's chest. He took his index finger, wiped up the tear and kissed the salty liquid. His heart ached for his lovely bride. His heart was also heavy, but they needed to do this right, so that their life together began with honor, and with all people involved taken into consideration.

"I will be in Columbus soon to look for work. I need to request vacation time from my current job. I'll tell them that I am moving. My boss is a good man, he'll give me the time, and keep me on until I find something else."

Lena interrupted. "Mihinga! I don't know what you do!" she exclaimed.

Michael chortled. "I'm a chef. I have a degree in the culinary arts," he added.

This time Lena managed to sit up. Her eyes were blazing, their deep brown depths sparkling with excitement. The pupils of her eyes dilated, causing her eyes to appear to be of the same deep, brown color.

"Michael!" she exclaimed, "Michael, this is perfect!" she continued excitedly, grabbing his hand and pressing it to her breast. "I run a restaurant. Vicki, the lady for whom we had the Wopila today, has just become Unci's sister. She's the owner, and she is looking for a chef!"

Michael was dumfounded.

"Why do I feel that Wakan Tanka is behind all of this," he queried with wonder.

"So, you can leave with us tomorrow!" Lena exalted.

Michael drew Lena into his arms again, and digested the latest bit of information. It was extraordinary how the day had turned out. He'd gotten up, made coffee on the camp stove, wakened Sonny, and prepared for the powwow. Now, here he was, a married man, at least in the eyes of The People, and about to move, lock, stock and barrel to a new city, a new state, a new job and a new family.

Michael noticed the circular opening of the tipi beginning to grow light.

"Lena," he whispered, "dawn is almost here."

Lena gave a small cry. She didn't want the dawn. She wanted to stay here, with her new husband, make love again and stay within the circle of his arms forever.

"Lena," he continued, "I will come to you as soon as I can. I have to give notice and close up my apartment." Michael was quiet for a few seconds.

"Sonny can help me. I know he will. That may expedite the move. Do you live with your parents?" he asked, almost as an after thought.

"No, I live in my own apartment. It has a small living room, two bedrooms, a bath and galley kitchen," she offered.

"See if you can move in with your parents," Michael instructed. "No," he interjected as Lena began to protest. "We will do this right. We will not live together until legally man and wife."

Lena showed her disappointment, but knew that he was right. Truthfully, she didn't think she could live with Michael openly until they were legally married. Her mother and father would not wish for her to, and she wanted to start her marriage off right.

"I will move into your apartment," Michael continued. I can use the second bedroom to store anything that I can't find room for in the living areas. Then, we can search for a new home while we wait for your 18th birthday. When would you like to be legally married, Little Bird?" he questioned, reverting to the pet name he had selected for her that morning.

"Well," she mused, "my birthday is December 2nd. Can we marry on the 5th? It's Vicki's birthday."

Michael smiled and pulled her close again. We shall be married on the fifth then," he affirmed. Drawing her close, they made love again as the opening of the tipi filled with dawning light.

Chapter Thirteen

Dedicated to the real neighbor, my beloved friend
Jo-Ann Glockner
1939 - 1998

Half Sides

Now you will feel no rain,
For each of you will be
Shelter to the other.

Now you will feel no cold,
For each of you will be
Warmth to the other.

Now there is no more loneliness,
For each of you will be
Companion to the other.

Now you are two bodies,
But there is only one
Life before you.

Go now to your dwelling place,
To enter into the days
Of your togetherness.

And may your days
Be good and long
Upon the earth.

Apache Wedding Prayer

Lena stood in the kitchen of a ninety-year-old condo, which she had moved into only the week before. She leaned against the stove sipping a glass of iced water. Before her loomed her latest project – an old, Hoosier style hutch, complete with a white porcelain countertop. Found in a flea market, Lena bought the antiquity in spite of the fact that someone had removed the flour bin and pounded in a metal medicine chest in its place. *I wish they had left the bin*, she mused, *Oh, well. At least I can put spice bottles in there for now, and use the top as extra counter space. Besides, I couldn't have afforded it if it had been complete*, she reasoned.

Michael, as promised, arrived in Columbus two weeks after Lena, Vicki and Reva returned from the powwow. By then, Lena was temporarily installed in her parents and grandmother's home. For now, their couch would do well for sleeping, immersed as she was in her dreams of another bed, soon to be occupied by both her and her handsome husband.

Michael arrived in the early evening. Lena rushed to the door of her parent's and grandmother's home, and threw herself into Michael's arms. Michael chuckled and held her to him, as he quickly lowered a wicker laundry basket to the porch.

"You almost made me drop my bride price!" he chortled with glee, so happy was he to hold her small, shapely form in his arms again.

Lena took his hand and led him into the home. She brought him first to her father, and introduced Michael to Peter. Lena then guided Michael toward Mary and finally to Reva, to allow them to greet each other after the two-week separation. Michael excused himself and returning to the porch, re-entered with a wicker laundry basket full of foodstuffs.

Michael walked directly to Peter, and placing the basket at his feet, announced:

"I wish to marry your daughter. I promise to provide for her, both in the old and the new ways. I promise to honor her as my half side and to care for our children.

Peter's eyes welled, and he fought to hide his emotions – difficult to do since his injury, as he still had some problems with controlling his facial muscles. But, he managed, and asked Mary to show him what the basket contained.

Nestled within the Indian blanket lined basket was a smoked ham, bags of flour, cornmeal and boxes of baking soda, baking powder and packets of yeast, for the making of fry bread.

A tin of coffee, and one of tobacco, nestled side-by-side in the basket, beside a large bag of potatoes. Sweet potatoes as well as ears of corn were scattered throughout the basket, and in the center, safe from being squashed, was a large bag of tomatoes.

A plastic container of green beans, as well as a package of kidney beans, were included, along with a zucchini, a large head of cabbage, lettuce and kale. Blueberries, strawberries and a fragrant melon, encased in plastic, rounded out the presentation.

The message was clear: Lena would never go hungry while Michael was taking care of her.

Peter gave a crooked grin, nodded, and looked to his wife with pride glowing in his eyes. Peter had given his blessing.

Upon Michael's insistence, he interviewed with Vicki for the position of head chef, and spent the week cooking for her on approval. Said approval swiftly given, as Vicki realized what a gem had fallen into her lap. His cooking was inventive and delicious. Inspired by Native American cuisine, his style not only fit in with the theme of her restaurant, but enhanced it as well. She could not wait for him to return and set up permanent residency, marry Lena, and begin as head chef in her restaurant.

What a fantastic series of happenstance she thought to herself, overjoyed that Lena would soon be happily married, and she would have an accomplished chef to add to her staff.

Wait a minute! Vicki realized to herself. *According to tradition, he is my son-in-law!* Vicki couldn't believe her luck. Childless, and bereft of her husband just a few, short years ago, she believed that any happiness was in the past. Now, here she was, surrounded by people she loved, and who loved her, and actually invited her to be a part of their warm and loving family.

At the end of the week, Michael returned to Iowa to close up his apartment and work out his notice with his employer, but not before he and Lena went house hunting. As luck would have it, they found exactly what they wanted within a couple of days. The townhouse, converted to a condominium, was situated in the Short North, so dubbed because it was a short distance from downtown Columbus. Once a distressed area, the vibrant neighborhood was on an upswing, as home and business owners spruced up their properties and brought the area back to life. The Short North was close to theaters, art galleries and high-end restaurants. Indeed, the area itself was soon opening its own galleries and eating establishments, and residents gained satisfaction in seeing the value of their properties rise.

The two-story condominium was listed at a very affordable price for the young couple, due to its rough condition. Built in 1890, the end unit of a four-unit townhouse, had once been home to a patriarch whose children and their families resided in the other three residences. Around the 1950s, the townhouses were converted to rentals, until purchased by an investor who put the units up for sale just a few months before. The other three condos were sold, the last remaining empty because of its condition.

The walls were unpainted and in need of repairs, the floors scuffed and scarred. It was rough, it needed a lot of work, but it was so – comforting, solid, homey, safe. The brick walls were a good foot thick; the ceilings were high, and the rooms spacious. Lena was sure that she could make it into a comfortable home for herself and Michael. In any event, she was going to give it one heck of a try!

Michael purchased the condominium, and as soon as he closed on it, Lena moved in.

So, here she stood, painting her abused hutch and daydreaming of the day she and Michael would live together as man and wife.

Lena turned and looked out the back door, which stood open to a glorious fall morning.

Our tree is full of apples! she congratulated herself! *I'll make an apple pie!*

Just then, she noticed one of her new neighbors coming up the walk. She had met the owners of the other three units on moving day, and instantly hit it off with Jo-Ann Glover who owned the unit at the opposite end. Jo-Ann had invited Lena over for a "martooni" and dinner for the following Saturday night to celebrate the move-in, and Lena and Michael's upcoming marriage. Anxious to get to know the neighbors who shared the large, undivided back yard, she accepted the invitation, and promptly arrived at Jo-Ann's back door at 5:00 P.M. on the appointed day. Lena was pleased to have made a new friend; *it'll be nice to have a someone so close by*, she reasoned, and accepted the invitation in the hopes that she and Jo-Ann might become good friends.

As with her own unit, the back door led directly into Jo-Ann's kitchen. Whereas Lena's condominium was a shell, not a wall in the place was without need of plaster and paint, Jo-Ann's unit was carpeted, painted, and finished. Lena stood in the middle of the kitchen, looking around. Like her condominium, it was laid out in a shotgun floor plan, that is, she could stand in the kitchen and look through the connecting dining room and into the living room. Jo-Ann's home was decorated in the Victorian style, and was very charming, the period furniture blending well with exposed brick walls, carved mantelpieces, and marble hearths.

"Have a seat." Jo-Ann offered, gesturing toward a wooden armchair beside the kitchen's door.

Lena sat and was immediately handed a red, plastic juice glass, filled with a clear liquid, which emitted a sharp odor. A green olive stuffed with an onion and a lemon twist, floated in the water-like liquid, as did several ice cubes. Dismissing the mystery drink for a moment, Lena continued to look around the room.

Although the counterpart of her own kitchen, Jo-Ann's was much different. Fake wooden beams extended east to west across the ten-foot high ceiling, giving the room a rustic look, as if one had just stepped into either an English hall or a log cabin, Lena couldn't decide which her new friend had been trying to emulate. Dark cabinets lined the east and south walls, topped with various baskets, vases and memorabilia, accompanied by a pair of green, blue, or yellow eyes tucked in here and there. Jo-Ann was obviously a cat lover.

Black textured Formica counter tops wrapped around the east wall to the south where the kitchen sink sat beneath a cat-bedecked window, placed in mirrored fashion to Lena's own, complete with the view of an apple tree – this one sporting red apples instead of Lena's green. Red checked gingham café curtains decorated the window above the sink and another behind a green, cat clawed, vinyl lounger, which sat in a place of honor beneath a brass floor lamp. Lena noticed that Jo-Ann had a dishwasher, an appliance Lena wished she had, as well as a larger refrigerator and a pantry. Compared to the dirty, yellow linoleum of her kitchen, Jo-Ann's brick patterned vinyl flooring looked brand new.

Jo-Ann walked over to the cracked, scarred, green vinyl lounger, and groaning, sank into her chair, her right hand holding an identical glass to the one containing the untouched drink in Lena's hand.

"You have a lot of work to do, Lena, but in a way you're ahead of me. I have these nice appliances, my fake beams, cheap carpeting and vinyl flooring, but I paid a lot more for my unit. By the time you came along, the owner just wanted to get the units sold. In the end, you'll come out on top."

Lena looked at her and smiled.

"You think so? Well, thank you, Jo-Ann. It is a bit overwhelming, but I think I can.....handle.....it. Jo-Ann, there's a cat sitting on your stove with its back to me. It looks like it's angry or something!"

Jo-Ann lit a Marlboro and glanced to her left where the stove was situated. Indeed, yet another feline, this a grey, striped, longhair, sat in the middle of the stove, back toward Lena and very definitely in a snit, her hairs standing on end, and a faint growl emitting from her throat. Jo-Ann laughed, taking a generous sip of her drink.

"Oh, that's Maude. She's angry with you because you're sitting in her chair!" Lena looked at Jo-Ann, who countered with a large, toothy grin.

"You have got to be kidding!" Lena responded, laughing. "Well, please extend my apologies, if you don't mind. I certainly didn't mean to take Madam's chair!" She chortled.

Jo-Ann raised her glass.

"Salut!" she exclaimed, and quaffed another portion of her drink.

Lena lifted her own glass to her nose and smelled. It had a faintly floral aroma, overridden by a strong smell of alcohol, definitely pungent, but Jo-Ann was drinking it so smoothly, it must be fine. She tipped the glass to her mouth and took a long sip. Her first reaction was that the liquid tasted like perfume – flowery or something. Then it hit the back of her throat! She felt as if her esophagus were closing! Her ears burned and her throat spasmed. She coughed, sputtered and fought to regain her breath. Jumping from her chair, Jo-Ann raced over and began patting Lena on the back.

"What is this stuff?" she finally choked out as Jo-Ann resumed her seat.

"A martini! A dry martini! You mean to tell me, Lena Catcher, that you've never had a martini?" Jo-Ann exclaimed, clearly unaware that she was serving alcohol to a minor.

"Oh, I am sorry. I just assumed...well, drink it slower. I promise you'll come to love it!" Jo-Ann rose from her green, vinyl chair again and refilled her glass.

"Now, I like my martini's dry – very dry. To some that means a splash of vermouth over ice and then add gin to the rim. Others will take a pitcher full of ice, fill it with vermouth, pour the vermouth back into the bottle and then add the gin. Me...well, to me a dry martini is the vermouth is allowed to sit on the same shelf as the gin!" Jo-Ann smiled and waived her glass in salute, splashing some of the liquid onto the floor as she again plunked into her lounger while taking a long drag from her cigarette.

"You mean," Lena looked at her glass and back at Jo-Ann, "I'm drinking straight gin?"

"Sure!" Jo-Ann said. "It won't hurt you. Now, I have to go upstairs and do a few more things, and then we're off to dinner. Remember, I'm buying!"

With that, Jo-Ann stubbed out her cigarette, rose from her chair, and headed toward her stairs that led to the second floor, which Lena knew she would recognize, as the layout would be a mirror copy of her own – minus the falling plaster.

She leaned back in her somewhat uncomfortable, wooden chair, and contemplated Maude's stiff back. Still affronted, the cat continued to sit in the middle of the stove in silent umbrage at Lena's audacity in using her chair. Rising quickly, she walked to the kitchen sink. Placing her index finger over the rim of her glass, she poured out the gin, retaining the olive, lemon twist and ice. Refilling her glass with water, she returned to her seat, all the while chuckling to herself, and contemplating her absent hostess.

Jo-Ann Glover was an eccentric, this was clear. She had greeted Lena at the door in a brown, fuzzy garment, which she called her "Fozzie Bear Robe," after the loveable, brown Muppet on *Sesame Street*. Completing her wardrobe had been lime green, fuzzy slippers, and a large, diamond ring.

Jo-Ann Glover was forty years old and single. Her life, however, was not without excitement. Born in West Union, Ohio, she had traveled to Columbus at the tender age of eighteen to "seek her fortune," which consisted of taking the first job she was offered with an Ohio State University affiliated Ophthalmologist; it was the only job she would ever hold. Her youth was spent in anticipating her two-week vacation slots, in which she would board a plane to New York, and seek out sundry friends and acquaintances with whom she planned somewhat unusual adventures.

During the ensuing years, Lena would spend many evenings in that uncomfortable wooden chair, pretending to sip the pungent, fragrant "martoonies" Jo-Ann always served, contemplating Maude's indignant back, and listening to what she would later call "Jo-Ann Stories": madcap adventures which many times seemed as if they should have been played out in some crazy sitcom on television. Lena would remember stories such as the "Uninhibited Island" in which Jo-Ann would explain that she and a friend had flown to his privately owned island and decided to skinny dip. Once in the water, they heard whistling and cat-calling. Turning, and looking up, they found a construction crew cheering them on.

"I would have sworn the island was uninhibited!" She exclaimed.

"Uninhibited?" Lena questioned – and then they had laughed, holding their sides and rocking when she and Jo-Ann finally realized that she meant uninhabited.

Then there was the story of when Jo-Ann was twenty-one and made her first trip to New York. She had been so proud of herself: flying on an airplane! Placing her foot on the first step of the roll away stairs, which had been pushed up to the plane's exit door, she noticed her date waiting there to meet her. Giving a toss of her chic, veiled hatted head, she lost her footing, promptly rolling down the entire length of stairs, and landing at the feet of her escort.

What would have devastated others did not faze her in the least! Eccentric, outrageous, generous, and full of humor, she attacked life rather than lived it, and survived in a world too harsh for her fragile psyche, with the aid of wit, cigarettes, large doses of alcohol, and her pets.

She was owned by five cats: Maude was a longhaired grey tiger of imperious attitude. Schnee, German for Snow, was a sapphire-eyed white longhair who considered herself the beauty of the family. Sherman, a one-eared orange and white tabby found on her doorstep one day, bloody and half-dead, was the buccaneer of the family. Herman, a black and white tom, who could possibly have been Errol Flynn in another life, was personally responsible for the entire repopulation of black and white cats in the Short North area. Then there was Oliver, a sleek, grey aristocrat with yellow eyes, who could never become reconciled with the fact that he was forced to live among such commoners. They were her loves and her source of affection in an environment fast becoming unendurable. She drank too much, smoked too much, ate to her fill with gusto, and gave of herself so completely, that all who knew her loved her, though they feared for her health. All of this Lena was later to learn. In the meantime, she sat patiently, waiting for her hostess to join her, gazing at Maude's back, still erect with indignity, a low growl emitting from her gray-furred throat.

"A pretty giiiiiirrrrrrrl, is like a melody!" came ringing through the condominium's corridor as Jo-Ann "floated" into the kitchen, dressed and ready to go. Standing at 5'4". Jo-Ann weighed approximately 140 pounds and had, as Lena would later describe, the build of Julia Child, the face of Judy Garland, the hair of Liza Manelli, and the voice of Carol Channing. Dressed in black slacks and black tunic top, sewn over with small seed pearls, she topped off the outfit with a plain, worn, black trench coat, which Lena was later to call her "signature coat," and a large tote, used as a purse, which Jo-Ann laughingly claimed gave her the official status of "Bag Lady." She still wore the large, diamond ring, a circle of four trumpet-like scrolls of gold, each inset with a quarter carat diamond and a half carat diamond in the center. It was garish and oversized – and it fit her to a tee.

Jo-Ann never learned to drive.

"I tried to drive twice. The first time...okay...the sisters where I went to high school decided that I should learn, and so off we go in the convent car with me at the wheel. I did fine until a beer truck got in my way! There we were, looking up the ass-end of this truck, and what happens? Some kegs burst, and we're flooded with beer! Probably the best time those nuns had in years!

"Then, oh, a couple of years later, after I'd moved here, I was dating this guy in the south-end, and he decided that **he** could teach me to drive so, once again into a car and off we go! I really thought I was getting the hang of it. I still to this day don't know what happened, but all of a sudden, there's this crash, tinkling glass and I'm nose to nose with a poster in front of the Paris Theater facing this chick wearing nothing but a couple of black rectangles. After that, I gave up and said 'No more!'"

All of this flashed through Lena's mind as she watched Jo-Ann walking along the sidewalk, which led to her back door.

"Jo-Ann! Good to see you!" Lena smiled, opening the screen and inviting Jo-Ann in.

"Howdy, neighbor!" Jo-Ann chirped.

"Oh, your new hutch you were telling me about. Veerrry nice!" Lena smiled.

"Thanks! Michael and I like antiques, as you have probably guessed," Lena replied in reference to the few pieces that she had bought to augment the furniture Lena had kept from her family's three-room apartment, combined with Michael's pieces from his soon to be former

93

residence.

Jo-Ann nodded. Clearly, she had not come over to discuss furnishings. She walked over to a small kitchen table and sat down, drumming her fingers on the Formica top.

"Lena," she began.

"Yes?" Lena replied.

"When are you getting married?" Jo-Ann questioned.

Lena regarded her friend. She was amazed at how close she had become to Jo-Ann in the few months she had lived here. With Jo-Ann, you were never bored, and she could keep you laughing with her stories until you begged her to stop.

Lena recalled Jo-Ann's horror when she realized that she'd served alcohol to a minor. Within sixty seconds, her face had registered disbelief, shock, consternation, and finally, self-ridicule.

"You'd think I was dropped on my head!" she exclaimed.

I think that one of the things I love about her the most – is her ability to laugh at herself, admit her mistakes and move on, Lena mused, and her admiration for her friend heightened.

Lena walked to the sink and washed her hands. Grabbing a dishtowel, and drying them, she turned to Jo-Ann and smiled.

"Well, girlfriend, I'm glad you asked. It's a month away, and I want you to be my matron of honor."

Jo-Ann's jaw dropped; she clearly was not expecting the offer. Then, a small tear coursed down her left cheek and she sniffed.

"Are you sure?" she asked, voice quivering.

"Absolutely," Lena affirmed. "I can think of no better person.

"Nickie is a dear friend, and she will be my bride's maid. As the elder of my friends, I want you to have the position of matron of honor. I've grown very close to you, Jo-Ann. I've talked about this with Nickie, and she completely agrees with my choice. What do you say?

A smile slowly spread itself across Jo-Ann's face.

"Sure! But I don't have a dress!"

"Wear whatever you've got. The wedding is going to be very simple. Vicki has offered the restaurant and Julie, I've told you about her, is driving in from Iowa to do the legal ceremony – she has already performed the traditional and is licensed to perform marriages here in Ohio.

"Good. It's all set!" Lena clapped her hands and sat down across from her friend.

"Well, then, what I was about to do is even more appropriate," Jo-Ann stated, giving Lena her toothy grin.

"I want to give you something special, something very special," Jo-Ann stated, placing a small package on the table.

"Please," Jo-Ann entreated, "accept this with all of my love."

Lena took the small offering and carefully unwrapped the parcel. It was a ring box. Upon opening it, Lena beheld an exquisite turquoise ring. The marquise-shaped stone was set in a beautiful, silver fluted setting. Mother of Pearl traced its way through the vivid, blue stone. It reminded Lena of the earth, like the maps you see where the earth is represented as an oval. The workmanship was beyond compare. Lena gasped, and looking up at Jo-Ann, shook her head.

"Hey, Missy," Jo-Ann interjected, "don't you dare say no." She smiled affectionately and continued:

"This was my mother's, and I want you to have it. Wear it at your wedding...something old and something blue! Plus, I know that it is your birthstone, and so it will be good luck."

Jo-Ann stood up and walked to the door. Before Lena could say a word, she pushed the screen door open and left.

The day was a crystal white. Bright sunshine shone through ice-rimed windows, reflecting intricate lace-like patterns on the shining hardwood floors. Linen draped tables were graced with bouquets of day lilies, Lena's favorite flower. Silky, linen napkins in an amber color-on-color chevron pattern were nestled within simple, silver napkin rings.

Twinkle lights sparkled on doorways and a small arbour, which Julie constructed the night before from grape vines, to set off the area in which the couple would be wed.

The restaurant was closed for the night to the general public, but it would be full nonetheless. Michael's family would be there, as well as favorite patrons, friends of Vicki's, and of course, the Catchers and their friends, including Dean and Nellie and Dean's brother, Gary who now rented the apartment to Sonny.

Sonny walked through the restaurant, assuring that all was in order. In the four months since the powwow, Sonny was an indefatigable help to Michael. He helped Michael move, first from his apartment in Keokuk to the apartment on Front Street, and then from there to the condo in the Short North. In addition, he closed his own apartment and moved into the Front Street address, once Michael moved his furnishings to the condo which he was to share with Lena. The two then roomed together until Michael and Lena's marriage was legally solemnized.

A stroke of luck landed Sonny a job with Vicki as well. Remembering his performances at the powwow, and observing his organizational skills, she offered him a job as Night Manager. Sonny did not disappoint.

Cowboy boots echoing on glistening, hardwood floors, Sonny made a final run through the restaurant. Everything was in order. He stopped to straighten a lily half fallen from its vase and made his way to the kitchen.

Michael, of course, would not be working tonight, and Sonny volunteered to step in and make sure that all was in order.

He walked through the kitchen area, careful not to get in the way of the sous chef, who was in charge of the food tonight, and his various assistants. Grabbing a spoon and dipping it into a poblano sauce, he tasted it and rolled his eyes. Delicious! Smiling, Sonny exited the kitchen and returned to the main room for a final, double, double-check.

Sonny was not sure how he would react to the wedding of his brother/cousin to Lena. So far, he'd managed to avoid seeing too much of Lena – his new job, and moving, being the perfect excuse. But in the deep, dark hours of the night, his heart would ache, and his soul cry out for the winsome, beautiful girl he'd fallen in love with in Keokuk. Still, Michael was his childhood friend, playmate, brother, cousin. Michael's happiness was important to Sonny, and he had to admit to himself that his love for Lena made him feel responsible for her happiness as well. Therefore, he was resolved to be reconciled, and to rejoice in the marriage of the two people he loved more than anyone else.

Lena prepared for her wedding in her office. Lena's mother's ribbon dress, worn at her own wedding, fell just above Lena's ankles. Exquisitely beaded white moccasins, lovingly fashioned by her unci, with red and gold beads, graced her tiny, narrow feet. Her mother's wedding wreath encircled her shining hair, a duplicate of which Michael would be wearing. Michael and Lena's mothers had fashioned the wreath, becoming fast friends during the process.

Her bouquet was four Artic Snow day lilies, their creamy, ruffled, white petals edged in gold, complimenting the flowers in the dining area. Tucked within their silky petals was her prayer feather. Her wedding band was silver, fashioned into the shape of an eagle's feather.

Michael finished dressing in Vicki's office, and proceeded to the arbor to await his bride. He was dressed in a fringed, white buckskin jacket. A turquoise bolero tie, worn in honor of his bride, encircled the color of a crisp, white, cotton shirt. Black jeans and black cowboy boots finished off his wedding attire.

The sweet soaring notes of a flute drifted to Michael's ears. Brent Blount,[84] a musician of high regard who played tenor sax, clarinet, blues and jazz guitar and the Native American flute, was playing "Wankan

---

[84] http://www.brentblount.com/

Tanka,"[85] a song about new beginnings. There was a hush, and slowly the flute began again. This time, it was "Sunrise Song."[86] A lilting vibrato filled the rooms. It was time.

Lena gave a start and smiled. Brent was playing the song she chose for her entrance. Taking a deep breath, Lena opened the door to her office, and began her journey as a wife.

---

[85] http://www.youtube.com/watch?v=17h34SywAHY
[86] http://www.youtube.com/watch?v=7Ki9qeH8Oeo

Chapter Fourteen

May the Warm Winds of Heaven
Blow softly upon your house.
May the Great Spirit
Bless all who enter there.
May your Moccasins
Make happy tracks
in many snows,
and may the Rainbow
always touch your shoulder.

Cherokee Prayer Blessing

She loved the smell of him, the look of him, the feel of his firm, muscular thighs against her softer, pliant flesh.

Lena turned to her sleeping husband. Cheek nestling on her left palm, she gazed down upon his slumbering form. *Such a handsome man* she mused, *so sweet and thoughtful – so beautiful inside and out.* Lena rolled to her back, and cradling her head in her small hands, she smiled, gazing at the cracked ceiling above.

We need to strip the wallpaper from the ceiling, she though sleepily. Lena loved her new home, in spite of its flaws. Large rooms filled with diffused light gave the spaces within the condo a soft, mellow feeling. The high ceilings, tall windows and ornate mantles spoke to her of years gone by. She often wondered who had lived within the walls of her beloved domicile before she and Michael purchased it.

They must have been happy, she reflected, *because the house feels happy.*

Lena turned onto her right side and observed the antique mantelpiece that graced the east wall of the bedroom. Carved wood, blue, Victorian tiles, and a cunningly wrought cast iron surround, spoke to her of a pride of workmanship often absent in today's world. She loved her new home; loved her husband; loved her life.

Turning to Michael again, she kissed him on the tip of his nose, then proceeded to rub it with her tiny one.

"Wake up, sleepy head!" she commanded, melting into his broad chest as muscular arms enfolded her, drawing her to him with a long, contented sigh.

"Good morning, Little Bird," Michael whispered drowsily. "It's good to awaken this way."

He smiled at his wife tenderly, and with seemingly no effort, rolled over until she lay against the mattress and he was atop her small, shapely body. Michael bent to her lovely lips, kissing them lingeringly, drawing her into him, into his heart, his soul. Lena melted against him, sighing with happiness.

Michael reluctantly released her and rose from the bed.

"We must get started, Mitawin," Michael grinned.

Lena pretended to pout, and rising from the disheveled bed, jumped into his arms, laughing and wrapping her lovely legs around his waist. Chuckling, Michael spun around, holding tightly to his beloved wife, her wondrous hair fanning out in a silky, glossy crescent. It was a new day, they were more deeply in love than when they married eight months before, and they were facing a day doing what they loved most, working together to provide delicious food for the people who honored Vicki's table.

Michael added sliced apples and tomatillos to the sauté pan, and with a tilt of the vessel, first forward and then back, expertly flipped the fruits, coating them with the cooking oil. The kitchen of Vicki's filled with tantalizing smells as the flavors of the sweet and tart fruits married.

Sous-Chef Ed Soaring Eagle Chenoweth, was busy preparing his famous Elk Meatloaf, while the pastry chef worked with an intern, preparing the most popular dessert of the now famous eatery: Cedar Woman's Aztec Chocolate Cheesecake.

Inspired by the historical accounts of Montezuma's favorite drink of chocolate, mixed with hot water and peppers, Lena worked diligently on the recipe, until she attained the perfect mix of sweet chocolate, combined with the heat of cayenne. The restaurant couldn't make enough of them, as the demand rose almost daily.

Sonny sauntered in and walked toward Michael. Peeking over Michael's left shoulder, Sonny pronounced,

"Man! That's my lunch you're making, Cousin." Laughing, Michael returned,

"No way. This is for table five." Sonny chuckled, and patting his brother/cousin on the back, left the kitchen. He knew that soon Michael would prepare his dinner, and he was anxious to relax and enjoy the meal.

He walked over to where Nickie stood at the hostess booth, and uttering a few pleasantries, strolled away.

Nickie Makoche` Wanblaka Tuwa Ista Numpa Winyan, or Ista Numpa[87] for short, Greene stood completely still. Outwardly, it appeared

---

[87] Mah-koh-cheay wahn-blah-kah tdoo-wah eesh-tdah noom-pah ween-yahn
– Two-Eyed Woman Who Sees in Both Worlds

as if nothing had changed. Were someone to observe more closely, however, they would see that she was, to say the least, agitated.

Sweat formed along her hairline, and her breath caught in her throat. Her stomach clenched as a feeling of hopelessness filled its cavity, and the pounding of her heart was drowned out by the roaring in her ears. Nickie was hopelessly in love with Sonny.

Daughter of the Comanche, Nickie stood at 5'4". Her round face, and slightly plump body, did not answer to the modern American ideal of beauty. Most women wrote her off as unattractive. Men found her fascinating.

Quick of wit and sharp of mind, she could converse on many subjects, her dry sense of humor adding to the conversation as a delectable sauce adds to a well-prepared dish. Her large, brown eyes would sparkle, and her white smile flash, as she savored conversation as one does a delicious meal. More importantly, she made those around her feel important, well liked, and desirable as human beings.

Her most attractive feature was her waist-long, abundant, black hair. Shimmering with blue highlights, it brought to mind an ebony waterfall, and many a man wished that he could touch it, perhaps wrap it around his neck and breathe in its heady perfume.

Nickie was oblivious to the effect she had on men. She saw no one but Sonny, and Sonny was in love with Lena.

Nickie had once hoped that Sonny would notice her, but at Lena and Michael's wedding, Nickie glanced toward Sonny, and saw the look of utter devastation on his face. Her heart plummeted. She recognized the same hopeless love she felt for Sonny on his face.

She contemplated leaving the restaurant and getting a job elsewhere, but she owed Lena so much; loved her like a sister. Hell, if anyone could understand why Sonny loved her, Nickie could; she could easily see why anyone, male or female, would love Lena. But it was so hard! Whenever Sonny approached her, a heat would rise in her body, and a longing in her heart for this beautiful, talented man.

She wished with all of her heart that she could have a relationship with Sonny like Lena had with Michael.

Chapter Fifteen

When your time comes to die, be not like those whose hearts are filled with fear of death, so that when their time comes, they weep and pray for a little more time to live their lives over again in a different way. Sing your death song, and die like a hero going home.

Tecumseh

Lena lay with Michael encircled in her arms. She began to relax, the comfort of the warmth of his body easing her into a soporific state. She could feel his heart beating, could sense his breath as if it were her own. She snuggled closer to him, smelling his special fragrance, reveling as her heart filled with love.

Without warning, a cold humor ran through her body, as she felt his heart stop, felt the disconnection of their souls. With a startled cry, she turned her husband's face toward her own and saw that he had left this world.

Turning her face to the window, a smile of relief formed upon her lips, as through the rectangular opening, she beheld the Thunderbird. Her spirit lifted from the bed, and passing through the window, she stepped upon the giant bird's wing. Michael was there, waiting for her. Hand extended, he helped her upon their transport: the wings of the Thunderbird, which would take them to the edge of the universe together, and un-separated, they would walk the five steps to the Spirit Path and into the Spirit World.

She gazed into her beloved husband's eyes. She loved him so completely, and now they would be together forever.

Michael pulled her to him and held her. Lena felt the strength of his arms, the fullness of his love, his hand stroking her glorious hair.

"We will go together, Mihinga," Lena whispered, clutching her husband to her.

With a feeling of panic, Lena felt Michael's arms relax as he slowly moved out of their embrace. His hand loosened in hers. He shook his head slowly, his face full of mourning.

"No, Little Bird, it is not your time. I will wait for you in the Spirit World."

Lena felt herself flying back through the window, her spirit returning to her body against her will. Her soul cried out as the Thunderbird flew into the horizon, taking Michael from her.

Lena wakened with a startled cry. Pillow clutched within the circle of her arms, she searched the room frantically. Slowly, slowly, her pounding heart returned to its normal beat. Lying down, she closed her eyes breathing deeply.

It was a dream. Thank you, Creator, it was just a dream!

Lena rose from her bed and raced for the shower. It was August, and hot, as the condo had no air conditioning. Conversely, in December, the upstairs was freezing; the ancient forced air furnace provided heat only to the first floor. A two-way vent allowed whatever weak heat could find its way to the spacious master bedroom, but Lena noticed that the curtains often froze to the windows, and any beverage she happened to bring up to the room sported a rime of ice the following morning. But today the air was stifling, although it was only five a.m.

Jumping quickly into the shower, Lena felt the cool water begin to slough away the remnants of the nightmare.

What a crazy dream! she thought to herself.

Mentally shaking her head, she applied shampoo, and washed her long, glossy tresses. She had a busy day ahead of her, and tonight Michael would be coming home after a weeklong absence, their first separation since their marriage.

Lena longed to see him. The week had dragged by in a seemingly endless progression of long, lonely hours, and nervous excitement filled her heart at the thought of holding him in her arms once again.

No wonder I had that horrible dream, she mused. *It has seemed like years since Michael left for the powwow.*

An award-winning grass dancer, Michael made the decision that, in spite of the fact that he would miss his beloved wife, he needed to go to the powwow held in Keokuk, Iowa. Boy Ladd was the headman this year, and Michael wanted to combine the trip with seeing his old, boyhood friend and that of seeing his family. Upon learning of his plans, Vicki asked if she could travel with Michael. There was a distributor of elk and buffalo meat in the nearby city of Fort Madison. She wanted to meet with the general manager in the hopes of getting a better deal on the specialty meats so important to her restaurant. Happy for the company during the long drive, Michael immediately agreed to bring her along.

Turning off the tap to the shower, and stepping from the molded tub, Lena selected a towel and began drying her long, lustrous hair. There were many things on her agenda today – there was the menu for next week to complete, and three potential interns to interview. In addition, there was a celebratory meal to plan to honor Michael and Vicki's return.

Lena wrapped the large bath sheet around her small, curvaceous body, and ran on tiptoe to the bedroom.

I must talk to Sonny as soon as he gets in. Lena reminded herself. *I think I miss Vicki almost as much as Michael!* She inwardly exclaimed.

Opening her closet door, she selected a crisp, white blouse with a crocheted lace collar, a simple, black pencil skirt, and a black pair of pumps. Turquoise earrings, with a matching necklace, and Jo-Ann's ring, completed her ensemble. Turning around, and viewing herself at different angles in the floor length mirror of her antique vanity, Lena nodded her head in satisfaction. Grabbing her black, clutch purse, she extricated the keys to her 1974 Capri 2000.

She was exhilarated every time she inserted the key and it started. Now 19-years-old, the Competition Orange automobile, christened Punkin' because of its color, was as faithful as the day she bought it shortly after her marriage. She loved driving it and enjoyed its sleek lines and stability. Patting the dashboard, she murmured, "Good baby," and pulled out of the one car garage off the communal back yard of her condo.

Lena pulled into her reserved spot in a nearby parking lot, and stepped from her car. Smoothing her skirt and grabbing her purse and brief case, she locked the door, and turned toward Vicki's, just two blocks away. The air was fragrant as morning dew kissed grass and flowers; dawn was just breaking as Lena unlocked the door to the restaurant.

She closed and relocked the door. Moving toward the back of the restaurant, she headed toward her office. Lena liked to arrive early and get most of her paperwork done before phones started ringing, and people started poking their heads in her door for various questions or announcements. She missed Michael, who usually arrived with her for similar reasons. He liked to get the kitchen organized and ready to go before anyone else showed up. Were he here with her today, he would soon bring her and Vicki, who always arrived shortly after, a cup of coffee, and they would sit and plan the day.

Lena permitted herself a small frown. God, she missed him! The five days he'd been gone seemed like an eternity.

Walking passed Vicki's office, Lena saw her friend and employer sitting at her desk. Lena grinned,

"Good morning, Taskmaster," she joked.

Looking up and smiling, Vicki answered,

"Love you, Baby."

Lena smiled her answer and walked another few feet before realization hit her. Vicki was back! That meant Michael was back! She must have just missed his return to the condo! Turning on her heel, excitement lighting her beautiful face, Lena rushed into Vicki's office.

It was empty.

The story unfolded like a James Dean movie. Michael and Vicki enjoyed the powwow and Michael his reunion with his family and Boy Ladd. They stayed the full three days, and took a day to investigate the warehouse from which they were thinking of ordering their specialized meats. Eager to return home, they decided to leave in the late-afternoon, instead of staying over. Deciding to surprise Lena with their early arrival, they set off in Michael's automobile and headed home.

They almost made it. A drunk driver slammed into Michael's car a mere 18 miles from their destination. Michael threw himself in front of Vicki, but the airbag malfunctioned, and both were crushed. They died instantly.

Listening attentively to the police officer, Lena quietly fainted.

Chapter Sixteen

Only the Rocks Live Forever

Arapaho Quote

The smell of flowers overwhelmed her. Lena was vaguely aware of Sonny's arm around her small shoulders, of Nickie leaning against her as if for support.

On one level, she realized that Michael was gone forever, but her love would not let her accept that he was gone from her until she too rode upon the wing of the Thunderbird.

Sonny was numb. Like the victim of a gunshot wound to the heart, he felt nothing, but he knew the day, the hour, the minute would come when the numbness wore off, and the pain would be, literally, heart-rending.

His gaze wandered from coffin to coffin. The double funeral made sense: Vicki had become such a part of Michael's life that it was right that the two be mourned together.

Sonny gazed upon Vicki's still form.

Such a caring and giving woman, Sonny thought, clenching his eyes in order to fight back tears.

Memories of Vicki formed in his mind: Vicki, embracing him on his first day at the restaurant, assuring him that he was welcome; Vicki, smiling as she walked to her office, a skip in her step testifying to her joy in her life, her restaurant and her friends.

Sonny turned to Michael.

Brother/cousin, how will I live the rest of my life without you in it? How can I go on for a lifetime without hearing your laugh, feeling you slap my shoulder at the end of a joke?

Sonny, his mind again awash with memories, saw the living Michael at the powwow where he met Lena; remembered the young boy who played with him during long, humid nights; recalled the teenager roaring up to Sonny's house in his first "Rez Rocket." Clenching his teeth, Sonny forbad the memories to continue. He must maintain control; he could not let the pain enter his heart until he was alone!

Sonny turned his head to look at Lena. Dumb from the moment she awoke from her faint, she maintained her unspoken grief. Stoic and silent, she left the preparations of the double funeral to Sonny and Nickie, except for the reception. Lena focused on the food that would be served in Vicki's restaurant.

It's as if, Sonny mused, *she were preparing them for Vicki and Michael again...as if they would be there to eat and drink with their friends.*

Sonny bowed his head and once again fought back tears.

Not yet, he told himself, *not yet: not until this is all over and I am alone.*

Nickie placed a hand on Lena's right shoulder in an attempt to break through her stoic façade. Nickie gazed upon Michael – so handsome, even in death. Sonny had chosen to bury him in his grass dancer regalia. The effect was stunning. Even in death, Michael appeared to sing with life.

Now, with Michael gone, I absolutely don't stand a chance with Sonny.

Nickie gave a start, gasped and ran from the room.

Sonny heard Nickie's intake of breath, and looked just in time to see her run into the hallway of the funeral home. Turning to Boy Ladd, he asked that he stay near Lena, and walked briskly out of the room in search of Nickie.

Nickie ran to the parking lot. Fumbling with her keys, dropping them, and awkwardly retrieving them, she finally managed to enter her car. Bending over the steering wheel, she began to wail. How could she have thought such a thing?

Oh, my God, she screamed inwardly, *what kind of monster am I? My best friend has suffered a devastating loss, and I'm angry because now she is free for Sonny? What is wrong with me?*

A tap on her window caused her to jump. Turning a tear-stained face toward the sound, she beheld Sonny, motioning for her to open the door.

Lena sat stiffly in the leather cushioned, high-back chair. The man across from her was opening a file. She jumped as a young woman offered her a glass of water. Shaking her head, she declined the beverage, and returned her gaze to the attorney who sat across from her.

Larry Prince specialized in Estate law. Not a tall man, he was nonetheless imposing, and bore a striking likeness to the actor Mike Myers. His large, brown eyes were kind, and not without sympathy, as he looked up to address Lena.

"Lena, I am about to read the last will and testament of Vicki Compton, but first, I'd like for you to read a note which she particularly wanted me to show you."

Larry leaned forward and handed Lena a piece of paper. As if in a trance, Lena accepted the heavy, vellum document, and began to read, her eyes widening with every sentence:

My Dearest Lena,

I have come to love you as I would love my own daughter. Perhaps this is why I felt it so appropriate when your grandmother, your unci, adopted me as her daughter. It just seemed to fit.

You have brought me great joy. Knowing you has filled my spirit with such happiness, that I cannot express to you how wonderful being a part of your life has been. From the moment you walked into my restaurant, you have been a blessing to me.

And so, sweet daughter, I bequeath to you my other child. I want you to have Vicki's. It's yours, with all of my love.

Vicki

Lena was stunned! She knew that Vicki loved her, but it had not occurred to her that she would inherit the restaurant. Her amazement increased as Larry began to read the will. Lena was Vicki's sole heir; Lena was a wealthy woman.

Chapter Seventeen

There is no death, only a change of worlds.

Chief Seattle

The restaurant was closed to the public for the first time since Lena and Michael's wedding, but it was not a happy occasion this time. Tonight was the one-year anniversary of the deaths of Vicki and Michael.

Officiating in the Wiping of Tears Ceremony was Boy Ladd, childhood friend of Sonny and Michael.

Boy Stands With Wings Ladd stood 5'6" and weighed 130 pounds soaking wet. Quiet and kind, he was often asked to perform ceremonies where compassion and delicacy were required. He was asked by Michael's family to officiate at the Wiping of Tears ceremony because of these qualities.

Boy Ladd smudged the restaurant and guests, and performed the Canumpa, or Pipe Ceremony, in which the catlinite vessel was loaded and smoked, and prayers offered up to Creator. Walking up to each mourner and wiping their tears with red, one-inch square tear cloths, Boy Ladd reminded the attendees that one year had passed since the deaths of the two loved ones: it was time to move on.

"Tunkasila Wakan Tanka, hear me. It is Stands With Wings and I come humbly before you to seek healing for this family.

"Lena Cedar Woman Young Bear, with these tear cloths, I wipe away your tears. You are done with your mourning, and it is time to move on. Now is the time for healing, and a time to move forward.

"It is time to let go of those you loved, and allow their souls to move on.

"It has been a year since your loved ones made the Journey, and it has been hard for you who loved them. So now, I wipe your tears, and pray that the Grandfathers make you over in a good way.

"Allow your loved ones to move on to the Spirit World, their time here is done. Release the ties that bind them here to you, and allow them to complete their journeys. You *will* see them again when it is time, but you need to allow them to move on.

"It is good that you mourn your dead. It is a testament to their lives, but the Grandfathers tell us that life must go on. Honor the dead by celebrating your own life.

"And so I wipe away your tears, and pray that Tunkasila will make you over in a good way, and that your healing can be complete.

"Tunkasila Wakan Tanka, I ask you to watch over these pitiful ones, that you make them over in a good way. Allow them to heal, and to move on from this sorrow.

"Hau, Mikauye Oyapi, hetchetu yelo[88]."

Smiling, Boy Ladd cried, "Now, Indian, up and move on!"

Walking over to Lena and embracing her, Boy Ladd proceeded to offer hugs and words of consolation to the rest of the guests.

Nickie and Sonny prepared a Spirit Plate for the grandfathers. The platter contained a little of everything being served, and would be placed upon a small table set up in front of the restaurant's entrance so that the Grandfathers could eat without being disturbed. As they worked, Boy Ladd prayed over the food. That done, the mourners were free to eat, remembering stories about the departed, and reveling in the memories they shared.

One mourner was too young to take part. He was three months old, born nine months after his father's death.

Logan Singing Grass Young Bear was a healthy baby. Born May 1, 1995, he arrived two weeks later than his projected birth date. Reva bent and lifted the small child from his bassinet. Crooning, she examined the small, disfigured face of her great-grandson.

Logan, named for his great-grandfather, was born with a moderately severe clefting of the lip, gums and hard and soft palates. But, he was beautiful. The defect could not mar the fact that he was, indeed, a handsome boy, and Reva rejoiced in the fact that her life was extended to the point that she could hold her great-grandson in her arms.

Mary peered over her mother-in-law's shoulder, her eyes misty with love and protectiveness. Peter beamed his happiness, a slight droop still manifesting on the left side of his mouth.

"Cha! Did anyone ever see such a beautiful child?" Reva asked, swaying slightly in the universal way women rock when holding a baby.

Now 80, Reva Two Strikes Catcher still stood straight, filled her days with work, and was now caregiver for her great-grandson.

Along with the restaurant, Lena inherited Vicki's house in Westerville. Standing on a private lake, the serene atmosphere helped to calm the young widow when stress threatened to overcome her. She missed her beloved condo, but it wasn't the same now that Michael was no longer there with her. Renting it to a young couple, she moved to the house in Westerville, and there awaited the birth of her child.

Reva moved in with her granddaughter, and watched the young Logan while his mother worked at the downtown restaurant.

At age two months, Logan underwent lip closure surgery. He still needed a Mead Johnson Cleft Palate Nurser to eat; his hard and soft

---

[88] Hoh, Mee-kah-ooh-yay oh-yah-pee heh tdchey tduu yeh loh – Ho all of my relations. I have spoken and it is so.

palates were still open, and he couldn't form a vacuum to suck. The soft-sided bottles allowed anyone feeding Logan to gently squeeze his formula into his mouth. Logan was fed upright. His uvula was also split, and since its function was to stop a baby from choking while lying supine, the upright position prevented this from occurring.

Logan thrived, and was soon sporting chubby cheeks, his little legs filling out and kicking in the air with gusto. His eyes were large and brown, drawing everyone's attention to them. His little nose was canted to the left. Since his alveolar ridge, or upper gum line, was also clefted, the nose did not have the support it needed. This would be fixed in subsequent surgeries.

His mother adored him.

Chapter Eighteen

As I Walk with Beauty,
As I walk, as I walk,
The universe is walking with me.
In beauty it walks before me;
In beauty it walks behind me;
In beauty it walks below me;
In beauty it walks above me.
Beauty is on every side.
As I walk, I walk with Beauty.

Traditional Navajo Prayer

Lena was frantic about getting Logan to drink from a cup. Dr. Reuben, the plastic surgeon to whom Lena had decided to entrust her child, stated that Logan must be able to drink from a cup before palate surgery. Once the palates were closed, suction would be possible, and dangerous to the newly closed palates until they healed; a vacuum could rip the stitches and reopen them. Even a sippy cup could cause a vacuum to form, and put stress on new sutures.

Countless, frustrating hours were spent in trying to get the little imp to comply, until one day, tired of standing by and watching the drama, Reva got up from the table and walked to the kitchen which adjoined the family room. Opening a drawer, and extracting a spoon, she calmly walked to the child secured firmly in a high chair, dipped the spoon into the glass of water, placed it upon his lips and tilted. He drank. Continuing until the vessel was half way consumed, she lifted the cup and placed it against Logan's lips. Again, he drank.

"Cha! So much fuss. The child is thirsty – he will drink, ennit!" Reva proclaimed.

Relief swept through Lena's body, and then chagrin.

"Cha, Unci, I have been blinded by fear!"

Reva smiled, nodded, and continued the procedure until Logan emptied the cup.

Lena bent over the crib in which her 14-month-old son slept. Gathering him gently into her arms, she lifted him from the bed and held him to her. She was sick in her heart – this was one of "those" days.

Lena found her child adorable, and often wondered at those who saw his anomaly as something to be ashamed or afraid of. Indeed, on the day of his birth, her unci declared, "Cha! Creator has marked you for Himself, ennit?" Looking into the eyes of her great-grandchild, Reva firmly believed that Creator often marked people to protect them from the evil spirits that walked, not only the earth, but the spirit realm as well. In putting a special "stamp" on individuals, Creator boldly stated: "Stay away! This soul is special to me."

In addition, a person thus marked gained strength, which traditionally beautiful people might never know. In living with the anomaly, and in modern times, the subsequent surgeries and therapies, the individual born with the anomaly would learn a tenacity of spirit uncommon to those who walked the earth with no such challenges.

Creator's choices could be seen throughout the world: children born with dwarfism, aging at an accelerated rate, extra or defective limbs or, in Logan's instance, craniofacial anomalies.

But, society had its preferences, and they did not include a person whose face did not live up to accepted standards.

Today was one of "those" days – the day of Logan's second surgery – hard and soft palate closure.

The hours crawled by.

If only Michael were here, Lena mourned to herself.

She missed him, missed him passionately. Their time together was so short:

How could I have known that I had to get a lifetime of love in eight, short months? she wondered to herself.

Sitting in the waiting room at Children's Hospital, Lena, Reva, Mary, Peter, Sonny and Nickie, waited anxiously for the surgeon to call. An hour passed, and they knew that it would be longer before they heard. The telephone on the attendant's desk finally rang. She answered and nodded to Lena. Rushing to the phone, Lena clutched the receiver to her ear: it had gone well. Logan was on the way to his room.

Lena reclined on the sofa in her family room, which overlooked the back deck. It was sunrise, and an ethereal mist lay upon the dawn-struck waters of the lake. Logan lay in her arms. Now four, he was recovering from his third surgery: lip revision, in which his upper lip was plumped out by taking flesh from the inside of his mouth, and filling in the inverted v-shaped notched left behind; tip rhinoplasty where his left nostril was sculpted to match the right, and ear tubes.

Being male, Logan's Eustachian tubes lay more vertically than a girl's. To make matters worse, the structure of the bones of his skull were compromised by the clefting, and his Eustachian tubes lay more vertically than was typical, even for a male. Ear tubes were a simple solution in the attempt to prevent repeated ear infections, which could result in possible hearing loss. They would drain any collecting fluid, and help to prevent ensuing problems.

This was their first day home after a two-day stay at the hospital. As with his other two surgeries, Logan spiked a high fever after his operation. The hyperthermia kept him in Children's until it could be kept under control.

Lena spent most of their stay in the hospital lying in the crib Logan occupied. Cradled within his mother's arms, he made it through the ordeal. Now, at home, exhausted, he rested quietly.

She looked down upon his sleeping form. Soft, round baby cheeks, shadowed by a crescent of eyelash, pulled at her heart.

I love you so much! she whispered to herself.

Lena lay back on the pillows placed to support her back. This was one of her favorite places to be – especially in the early morning hours. She could watch the dawn while holding her sweet boy. Soon the ducks would begin their quacking, the geese their honking, the birds their singing, and sun would spill out upon the lake like a liquid rainbow, poured from a giant pitcher by the hand of Creator.

Lena shifted her body a little and repositioned Logan. Glancing down upon him once again, her breath caught in her throat:

What you have taught me! she marveled. *Your beauty transcends your anomaly.*

How could anyone *not* see his beauty? It was there in the way his bright hair curled, his lovely, large, luminous, brown eyes, his chubby cheeks, dimpled, star-like hands and vibrant smile. A faint, white scar gave testimony to the lip closure at age two months, and now the stitches below his left nostril from the tip rhinoplasty.

Lena drew her child to her. She remembered how she frantically tried to get him to drink from a cup, only to watch as her unci solved the problem with common sense. She laughed to herself,

My unci! Only she could see right to the heart of the problem and quietly fix it.

Unci!

Lena felt a tear slide down her cheek. Her wise and gentle grandmother had passed to the spirit world just six months before. Upon wakening on that fateful day, Lena walked to the kitchen to find it dark: no coffee brewing, no clatter of pots and pans. Returning to the upstairs, she opened the door to her grandmother's bedroom. There Reva lay, her face toward the window, a smile upon her aged face. Lena looked out of the windowpane, following her grandmother's gaze. There, on the shore, stood two blue herons, their necks entwined. Reva was now with her husband; she had ridden the wing of the Thunderbird to the edge of the universe.

Chapter Nineteen

Ho, Thunder Being Nation, I hear you singing.
I greet you as a relative, and thank you for the gifts that you bring.
Ho, Thunder Being Nation, I come singing.
I gift you with tobacco as a thank you for your gift.
Ho, Thunder Being Nation, the skies are singing.
Ho, my relations, I have spoken and it is so.

Julie Spotted Eagle Horse Martineu

Sonny unlocked the door to the restaurant. Ducking in quickly, he closed the door against an early August thunderstorm.

He liked this time of day, when he was alone in Vicki's. He could pretend that Michael would show up shortly with Lena. Soon Vicki would follow, and the day would slowly begin. In the five years since Michael and Vicki's deaths, Sonny never ceased to miss them; he never quite got away from the pain their memory caused. Then, there was Nickie.

Sonny winced inwardly at the picture of her that came to his mind's eye: hurt, confused, broken.

The scene played out before him like a home movie gone bad: his running after Nickie as she fled from the funeral home; Nickie in her car sobbing; Nickie opening the door as he rapped on the window, scooting over for him to enter the car, her face distorted with pain; Sonny driving her home and helping her into her apartment.

I should never have gone in, he scolded himself, for once through the door, she was in his arms.

Sonny remembered looking down upon her as they lay on the floor. Nickie's eyes closed, her lower lip caught between her teeth, tears flowing down her temples and into her hair. Moved, and driven by compassion, and yes lust, he had to admit, he made love to her right there on her antique, braided rug.

Later Sonny made a hasty exit, hating himself, hating what he knew he was doing to Nickie.

She didn't understand, and the look of hurt and anguish on her face would remain in his memory forever. She allowed him to see it once, when her guard was down, but only once. It made it even worse for him to bear.

It took some time for Sonny to realize that they both reacted out of grief. The death of their friends was unbearable, and somehow, they needed to celebrate life, celebrate it in the most primal way possible – making love. But, it didn't make Sonny feel any better about what he'd

114

done, and definitely had not eased Nickie's grief. Truth to tell, it increased it.

Slowly, Sonny came to realize that Nickie loved him, and his heart clenched anew at the knowledge. He could never love Nickie, not that way. His only love walked in the diminutive form of 23-year-old Lena Cedar Woman, the widow of his brother/cousin.

Lena drove passed the Whetstone Park of Roses on her way to pick up Jo-Ann.

I need to remember to bring Logan here, she mused, thinking of how her four-year-old dynamo would love the many varieties of roses displayed in over 11,000 rose bushes and herb, daffodil and perennial gardens set on 13 acres of Clintonvile's Whetstone Park.[89]

Lena drove another block and pulled into the parking lot of the three-story office building where Jo-Ann worked for an opthomologist, the only job she'd ever held. Jo-Ann was coming to spend the weekend.

Their friendship remained intact, and Jo-Ann was a frequent visitor, especially on weekends. Jo-Ann could no longer afford to get away on vacations, and considered Lena's lakeside home her own, personal, weekend retreat. She would sit on the deck, drinking her "martoonis," reveling in the quiet, bucolic atmosphere of the secluded neighborhood.

Jo-Ann was coming out of the building just as Lena pulled in.

"What, no Logan?" she queried, disappointment in her voice.

"We'll be picking him up at day care," Lena informed, "It's just about time for the school to let out. From there, we're going to this restaurant I want you to check out. It's called Carsonie's. We love it and they're very nice to Logan," Lena finished.

"How is the school turning out?" Jo-Ann asked.

"Beautifully!" Lena smiled.

Pulling out of the parking lot, she directed her faithful Punkin' toward Cooke Road. Lena found it amusing that, like her mother, she preferred the back roads to the freeway. Perhaps it was because of Michael and Vicki.....shaking off the thought, she immediately began to bring herself up to date on Jo-Ann's life and friends. Although they spoke on the phone often, face-to-face conversations were by far more satisfying.

Soon, they were pulling into the restaurant's parking lot located in the Glengary shopping center. Logan, secured in his car seat in the back of the ancient car, clapped his hands in joy. He knew what awaited him. David, the chef/owner, had created a special dish for him called "The Logan Special," which consisted of spaghetti, extra sauce and extra bread.

---

[89] http://www.clintonville.com/parkrec/rosegarden.html

Logan waved to the server on duty, and the three friends selected a booth. Soon menus, flatware and water, with Logan's obligatory glass of chocolate milk, were presented. Lena immediately placed her hand around the tumbler of milk so that Logan's lunge for the tasty beverage did not upset the glass.

"Okay, this place is cool. I like it," Jo-Ann offered.

"It has given me an idea," Lena informed. "I like that it is ethnically identified, it's well run and organized, and the menu offers a nice selection without going overboard like many do. Jo-Ann, I want to open my own restaurant right here in Westerville."

There was a flash, a crack of thunder and a curtain of rain.

"Wopila!" Logan crowed, his chubby arms held heavenward!

Lena laughed and pulled her son toward her, kissing his silky hair.

"Wopila, indeed!" she laughed. "The Thunderbirds approve!"

Chapter Twenty

Honor the sacred.
Honor the Earth, our Mother.
Honor the Elders.
Honor all with whom we
share the Earth:
Four-leggeds, two-leggeds,
winged ones,
Swimmers, crawlers,
Plant and rock people.
Walk in balance and beauty.

Native American Elder

Endrit[90] tossed roasted poblanos, garlic, spinach and honey into a blender and hit the pulse button. Since his arrival in the U.S., Endrit, or Diti[91], as his friends called him, had immersed himself in the ethnic cuisines of the Americas, especially Cajun, Creole, African, Hispanic and Native American. He landed his job at Vicki's shortly after his graduation from the Columbus Culinary Institute.

Diti removed the buffalo shanks that were searing in a cast iron skillet, and added diced onion, celery and carrot, or mirepoix,[92] and chopped garlic. To this, he poured some buffalo stock, to deglaze the pan, and finally tomato paste. Placing the shanks into the mixture, he brought it to a boil, then lidded the skillet and placed it into an oven.

Diti stopped for a moment, and lifting a glass of water from his workstation, drank deeply. The kitchen was a little warm, but he had been so engrossed in his cooking, that he hadn't noticed his growing thirst.

Diti loved his job, and was profoundly grateful for his luck in starting his career in such a top-notch establishment. He believed in Lena, and knew that his career would continue to flourish.

Beginning at Vicki's as a prep cook, then Sous-Chef, Diti was ultimately promoted to his present position as Executive Chef. Cooking was like breathing to him, and his dedication to his craft was apparent in the food he prepared, as well as his manner of presentation.

---

[90] En-dree – Albanian meaning light

[91] Dee-tee

[92] Meer-pwah – a combination of one part diced carrots, one part diced celery and two parts diced onions used as a base for many types of cuisine, especially in French dishes.

Diti walked to the sink and refilled his glass, drinking thirstily again. Delicious aromas were wafting through the kitchen, embracing him in their succulent vapors.

Endrit Kastrioti was a thirty-year-old, dark haired man from the capital city of Ballsh in the province of Mallakaster in Southern Albania. He often traveled to Southern Ohio for micro-vacations with his family, enjoying the hills of Hocking County, which reminded him of the rolling land of his mother country. However, the clean, green smells of Old Man's Cave, for instance, did not remind him of the smell of his hometown. Rich in petroleum and home to a refinery, the smell of gas permeated the air of Ballsh and seemed, according to Diti, to "punch the air right out of your lungs."

Short of temper, and quick to apologize, he adored his wife Besara[93] and daughter Era.[94] He was a kind man who loved children, women, his family, and good food.

Diti turned from the sink as the door to the kitchen opened and his brother, Dejan[95] entered. The day manager of Vicki's, Dejan arrived in America a few years before his younger brother. Married to Luli,[96] a petite beauty with a large personality, he felt extremely fortunate in all areas of his life: his family, friends, and working with his kid brother. Tall, with the same dark hair as Diti, Dejan walked with an air of confidence, presenting to the world an open, charming personality, which drew many to him. His larger hand held that of the eight-year-old Logan.

Face wreathed in smiles, Logan limped to a table and chair where he would spend the morning helping Diti prepare some of the ingredients for the lunch crowd.

Two weeks previously, Logan had endured yet another surgery to repair his anomaly. A sizeable piece of bone taken from his tiny hip was transplanted to his alveolar ridge, or gum line, where bone was missing. Once his surgeon was comfortable that the gum would not resorb, an orthodontist could begin straightening Logan's crooked teeth. Logan was missing an incisor due to the clefting, for which a new tooth would be provided where the now new gum existed, either by moving the tooth behind the empty space forward into place, and shaping it to look like an incisor, or by implant.

Logan faced a summer of restricted activities because of the missing bone from his hip, which needed to re-grow before he could ride his bicycle, jump, roller skate, or engage in any of the activities an eight-

---

[93] Baysa-ar – honor, trust, faith
[94] Air-uh – wind
[95] Dan – God is my judge
[96] Loo-lee – flower

year-old boy enjoyed during the long, summer vacation before starting back to school in the fall.

Lena knew that her parents would gladly watch their beloved grandson while she was at the restaurant, but wanted Logan engaged in something to stave off boredom. In addition, she felt that an opportunity to learn a life skill must never be passed up. Also, Logan would inherit the restaurant some day, and Lena felt that he should begin learning how to take care of his inheritance. Therefore, she recruited her staff to help her with her son, until her parents picked him up in the early afternoon for a much needed rest after the activities of the day.

Diti smiled at the little boy, wincing inside as he remembered the pain Logan had endured after his surgery. He was, however, pleased to see that Logan's limp was becoming less and less noticeable, which meant that the pain was abating.

Such a sweet kid, Diti thought to himself, preparing to enjoy Logan's company.

Logan was a little boy - for a while longer. His arms were smooth and round, his shoulders boney: the body of an active child gone from chubby and babyish to the coltish build of the adolescent who likes to fish, bullfrog hunt, run with his dog.

His hair was a luxuriant, shining dark, brown. His large eyes, the same color as his mother's, were luminous and full of intelligence, his forehead broad and high, but not overly so. His skin was a smooth bronze, his brows clear cut and slightly arched, his face beautiful in spite of his birth defect: the severe clefting of the lip, gum and hard and soft palates, now repaired. The surgeons had done their work well. His upper lip was plumping out and the hint of a cupid's bow was beginning to manifest.

Diti walked to the table and placed a bowl on its immaculate surface.

"Lale!"[97] he exclaimed with pleasure, "it is good to see you today. You're going to help me, yes?" Diti asked, his eyes sparkling with pleasure.

"Yes, Diti," Logan smiled. "You are kind to let me come and help. What do you want me to do?" the child queried.

"A very important job," Diti informed. "Our customers love our sweet potato hash and it is in big demand. It takes a lot of work to keep enough ready to throw into the sauté pan and have it out of the kitchen with the rest of the meal. So here is what I want you to do."

Diti placed a partially cooked sweet potato on the table. Handing Logan a plastic chef's knife, which he had bought the night before at the local GFS restaurant supply market, he showed the boy how to pull the

---

[97] Lah-lee – Albanian - little brother

skin off the boiled root vegetable, a task made easy by the cooking process. He then instructed him on how to cut the potato in half, each half into quarters and then to dice them into bite size pieces.

Logan smiled his understanding and set to work, his pink tongue peeking out of the corner of his mouth, as his mother's used to do, in the warm and loving kitchen in which she grew up in Southern Ohio.

The morning progressed serenely, with Logan dicing sweet potatoes, crumbling cooked bacon, chopping chives and performing other simple yet important tasks.

At one point, Diti had to suppress a smile when, turning to Logan he asked,

"Is it going well, Lale?"

"Yes, Chef," the precocious boy answered.

Diti was amused but pleased at the same time.

He'll make a fine restaurateur some day, Diti asserted, nodding to himself in approval of his statement, *a fine restaurateur, indeed.*

The morning progressed quickly for Logan. Busy with his duties, the morning hours flew, and before he was aware of the time, Diti placed a plate in front of him. Logan smiled with delight. His favorite dish of the restaurant, Elk meatloaf presented upon a bed of herb-scented quinoa. Spears of asparagus shone vibrant green and glistened with olive oil. The scent of rosemary tickled his nose and caused his mouth to water.

Diti smiled his appreciation and returned to the stove. As he reached the shining appliance, he heard Logan whisper,

"Waste, lila waste! Wopila, thank you, for giving your life that I may live."

Diti was touched. The young boy was thanking the animal and the plants that gave up their lives so that he may live.

Tunkasila! Logan cried! Peter smiled as he walked to the table where Logan was helping Nickie fold napkins for the evening service. It was mid-afternoon, and time for Logan to head home for some quiet time with his grandparents.

Peter was much improved from the man who sat at the "Spotted Eagle Table," so many years ago, not only mentally, but physically as well. His left arm was supple, his hand uncurled. An almost undetectable droop of the left side of his mouth, and a slight hesitance of speech, were the only apparent testaments to his head injury 15 years before.

Logan rose painfully from the chair. Walking to his grandparent's car would help to loosen his stiffened hip. Taking his grandfather's hand, and turning to give Nickie a shy smile, Logan thanked her for working with him. Walking into the sunlight with Peter, he gave a final glance back before the door to the restaurant closed.

"So, Takoja, what will we do when we get home?" Peter queried.

"May I go bullfrog hunting, Tunkasila?" Logan asked hopefully.

"Well, now, it seems that it isn't time yet for you to be trying something like that, ennit. How about if I hunt the frogs for you, you examine them, and then tell me if they are well enough to put back into the lake. If they're injured, you can help me set up the habitat, and I'll go buy some crickets. Would that be good?" Peter smiled.

"Oh, yes! We have to make sure that all of my babies are well, Tunkasila!" Logan stressed.

At age six, Logan chanced upon a teenage boy hunting bullfrogs along the lake's grassy shore. Questioning the young man, he obtained the rudiments of successfully hunting the fascinating creatures. He learned to handle them only when his hands were wet, so as not to tear their skin, to hold them gently and to return them to the lake as quickly as possible. Peter ruffled his grandson's hair, and slowly walked him to the car.

Mary was waiting, and exited the vehicle as Logan approached, hugging him to her. Burying her nose in his shining hair, she breathed him in, enjoying his clean, little boy smell laced with the fragrances of the kitchen. All piled in, buckled up, and headed for the lakefront house where Logan and Lena lived with their "pound puppy," Kelly, and the ducks, geese and frogs, which were a large part of Logan's life. He loved the lake, and considered the creatures whom he shared his life with his personal responsibility.

Peter pulled into the driveway, and they entered the spacious home. Kelly, a Yellow Lab, Terrier mix, ran to Logan, tail wagging with joy. Logan bent to hug her white, fuzzy head close to his heart.

"Hello, Sunka Ska![98] We're going bullfrog hunting!" he cried with joy.

"After a snack," Mary insisted, smiling with love at her glorious grandchild.

Mary prepared a plate of applesauce and fry bread, making sure, as Diti had, that the food was soft enough for the recovering youngster to enjoy without jeopardizing the bone graft, giving the requisite grandmother admonition:

"Bite and chew on the right side!"

Snack eaten, Logan followed his grandfather to the back deck and out to the lake, fish net in hand.

"Okay, Logan, you must tell me how to do this!" Peter laughed.

---

[98] Shoonkah Shkah – white dog

"It's easy, Tunkasila! Just lie down on the dock there and see if you can see some eyes. Then, use the net and sweep it slowly. When you feel a little, tender thing,[99] that is the frog. Just scoop him up gently and hand him to me."

"Yes, sir!" Peter smiled.

Peter was amazed at how quickly he managed to catch a bullfrog – a pretty good-sized specimen at that. Once pulled from the water, it was evident that the frog was in trouble. One of his back feet was missing, a bloody stump giving witness to a recent attack by a snapping turtle.

"This is a fine frog, ennit," Peter announced. "We need to get your habitat. There, over there, Tokaja. I have it ready for you."

Peter smiled at his grandson, indicating the plastic one-gallon fish tank, which he had found in the garage, complete with a few rocks for the frog to feed upon. Lake water was added to the tune of about three inches and the frog placed within his temporary "clinic."

Logan relaxed peacefully on the sofa in the family room, content with his day. He'd spent time with Diti and helped in the kitchen, gone over the evening menu with his ina and helped Nickie get ready for the evening service. Logan gave a small sigh. He kinda liked Nickie. Actually, he liked her a lot, and wished that she'd wait until he grew up. But, she wouldn't, would she – she was in love with Sonny.

Logan's smooth brow wrinkled in consternation. Nickie loved Sonny, but Sonny loved Ina. He knew he did. Whenever Sonny was around his ina, a soft light emanated from him, just like with Unci and Tunkasila, and a soft light shone from Ina, but she didn't seem to notice Sonny, except for restaurant matters. It was very confusing. Logan moved slightly and winced. There was still an uncomfortable pinch in his right hip. He settled a little more into the cushions until he was comfortable.

I sure don't understand it, he thought. *Nickie loves Sonny, Sonny loves Ina, and Ina loves...me!*

Logan smiled to himself and relaxed against the cushions again. Frogzilla gave a croak, and Logan turned his head to observe his amphibian patient. Ensconced on the hearth of the wood burning fireplace, the large, injured frog relaxed after a satisfying meal of six, large crickets. The stump had closed and stopped bleeding, and Logan was sure he could release him in a few days.

---

[99] *Christopher Bullfrog Catcher*, Christopher Shiveley Welch, Saga Books, page 27

Logan smiled to himself as his eyes slowly closed. Softly, sweetly, he drifted off with visions of fry bread, Nickie, and bullfrog hunts sweeping him away on a soft, soft cloud of dreams.

Chapter Twenty One

Our first teacher is our own heart

Cheyenne Proverb

Logan sat on the lower step of the back deck. Head in hands, he played the scene over and over in his mind. He had been naughty, and he didn't know how to make it right.

The day started out like any other. Ina was up and making him breakfast, when he slowly descended the stairs, following his nose. Carefully, he took one stair at a time, instead of his usual gamboling flight down the fourteen steps of the winding staircase. His hip still hurt a little, and he was careful not to do anything that could cause a fall.

I sure don't want to go through this again! he thought to himself.

The smell of corn mush drew him into the kitchen. It was one of his favorite breakfasts, and Ina made sure she made it for him often since the surgery.

Sometimes she fried it and served it with maple syrup, but since the bone graft, she made it like a hot cereal, like oatmeal. It was delicious!

Logan dug in hungrily, perching upon one of the stools at the breakfast bar.

"Logan, Unci and Tunkasila will be here soon. They are coming here again today instead of your going to their house or Vicki's. Until you recover, this is the way it will be. Sometimes you will be able to go to Vicki's, but sometimes you must stay here. That way, you are home on your lake, and can amuse yourself with fishing and watching your animals, when you're not helping at the restaurant."

Lena smiled at her son and ruffled his hair. He was taking the inactivity well, and was managing to get through each day without becoming too bored.

"Why am I not going to see Diti and Dejan and Nickie today?" Logan questioned, spoon poised halfway to his mouth.

"You are a big help at Vicki's, but today is a very busy day, and it's best if you stay here. I think you should have some quiet days, don't you? Perhaps tomorrow you can return.

"Oh!" Lena exclaimed, "I almost forgot to tell you. Sherri is bringing Happy over today. Now, be careful, she is a big dog. I don't want you wrestling with her or anything. In fact, why don't you brush her and maybe give her a bath on the back deck. I think she'll like that."

Logan was ecstatic! Happy was a beautiful Dalmatian, and he was crazy about her. Gentle of spirit, Happy was a welcome companion in the Young Bear home. Even Kelly enjoyed her company, and the two could be seen napping together or just "hanging out" on the deck, pink tongues lolling, tails thumping, as Logan explored his beloved lake.

Logan and Happy had something in common. Because of a problem with processing uric acid, the usually active dog had undergone a cystotomy for bladder stones. The two convalescents, therefore, kept each other company as often as Sherri could bring her.

Logan loved her glossy, white coat covered with round, black spots. Her nose, also spotted, was wet and cold and constantly nudging his hand for pets. Happy also shared something with his ina: heterochromia; Happy possessed one brown and one blue eye.

In addition, she was deaf, a condition known to the breed. Logan found that if he made certain motions while talking, like pointing to Happy and then a spot beside his feet and said, "Here," Happy would understand and come to him.

She was Logan's playmate, his friend, and he knew instinctively that he would remember her until the end of his days, that this time with Happy and Kelly, his ina, and his grandparents, would forever stay in his mind as a golden halcyon chapter in his life. In later years, the memories of his childhood would give him comfort, and a firm foundation of faith in himself.

Logan finished his mush and carefully slid from the stool.

"Ina, what can I do until Happy gets here?" he questioned.

"Why don't you color? You haven't done that for a couple of days, and the refrigerator is looking pretty empty!" Lena laughed, referring to the front of her French door fridge.

Logan would spend an afternoon coloring, and then proudly attach his work of art to the refrigerator door with magnets shaped like giraffes, dinosaurs and fish. The next day, the colorful artwork was taken away and placed in a box beneath his bed.

Lena once asked him why he removed his efforts so quickly and was surprised at his:

"Because it's been seen."

This confused her, but she couldn't seem to get him to express exactly what he meant.

In fact, the precocious child owned the heart of a poet and artist. He could taste the wind, smell colors, feel flavors. The world to him was a banquet of sensations and emotions in which he sometimes felt overwhelmed. He would create a drawing, and feel satisfaction in his work, but upon encountering it the next morning, believe that he had missed something...he could do better. Perhaps it was this tendency to aim for perfection, which led him to his current folly.

"Good girl, Kelly," Logan murmured.

Kneeling in front of a large, square coffee table, situated in the cedar-paneled family room, Logan lifted the hinged door which served as one half of the table top, extracting drawing paper and crayons. Kelly nudged him again, and Logan scratched behind her ear absent-mindedly.

"Just a minute, Kelly, I need to do this."

Logan closed the lid and arranged his supplies, intent on finishing his drawing before Sherri and Happy arrived.

Logan wanted to color Nurse Marengo. Her image was vivid in his mind, and he wanted to capture it. The bone graft surgery was the worst one he'd been through so far, and the images, sounds, and smells were still vivid in his mind.

He remembered waking up in a big room bustling with people, a little boy in the bed next to him beginning to cry, his head was completely covered in bandages, and Logan wondered what he had endured.

Logan's hip hurt! It hurt so bad, and his lip hurt. He could feel stitches hanging down in his mouth. He moaned, and a nurse was immediately at his side. Then he saw his ina.

"Hey, Little Man. How are you?"

Logan was very glad that Ina was there when he woke up. He didn't want to be scared. He was a man after all, but her presence helped him to stay brave. He was grateful.

He fell asleep, and the next thing he knew, he was in another room, and a nurse was bending over him. She had long, dark, wavy hair and incredible green eyes. But, the thing he noticed the most was her earrings. One was a flamingo and the other was a tiger! Logan blinked his eyes, sure that he was seeing things. Tossing her head, and making the earrings dance, Nurse Marengo laughed:

"You like?"

Logan smiled at the fascinating woman and murmured,

"Your earrings don't match, ennit."

"No, Dear Heart, they don't. I find that you little guys pay more attention to my earrings than the stitches and IVs, so I wear them to amuse and distract."

Logan liked that. He liked that someone would think enough to come up with something that would help kids get through those first few days after surgery. And so, he wanted to honor her by putting her image, as he remembered it, on paper.

He was coloring away intently, Kelly's head nestled in his lap, when Logan heard the slam of a car door and an excited yip. Using his hands to push himself upward, he walked stiffly into the foyer and gazed out the front door side light. Happy was here!

A crop of bright, strawberry curls caught the sun and burst into a halo of flame. Logan's breath caught in his chest as the now golden, red ringlets seemed to blaze in the sunlight.

How beautiful! he murmured to himself.

Sherri stepped onto the deck, Happy at her heals. Crossing her eyes and sticking her tongue out of the side of her mouth, she pretended to knock on the door. Laughing, Logan turned the knob, inviting Sherri and Happy into the foyer.

"Hello, girl!" he exclaimed, hugging Happy around her aristocratic neck.

"Hey! What about me?" Sherri laughed.

"Hello, girl!" Logan teased, grabbing Sherri in a similar embrace and scratching the top of her head.

"You goof!" she laughed, proceeding into the kitchen.

Smiling, Sherri caroled,

"Good morning, Mary, good morning, Peter."

She liked the Catchers, and felt that they were the quintessential example of a true marriage.

I hope I have something like that someday, she would often think to herself.

Maxing out at 5'3", pale, freckled, and slightly plump, the ingenuous red head was a welcomed addition to Lena's extended family. Sherri was Logan's dental hygienist, and had grown to love the young boy.

Generous of spirit, with a somewhat wacky sense of humor, she lived her life with both hands open, the latest testament of which was today's visit. Extremely energetic, and bursting with life, Sherri was continually busy, and her kindness in bringing Happy by, an hour-long round trip for her, underscored her giving personality.

Sherri exchanged pleasantries with Mary and Peter, and then, her body and mind in perpetual motion, was out the front door before anyone could take a breath. Logan watched as she left, eyes wide with hope. There it was again! Sherri's hair blazed in reds, oranges and gold as the sun hit the top of her head. Sighing, Logan turned and made his way back to the coffee table, two canine friends now standing attendance.

The morning passed contentedly. The sun moved across the room. Water shadows danced on ceiling and walls. Here and there light caught a piece of glass or prism, and rainbows played around the room. Logan colored away, stopping now and then to scratch a white ear, spotted chin or rub a dappled belly. He enjoyed the light in the room, and the rainbows, which were visiting him this morning.

He stopped for a moment to stand and stretch; staying in the same position too long made his hip stiff. He glanced at Happy, and then at a rainbow: Happy – rainbow, and was suddenly inspired!

Yes! he exclaimed to himself.

Lifting the lid to the coffee table, and burrowing amid its contents, Logan found what he was looking for. Holding it up to the rainbow and squinting one eye, he became excited. Sherri's fiery locks flashed across his mind's eye.

Perfect!

Walking across the back deck, Peter approached the sliding doors, which exited from the family room. He felt renewed.

There's nothing like a short nap in the sun, with the sound of ducks and fountains pleasing your ear, he mused.

Entering the family room, Peter noticed Logan and the two dogs.

Where is my Mary? he questioned silently.

Peter took a few steps toward the foyer and stopped. Wait a minute. Something was wrong. Turning slowly, he gazed upon Logan and his two friends.

"MARY!"

The sound of his wife's feet clattering down the stairs told Peter where Mary had been. He ran to meet her, pointing toward the foyer, his mouth flapping ineffectually. Alarm rose in her breast: was Peter stroking?

"Peter! Peter! What's wrong? Are you all right? Are you hurt? What's wrong?" she pleaded, concern growing with every passing second.

Peter shook his head and pointed again to the family room.

"Logan?" she cried, "is Logan hurt?"

Turning to fly into the family room, Mary felt Peter's hand clutching at her arm. Spinning toward him, she started to shout:

"Let me go!" when she noticed that, what she had thought was alarm and concern was, in fact, its exact opposite.

Peter was trying desperately not to break into explosive laughter. Clutching his sides, he bent and moaned. Covering his face, gulping, tears coursing down his cheeks, Peter again pointed to the family room. Mary stood before her husband, her look puzzled. A tentative smile began to crease her face. Slowly, completely confused, Mary entered the room.

Logan lifted his head and looked upon the lake. Today it offered no consolation. He had been bad. He had disrespected one of his best friends, and he didn't know how to make it up to her.

What was I thinking? he moaned inwardly. *What was I THINKING?*

Banishing him to the back deck, his grandparents ordered him to stay put until they called him in. They must be very, very angry with him, because they wouldn't look him in the eye. Whenever he tried to get them to look at him, they would turn away. Unci kept clutching Tunkasila, turning into him, her shoulders shaking.

Is she crying? he wondered in alarm!

Logan had never seen his unci cry. Head hanging, he went out onto the deck and sat on the bottom step. His mortification was complete.

Had Logan been more aware, he would have heard the closing of windows and shutting of doors, but he was too deep in his shame to take notice.

I can no longer walk this earth with honor, he grieved. *The grandfathers know my disgrace. Ate! Are you ashamed of me too?*

Logan sank into mute despair. Were he more aware of his surroundings, he would have been confused to hear unbridled laughter.

Logan slowly became aware of his surroundings. Sitting on the step, he heard his mother's car. He sank deeper into his shoulders, afraid, knowing how disappointed his mother would be with him.

She won't talk to me for years, he thought.

Tears spilled down his tanned cheeks, and he hung his head once more.

The sounds of the lake seemed to stop. The fountain sparkled, but there was no splash of water. The ducks swam but there was no hint of the quacking and peeping Logan had come to love. He sat upright and looked around…did he just hear…laughter?

He knew his mother's laugh, knew it as well as his own. He could hear her single whoop as she threw back her head, the clap of her hands. Single yelps of laughter followed.

Tunkasila was laughing. He could hear him, like a baloon leaking air. He would cover his face and then wheeze out his laughter, his face turning red.

He heard another car. Sherri!

Oh, no! he groaned.

There was the slamming of a car door and then he could hear her ring the doorbell.

Silence and then,
"Aaaaaaaaaaahhhhhhhhhhh!"
He listened intently: another scream and then Sherri's very identifiable hearty laughter. What *was* happening in there?
They've forgotten about me, he mourned. *I'll have to sleep under the deck with the opossum.*
Logan gave a start as he heard the *swish* of the sliding doors. Tunkasila motioned for Logan to come in. He rose and walked slowly toward his grandfather.
Logan was too upset to notice that each of the adults were still fighting back laughter.
Faces reddened with the effort, teeth clenched, they sat on the two couches in the family room. A dining room chair sat facing the four adults. Logan took a seat and awaited his sentencing.

Logan was so engrossed in his work that he did not hear his tunkasila enter the family room. When he heard him cry, "MARY!" Logan jumped in alarm, jerked out of his creative muse.
He heard his unci's rapid descent, the conversation in the foyer. Turning to Happy, Logan finally realized exactly what he'd done.
Mary walked into the room to see the dog standing beside Logan. Happy gave a yip. Lying down, she placed her muzzle between her paws. Logan stood frozen, his eyes wide. In his right hand, he held a permanent marker; in his left, he held two. Happy, once a beautiful black and white, now looked like a crazy quilt. Logan had colored in all of her white fur with the markers, using red, yellow and orange.

Unci cleared her throat and began to speak.
"Takoja," Mary bit her lip. Clutching Peter's hand, she fought off another spasm of laughter. She glanced at Peter and could see that he was clenching his teeth. She could feel a slight tremor go through his body and heard an almost imperceptible moan.
Her sides hurt, her stomach hurt and her jaws ached.
Cha! What a grandson I have! She laughed to herself.
"Takoja," she weakly began again.
Logan looked up and met his unci's eyes. He felt a wave of relief. Her eyes were stern, but kind, and a wave of love flowed from his heart to hers.
"Takoja, *what* were you thinking? Why did you do this to poor Happy? I thought she was your friend!"
Logan looked down at the unfortunate canine, lying by his chair, muzzle nested within her paws. Her beautiful coat was now a

kaleidoscope of colors seemingly set against a black background. She shifted her eyes up to his, and he could see embarrassment. Happy was embarrassed!

Logan was humiliated. Happy was his friend, and he had embarrassed her. He had made her feel that she wasn't beautiful by changing her colors.

I SHOULD sleep under the deck with the opossum, except that's too good for me too! I don't deserve any berry pudding either – not even fry bread. How could I do that to my friend?

Logan looked over at Kelly who was sitting on the opposite side of his chair. Her large, brown eyes gazed back at him and seemed to impart disappointment.

I promise, Sunka Ska, I will never do something like this again. I like you both the way you are.

Logan knew, deep in his heart, that he was responsible for Kelly and Happy. They trusted him, and he had betrayed that trust. Because Happy loved him, she let him ruin her beautiful coat. Logan looked at her again. Rising to a sitting position, she gazed deeply into Logan's eyes. They seemed to say,

"It's all right, Boy. I love you, and I know you love me."

Logan was forgiven by Happy, but not yet by himself.

What I did was unforgivable! he mourned.

"Cate sice hemaca,[100] Sunka Gleska.[101]" Logan hung his head, too ashamed to meet the faithful dog's eyes again.

"Logan?" Mary queried.

"I like Sherri's hair!" Logan exclaimed, fighting tears.

He was mortified again. His lips wouldn't behave and were trembling. He folded them into his mouth in an effort to control them, but his chin got into the act. He hung his head to hide the fact that he was on the verge of tears.

Face it like a man, Logan! he chastised himself.

Mary looked at Peter, then at Lena and Sherri. Everyone sat with mouths hanging open, completely surprised by his answer.

Clearing her throat, Mary tried to understand and said,

"Um, Logan, that doesn't make sense. You like Sherri's hair?"

"Yes, Unci. When she walks in the sunlight, it lights up like fire. It's really beautiful. That's why I run to the side light whenever I hear her car. I wanted to make Happy look like Sherri's hair in the sunlight."

"Well," Peter began, "she is a fire house dog."

Peter clamped his hand to his mouth, but it was too late. It was over; the pretense could no longer be upheld. A roar of laughter hit

---

[100] Chahn tday see chay hay mahn chah – sorrowing I am
[101] Shoon kah glay shkah – Spotted Dog

Logan full force, as the adults lost control completely. Lena leaned into Sherri and grabbed her arm. She threw her head back and whooped. Mary clapped her hands and gave a yip, pointing to Happy. Peter wheezed and turned almost purple. Sherri jumped from her chair, encircling Logan in her arms, and to his chagrin, planted a smacking kiss on his cheek.

"You *are* such a goof," she laughed and kissed him again.

Logan was amazed. *Are grownups crazy?* he wondered.

Chapter Twenty-Two

Wakan Tanka, Great Mystery,
teach me how to trust
my heart, my mind, my intuition,
my inner knowing,
the senses of my body,
the blessings of my spirit.
Teach me to trust these things
so that I may enter my sacred space
and love beyond my fear,
and thus walk in balance
with the passing of each glorious sun.

Lakota Prayer

Sonny bent over Lena's sleeping form. Gently, oh so gently, he drew his hand through her silky hair, its glossy tresses spread upon the pillow like a shimmering fan. Sliding down the bed until his chin was resting upon her fragrant shoulder, and nuzzling her neck, he breathed in her unique scent of wild sage. He drew in a deeper breath, endeavoring to pull the aroma of her flesh into the depths of his soul.

Sonny wished that he could draw her into him completely – or perhaps he had already, as there was never a minute that he was not thinking of her, longing for her, dreaming about her.

His soul soared with happiness. She was finally his! After years of waiting for this moment, craving her smooth arms about him, finally she was his!

The clash of trashcans in the alley behind his apartment woke Sonny with a start. The peace, which inhabited his heart seconds before, shattered. Sonny looked to his right. Lena was not there. It had been yet another dream.

Sonny was bereft. Each time he awoke from a dream where she was his, the devastation was more complete. His heart broke, and he threw himself upon the pillow, where just seconds ago, he dreamt his love had lain.

She is my half side Sonny mourned to himself, *and she does not know it. She thinks that Michael was her soul mate, but she is wrong. It is I!*

Sonny sat up in the bed, wrapping his arms around his knees and slowly rocking in an attempt to sooth his aching heart. Sweat broke out upon his brow and his long, dark hair fell across his knees, hiding his striking features.

Sonny remembered the day he fell in love with Lena and she with Michael. *She was so young,* he considered, *too young to know that Michael was the one.* Sonny ran his fingers through his hair, pulling it from his face, and stood up from the bed. He began to pace as he continued his monologue, the same internal conversation he had subjected himself to for the past 16 years.

How could she have known that Michael was the one? She was a baby, only 17 when they met. Then, they married and he introduced her to sexual pleasure. She was mesmerized, not in love!

*No, she **was** in love* he admitted to himself, *but it was the love of a young girl, not of a woman grown.*

"I am her half side!" Sonny cried aloud.

He stopped his pacing and sat on the edge of the bed, elbows on his knees, his hair once again cascading, hiding his face.

I am as Tutokanula[102] longing for his Tisayac[103], he groaned inwardly, thinking of the young warrior, Tutokanula who, upon gazing upon Tisayac, the spirit of Yosemite Valley, fell in love, but could not capture the heart of the shy spirit. He fled the valley, leaving his people to fend for themselves. Desolation followed.

Lena is afraid to love again, afraid that she will lose yet another one dear to her. How can I make her throw aside her fear as Tisayac did when Tutokanula returned and she saw his love for her?

Walking to the closet, Sonny roughly threw the sliding door open, grabbing the first thing he saw. He dressed quickly in a pair of faded jeans and a white tee shirt. Walking into the living room, he paused, reflecting upon the history behind the room in which he stood, and how it revolved around his love for Lena.

Sonny still lived in the three-room apartment once inhabited by Lena, her parents and grandmother, and later by him and his brother/cousin, Michael. Sonny had never seen the need to move: his life was simple and uncomplicated. He had no need of a larger space. Besides, remaining at the Front Street apartment made him feel closer to Michael – to Lena.

She had lived in these rooms, laughed, cried, perhaps daydreamed about her future love. Here, Sonny and Michael had begun their new lives in Columbus, Ohio. He could see Michael, smiling, full of hope and joy…longing for the day when he and Lena would wed.

Aaaahhhh, Sonny cried inwardly! *I can't keep it out of my mind for even a second!*

---

[102] The strong leader of the people who lived in the valley
[103] The guardian of Yosemite

Crossing the living room, Sonny sat upon the sofa, resolving to let the memories take him wherever they wanted to: the powwow, his performance and near faux pas during the Ugly Man Dance, Lena and Michael's wedding when Lena turned 18, and finally, his mind going back to Michael's funeral. There lay his brother/cousin, who had taken the five steps into the spirit world, and there stood his widow, Lena, his love. Remembering her pain made his heart break again.

He closed his eyes and took deep, long breaths in an attempt to calm his heart, still racing from the exquisite dream of him and Lena finally as one. Slowly, so very slowly, his heart stopped its racing. He opened his eyes, and there before him, stood Michael.

Resplendent in his Grass Dancer regalia, Michael did not speak, his black eyes shining like a sacred fire during a full moon, telling Sonny to trust what dwelt within the core of his being. Sonny nodded his understanding. He would not give up. He would continue to love Lena, for his love was good and strong and he believed in that love. It was not a desire that sprang from his loins alone, but from his heart as well, in fact, from his very soul. She was his life, and if the Grandfathers approved, he would make her his.

Chapter Twenty Three

Hold on to what is good,
Even if it's a handful of earth.
Hold on to what you believe,
Even if it's a tree that stands by itself.
Hold on to what you must do,
Even if it's a long way from here.
Hold on to your life,
Even if it's easier to let go.
Hold on to my hand,
Even if someday, I'll be gone away from you.

A Pueblo Indian Prayer

Now 36, Sonny was more handsome than he had been at the powwow in Keokuk those many years ago. His face, once that of an eager, young man, was changed. The pain of losing Michael, and his unrequited love for Lena, had left their mark, giving him a mysterious quality, irresistible to many, male and female alike.

Wide shoulders tapered to a narrow waist, accentuating the power of his muscled torso. Well-formed thighs seemed to burst from his Levi© jeans, his muscular arms causing many a woman, young and old, to sigh with longing.

Sonny worked out seven days a week, taking the frustration he felt from an almost celibate life, and pouring it into weights and barbells, dumbbells, and various bodybuilding equipment.

He would leave work, heading straight for the gym, working out until he felt that he could fall, exhausted, into bed, and hopefully, nothingness – except for those rare nights when Lena came to him, fulfilling his yearnings in passionate, sweet, dreams.

Occasionally, he would meet a woman whom he thought might break Lena's spell. The woman often looked like Lena, but never measured up to her in Sonny's eyes, leaving him more bereft with every failed relationship; Sonny could not escape his longing for the beautiful Lena with her magnificent, heterochromatic eyes.

Lena, my woman! How can I make you see that it is me you love?

Sonny sat in his office at Vicki's, lost in thoughts of Lena. The dream of the consummation of his love would not leave him. Tortured, deep in thought, he didn't hear the tap on his door. The squeak of an unoiled hinge caused him to look up, straight into the eyes of his half side.

136

"Son..."

Sonny's name fell short on her tongue. Her smile of greeting slipped from her beautiful lips, as she looked straight into the face of great suffering. She began to question her friend, to ask him what was wrong, when the look of torment slipped into that of deep longing. Lena faltered, tilted her head to one side in question, and then straightened, her glorious eyes widening in recognition. Slowly, she backed out of the office and shut the door. Leaning against it for support, her heart pounding, she finally acknowledged what she had seen in Sonny's eyes; she at last admitted to herself that she had recognized his love for her a long time ago, but had refused to admit it within her heart.

Turning, her shining hair fanning around her, Lena ran from the restaurant. Finding her car, she faltered with the keys until she finally unlocked its door, started the engine, and drove off.

Mary watched in surprise as Lena sped through the restaurant. It was not like her daughter to show extreme emotion. She wondered at Lena's obvious agitation until, remembering her mentioning going to Sonny's office, understanding filled her heart.

Mary recalled Sonny's arrival thirty minutes earlier. She knew instantly that Sonny was in great pain. Mary was a wise woman, capable of deep, abiding love. Therefore, she recognized it in Sonny; she knew of his profound love for her daughter. Her heart broke for the exceptional, young man whom she had come to care for as part of her family.

Hesitating, Mary walked to Sonny's door. Tapping lightly, she slowly opened it and peered into the space. Sonny sat, his head on his desk, fists clenched, knuckles white. Mary knew without looking that semicircles of blood were forming in the palms of his hands where his nails dug into his flesh. Sighing, Mary gently closed the door, and walked to where Sonny sat.

She could feel his mourning. Indeed, his suffering permeated her soul, cried out to her woman's heart. She knew why he suffered, had known for a long time.

It is time to put a stop to this, Mary thought to herself. *Michael is gone, and though we honor him in our hearts, he walks in the spirit world these 17 years past. I must speak to my daughter, and make her see that she is throwing away Creator's greatest gift – true love.*

Stepping to Sonny's side, and leaning toward him, Mary placed her hands on his shoulders, pulling him upright. Turning his swivel chair until he faced her, she wrapped her still lovely arms around him, pressing his tear-stained cheek to her bosom and beginning to rock. In the rocking, she offered comfort as women have done since The People first walked the earth. *Rocking, rocking, rocking*, Mary began to speak. Slowly, gently, she told Sonny of her knowledge, of her recognition of his deep love for Lena. Holding him to her heart, she vowed that she would help Sonny awaken Lena's love. Making small, comforting sounds, she gently calmed Sonny, the son of her soul.

Chapter Twenty Four

They are not dead who live in the hearts they leave behind.

Tuscarora

Lena pulled into the driveway of her Westerville home. Jumping from her car, she fled into the house, slamming the door behind her. Fleeing to her bedroom, she threw herself upon the bed. Following Lena's flight to the upstairs, Kelly slowly ascended. Walking to where Lena lay, Kelly gently nudged her arm. Her Ina did not seem to realize that she was there. Nudging again, Kelly sat, tail slowly thumping in the hope that Lena would respond. Kelly tilted her head to one side. She could hear the sounds her family made when their souls were in distress, and could feel her Ina's pain. Kelly's own heart began to ache. The thumping of her tail changed to one of confusion. She wanted to comfort her Ina, and in the only way she knew how, gently nudged her again.

Lena felt Kelly's wet nose against her arm. Rolling to her side, she found herself peering into the deep, brown eyes of the gentle canine. A weak smile creased her face. Reaching out, she began to stroke Kelly's soft, white fur.

"Sunka Ska, you wish to comfort me, but you do not know what is wrong, do you?" Lena queried.

Sitting upright, Lena dashed non-existent tears from her cheeks. Standing, she brushed her hands along the length of her clothing, straightening any wrinkles. Motioning to Kelly, Lena descended the stairs.

Walking to the sliding doors to the back deck, Lena gazed upon the bucolic scene before her. Ducks quacked; the fountains' spray arched toward the heavens and fell to the water in glistening bouquets of light. The sun threw diamonds across the surface of the water, as birds chirped and sang, and squirrels scurried. The sounds of the neighborhood reached her ears. The day was alive.

Alive.

Lena acknowledged to herself that she had literally lived with the memory of Michael as if he were still upon this earth, and allowed no other man to occupy the space he held. Upon entering Sonny's office, and seeing the pain on his face turn to that of longing, Lena was forced to admit that a living man wanted her, needed her, loved her.

Intuitively, Lena realized that she had caught him off guard. Stripped of his usual defenses, he did not have the presence of mind to mask his feelings as he usually did. What Lena witnessed, not an hour ago, was Sonny's naked soul.

She pressed her cheek against the pane of the door, her breath spreading a cloud of condensation across it. Within its wet, opaque cloud, Lena drew the letter M.

Michael!

How can I betray you? How can I cast you aside and make my life with another? You are my husband!

Lena moved to the loveseat beside the door. Head in hands, she sat, her heart in turmoil. Again, Kelly began to nudge her Ina's arm.

Kelly loved Lena. She remembered when her Ina and her boy, Logan, came into the big place where other dogs, some cats and other souls, were living, all of them kept in a small space that the people there called a cage. She hated not being able to run and longed to be free. There were few pets, even fewer scratchings and strokings, and even though the people there were kind, there was little love in the big place.

Logan was the first to spot her. She lay in the cage, her nose between her paws, depression permeating her very being, until she saw Logan's face light up. Kelly rose, her ears twitching as her heart filled with hope. "Ina! I found the one!" Logan had cried. Running to her, he dropped to his knees and opened the cage. Kelly jumped into his arms, tail wagging. She knew, she just knew, that she had found a way out of the big place and into a better life – into a family.

When she came home that day, her heart filled with joy. Her boy lay on the floor with her, petting and scratching behind her ears. Kelly turned over, exposing her belly, saying, in her own way, "I trust you, Boy." Logan rubbed her dappled belly obligingly and whispered, "I love you." Kelly did not yet know the words, but she recognized the tone, and inside, her soul exploded with joy.

Logan took her out to the big water, and they walked and played, Kelly filling her senses with the sights, sounds and smells of her new home. That day was vivid in her mind. Her elation and happiness since that time never left her, and her gratitude to her Ina, and her boy was boundless.

Kelly nudged Lena's arm again. Lena looked up from her cradling hands into Kelly's chocolate, brown eyes. Kelly chuffed, "Humpff," as if to say, "What is this all about?" Smiling, Lena caressed Kelly again as the loving canine laid her head upon Lena's knee.

"It's amazing how you know when I am in need of comfort," Lena offered.

She looked at Kelly and smiled. Lena loved her canine daughter with all of her heart, and at times, mourned the fact that Kelly would only be with her for a relatively short time.

I wish that our animal daughters and sons could live as long as we do, she would often muse. *Still, they live with us forever in our hearts.*

Lena sat upright, amazed and confused. It was if a thunderclap sounded in her ears. She sat still, emptying her mind, waiting for the grandfathers to speak.

A knock on her door brought Lena back. Sitting before her Ina, Kelly continued to stand guard, her chin on Lena's knee, as if to say, "I'm here. You're okay. I'm watching." Lena brushed her hand across her eyes as if to clear her vision. The doorbell rang and Lena, rising slowly, walked from the family room into the foyer. Through the glass, she could see her mother. Lena opened the door and stepped into her mother's arms. Murmuring soothing words, Mary held her child, and then gently pulled from the embrace. Passing through the door, she took Lena's face in her hands.

"We need to talk."

Chapter Twenty Five

Do not be afraid to cry.
It will free your mind of sorrowful thoughts.

Hopi

Lena motioned for Kelly to follow her upstairs. She lay on the bed with Kelly faithfully standing guard beside her. Lena needed to think, to sort out her feelings, to find an answer to her future. *Did I truly love Michael?* she wondered to herself? *Yes, I did. I truly did,* Lena affirmed to herself.

Her mind flew back, back to 17 years ago, to the day when she met and married Michael.

Lena remembered his vigil across from Julie Spotted Eagle Horse's lodge. A flash of memory, and there was Sonny as well. Lena sat up in bed, heat suffusing her face. In the excitement of the romance, she had forgotten Sonny's presence.

Lena lay down again. Turning on her side, she wrapped her arms around her shoulders, as if to comfort herself, as the memories came hard and clear.

Lena recalled the Wopila, and her inability to breathe, as Michael walked up to her, his presence sending shock waves through her body.

She remembered Julie pushing her and Michael into the arena, Michael's arm about her waist and holding her hand, her breathless confusion as they began to dance around the arena. Lena stiffened – again a memory of Sonny, charging Michael with the broom. His excuse of dew-slicked grass seemed to ring true at the time, but now she understood.

Michael.

Michael walking her to Julie's lodge, asking her to marry him, the ceremony and their first lovemaking, breathing in each other's fragrance, eager hands and mouths as the evening slowly, ecstatically, drifted into dawn.

Lena sat upright again and swung her feet over the side of the bed. She glanced down at Kelly and asked,

"Did I marry him because I truly loved him, or was it because I was so in love with the story of my parents meeting on their wedding day? What is the answer, Kelly?"

The thought disturbed her. She had never questioned her love for Michael, why did she do so now?

Lena rose and began to pace the room. Kelly sat, alert, watching her ina. She felt Ina's agitation and gave a low whimper. Lena turned, and dropping to her knees, hugged the valiant creature to her.

"It's all right, Kelly. It's all right. I need to think, but I'll be okay."

Kelly responded with a thump of her tail and a nudge of Lena's hand. Lena sat on the floor, her back against the bed frame, and slowly pet Kelly's fuzzy head, once again reposing on her ina's lap.

I did love Michael, but was it before or after our wedding?

Memories of their time together in the Short North condo flooded back. It was a good time, a happy time, the days filled with working together at Vicki's, the late nights filled with lovemaking and endearments.

Did I fall in love with him then?

Yet, within those memories of Michael, dwelt those of Sonny as well: Sonny, always there, especially after Michael and Vicki's deaths; Sonny, stepping in as father to Logan, continually checking to see that both were safe and cared for.

Sonny.

Lena looked down into her loving companion's eyes and sighed.

"Does it matter, Sunka Ska?" she asked. I loved him, and that is what matters. But, he is gone now, and I have mourned these 17 years. It is time to love again?

Sonny.

Lena remembered her father and his valiant struggle to regain his mobility, his strength. She remembered the lessons she learned from him during those hard times. Ate was not afraid to love. Ate triumphed for love.

"Yes, it's time to love again."

With that, Lena slipped to the floor beside Kelly's warm body. Wrapping her arms around her loving form, after almost two decades, she finally wept. She wept for the loss of young love, for the death of a young man in his prime, her loving adopted mother, and finally, for the joy of love renewed.

Chapter Twenty Six

What is this that I am feeling?
I am as Tisayac
When she first looked upon Love.

Gazing shyly, she beheld him,
Awe filled her trembling heart,
And she fled from him in fear.

Tutokanula – his heart bereft,
Cried out to his half side,
As she ran from his embrace.

I must find the courage, My Heart,
Open my arms to you,
And joined, we will ride the clouds.

Stands With Eagle Wings
Inspired by a Miowak Legend[104]

Lena rose early after a fitful night of interrupted sleep, her mind whirling with all that had occurred the day before. Arriving early at Vicki's, she walked directly to her office, thankful for a small span of time to prepare for her meeting with Sonny. *There is a lot on my plate today, but I must talk with Sonny,* she thought to herself, grimacing at her appalling, albeit accidental, pun.

Her thoughts returned to the morning before. She had been eager to talk to Sonny about her idea for a new restaurant. Excited and full of plans, she was finally ready to announce her intentions. Rushing to Sonny's office, and gently tapping on his door, her anticipation of his reaction got the better of her. Opening the door without the prerequisite, "Come in," she beheld the face of a tortured man, whose countenance turned to one of profound love once he beheld her.

Lena laid her head on the backrest of her chair. Mind whirling, she went over the entire scene again for what seemed the hundredth time. *I must talk to Sonny as soon as possible. This can't be left to work itself out.*

During the seemingly endless night, Lena wrestled with her feelings, and the implications of that which she was about to do. She still loved Michael, and always would, but she now admitted to herself that it

[104] http://www.americanfolklore.net/folktales/ca7.html

was Sonny who was her half side, the love of her life. She must tell him at once.

But, she was afraid. Michael's death had devastated her. Only the impending birth of her baby kept her in balance. Once Logan was born, the surgeries required to repair his cleft lip and palate gave her something to focus on, and the resulting added closeness between her and her son, partially filled the gap left by Michael's passing.

Lena realized with surprise that she had been able to mourn Vicki completely. Her love for the kind woman, who set her feet upon the path she now followed, helped her to celebrate Vicki's life instead of dwelling upon her death. Not so with Michael.

Did I continue to carry the weight of grief because I felt guilty? she wondered. *Was my continued grief a sentence I imposed upon myself to assuage my conscience?*

Her self-examination tore at her heart, but Lena knew that, if she did not look into her heart with all honesty, she would never get beyond the death of her husband; would never be able to move forward to a full and happy life.

And, there was Logan. *What an example I have set!* Lena thought with alarm. In keeping Sonny at a distance, she had taught her son to fear commitment, to push away love. Another revelation hit her like a thunderbolt.

Logan knew!

Armed as she was with the commitment to be brutally honest with herself, she sent up a small prayer to the Thunderbirds, begging for their aid in her quest for the complete truth, which dwelt in the core of her heart, her soul.

She again remembered her father and his valiant fight to recover from disaster. All of his efforts spawned by love, by commitment. She remember Zitka Mine's pronouncement, "He will waken and he will teach."

"Ate! I had forgotten!"

She began to recall little things Logan had said over the years: "Ask Uncle Sonny, he'll do anything for you, Ina," "Talk to Uncle Sonny, he cares about what happens to you," and many more besides.

Logan knew!

Finally, she allowed her mind to go back to the day Michael died. He had stopped on his journey to the edge of the universe to say goodbye to her. Lena had told him that she would go with him to walk the five steps to the Spirit Path and into the Spirit World:

"No, Little Bird, it is not your time. I will wait for you in the Spirit World."

Michael wanted her to move on, to be happy.

145

I must see Sonny as soon as possible and let him know that I love him!

She had no idea what she would say, if she would say anything at all for that matter. *Maybe I will just walk into his arms,* she wondered, and then blushed at the idea.

I am a woman of the Lakota and must always be a lady. Sonny must make the first move. Oh, how can I show him that I do love him and have these many years?

Her thoughts were interrupted when Nickie flung open the door to her office:

"Sonny's missing."

"What do you mean he's missing?" Lena cried.

"I mean he's missing. Diti said that he stopped by Sonny's apartment yesterday afternoon, later last night, and then this morning. Sonny isn't there and he is a half hour late. Sonny is never late."

Lena crushed down a feeling of panic.

"Listen, I still have the key to the apartment. Come with me."

Lena and Nickie ran up the iron stairs to the second level of the apartment building. Knocking on Sonny's door, Lena called his name. Five minutes passed until, finally, Lena inserted the key to the apartment door. Opening it slowly, both women gazed inside. The apartment was empty.

"Okay, look, he's probably grocery shopping or at the gym, let's go back to the restaurant. I'm sure he'll show up in time for work," Lena said, her tone belying the lines of worry on her brow. Nickie nodded reluctantly as Lena relocked the door.

Returning to the restaurant, Lena asked Nickie to come to her office.

"I've wanted to talk to you and Sonny about something for a month or so now. Why don't I brief you, and when Sonny arrives, we can all discuss my proposal."

The need for distraction was paramount in Lena's mind. Her new project, exciting, thrilling and very ambitious, afforded just the diversion her mind needed until Sonny finally arrived.

Nickie nodded, seating herself in a leather side chair, glancing at the clock nervously. Sonny was now two hours late; Sonny was always early. In fact, he was obsessive about, not only being on time, but early to the job.

"Okay, Lena, what's the scoop?" Nickie asked.

Lena was nervous as well. Like Nickie, she constantly glanced at the clock. Where could he be? She knew that he wasn't shopping or working out. This had to be related to what happened the day before.

Maybe he's just embarrassed and will call in sick soon, she mused. Lena shoved the thought aside and continued.

"Nickie, I have an idea for a new restaurant. I have an appointment this Wednesday with a real estate agent to look at an available site in Westerville, not far from my house, in fact. It's a great building – mid to late 1800s is my guess, and room enough for all that I've envisioned.

Lena and Nickie concentrated on the plans for the new store, discussing start up costs, staffing, menus and décor. Both were aware of the clock's hour hand's slow decent as the hours ticked by.

By 5:00 P.M., both Lena and Nickie were frantic.

"Nickie, I'm afraid something has happened to Sonny, and I think it may be my fault."

"What?" Nickie answered. "What could you have done to Sonny to cause him to disappear?"

Looking intently into her friend's eyes, searching for an answer, understanding dawned. Nickie's face registered her thought process, and Lena slowly nodded in agreement.

"Yes, Nickie, I discovered yesterday that Sonny is in love with me, and instead of talking to him about it, I fled. I spent all of last night meditating and thinking about it, and discovered that I love him too. What am I going to do, Nickie?"

Nickie gazed at her friend, wonder filling her eyes.

"How can you be so dense?" Nickie queried, disbelief and a touch of anger tingeing her voice.

Taken aback, Lena responded, "Dense?"

"Lena, the man has been in love with you since God was a boy, and you're just now catching on? He's done everything but collapse at your feet. Are you really that blind? Those eyes of yours may be incredibly beautiful, but they don't see very well as far as I can tell!"

Lena stared at her friend, mouth agape. An epiphany, like the clap of thunder heralding the arrival of the Thunderbirds, filled Lena's mind with clarity. Nickie loved Sonny. *How could I have not seen it?* Lena asked herself.

Groping for her chair, Lena slowly lowered herself onto its cushioned seat. Her head spun, her heart trip hammered, *How could I not realize the truth?*

Nickie rushed to her friend's side.

"Are you all right, Lena? What's wrong?"

"Nickie, you love Sonny and have for years. How was it that I didn't see it? Now, I have hurt you as well as lost Sonny. I'm a fool!" Lena cried, pounding her clenched fists on her knees. "A fool!"

Bursting into Lena's office, Boy Ladd faltered. Indeed, he almost fell over his own feet as he attempted to restrain his heretofore explosion into the room. Lena, still seated in her office chair, was stroking Nickie's shining hair. Leaning against her life-long friend, tears streaming down her entrancing face, Nickie clutched at Lena's waist. Crying quietly, she at last exposed her love for Sonny. Boy Ladd's heart swelled with love and protectivness. He felt that he should leave the room, but something made him hesitate. His ear caught Sonny's name, and as realization came to him, his heart shattered.

Lena looked up and into Boy Ladd's eyes. Her own glowing orbs, now opened to the truth, saw Boy Ladd's complete devotion and love for Nickie. Lena signed inwardly: *What a puzzle. What confusion we bring into our lives.*

Lena lifted Nickie's chin and said, "Boy Ladd is here, Nickie. We must see what he wants. *He wants Nickie,* Lena's inner voice answered back.

Turning to Boy Ladd, Lena looked her question, eyebrows raised, her head slightly tilted.

"I finally got away," Boy Ladd stuttered. "Sonny. He's at my apartment."

Jumping from her chair, Lena took Nickie by the hand. Walking to where Boy Ladd stood, confused and uncertain, she placed Nickie's slender hand into his larger, capable one.

"Take care of her, Friend," she muttered. Grabbing her purse and car keys, Lena left the restaurant.

Pulling up in front of Boy Ladd's apartment, Lena sat for a moment. Gazing at the windows of the front room, she envisioned the layout of the space, imagining where Sonny would be when she walked through the front door. Her heart clenched. *What if I'm too late? What if he has decided that he doesn't want me?* Stepping out of the car, Lena took a deep breath. Chin high, she walked up the pathway to the front porch and opened the door.

Chapter Twenty Seven

According to the Native People, the Sacred Space
is the space between exhalation and inhalation.
To Walk in Balance is to have Heaven and Earth
in Harmony.

Cherokee Prayer Blessing

Lena stood in the middle of the first floor space of the 19th century building. Her heart was light and filled with the promise her future held. Slowly, she began to turn, arms wide, as if to embrace the building and make it her own.

Completing her turn, Lena walked into Sonny's arms. Smiling with joy, she lifted her face to his and savored his lips as they met hers. She had never been so happy.

Lena rested her head on Sonny's chest, enjoying the *thump, thump, thump* of his heart. His hand moved to caress her, his soul rising as he enjoyed the feel of her silky hair entwined within his fingers.

Lena sighed as she recalled the events of the week before. *Where did I find the courage to walk into that apartment?* she asked herself with wonder. *From love,* she resolved. *Of course – from love.*

The walk up the path to the front door had seemed endless. Upon reaching the front stoop, Lena took yet another deep breath. Turning the doorknob slowly, she opened the door and stepped into the dimly lit interior of Boy Ladd's living room.

Sonny sat at the far end. Gazing through a shade-dappled window, he appeared to be contemplating the scene before him. As Lena slowly approached him, she became aware that Sonny, in fact, was unaware of his surroundings.

Gray from lack of sleep, his skin shown pale under a layer of perspiration, his eyes were red, the lids swollen. She could feel the despair spilling from his soul, and the air in the room was heavy with his grief.

Walking slowly, Lena approached him, no longer in a quandary as to what to say or do. Gently, she moved to stand before him. Kneeling, she gathered him into her arms and whispered, "You are my heart."

"Is this it then, Lena?" Sonny questioned.

Filled with joy, and the fulfilment of his love and longing for this glorious woman, Sonny would have given her the Taj Mahal if he could.

"Sonny, it is perfect! I can see exactly how it will be laid out, I can hear the music, see the people. It's just how I envisioned it!

Lena turned to the real estate agent waiting patiently at the entrance to the building.

Gayle was a slendar woman in her early 70s. Smokey, almost black eyes peered wisely at the world under a cap of dark, brown hair. Standing at about the same height as Lena, she joked in a rich, Texan accent, "It's good to be able to look eye to eye with someone over 12!"

"Gayle, this is it. Thank you so much for finding this lovely building."

"You're welcome. I knew the minute I saw it come up in the MLS that is was perfect for what you told me you needed." Smiling, she offered her hand to Sonny and then Lena.

"What are you going to call it, then?" Gayle quiried, happy with her client's enthusiasm and her success in finding just the right building. Lena returned her smile and answered:

"Cedar Woman."

Sonny stood at the entrance of the restaurant, allowing himself the pleasure of savoring the space before him.

Spacious and airy, its buff-colored walls soaring to a high ceiling painted in the same amber-like color, the room was warm and inviting. Glowing with golden light, beckoning one to come in, to relax, to enjoy, the entire space promised good food, good times and good memories.

Walking to a small station where the hostess would greet arriving guests, and escort them into the dining room, Sonny placed his left elbow upon its polished surface and continued to contemplate the spacious area.

Lining the north wall, six top, fan back booths of polished cherry, upholstered in a Native American print of gold, plum, turquoise and tangerine chevrons, sat upon a slightly raised platform. Matching tabletops of solid cherry completed the six-person banquettes.

Each seating area was lit by a small imitation rush light, set upon a shelf, which ran the length of the room, the exquisite bowls carved from catlinite, or pipestone, highly prized by Native Americans for carving peace pipes. Considered a sacred stone, it often represented the blood of the earth or the blood of The People. Illuminated by a small, flickering bulb, the reddish-amber reflective stone gave a feeling of warm candle light.

Hanging from the ceiling in the center of the room were three four-uplight ring chandeliers, repeating the catlinite bowls in a slightly larger size.

Filling the generous space beneath the fixtures, were four top and two top cherry tables with matching ladder back chairs, each table dressed with a single daisy placed in a cream-colored, ceramic bud vase.

A selection of condiments: mustard, catsup and Tabasco sauce, awaited hungry patrons who would soon honor Cedar Woman's table. The flooring was of gleaming cork in two shades. The main expanse was the color of honey. Marking the four corners of the main dining area was the Lakota Sioux holy symbol for the earth and four winds that blow, a simple square with a line radiating from each corner, symbolizing the blowing winds. Represented in rich sienna, the symbols helped to define the main seating area of the floor space.

Lena chose cork flooring for several reasons: it was environmentally friendly. The cork oak tree did not die when its bark was harvested every nine years. Indeed, some oaks lived well passed 200 years, still producing useable bark. The springy surface was much kinder on legs and backs, and Lena felt she owed this to her employees. In addition, the flooring was noise resistant, antiallergenic and very durable. Of course, there was the beauty of it.

Cha, it is beautiful, Sonny exclaimed to himself, *A truly breath-taking display,* he mused, his eyes roaming the main floor with its polished cherry, glowing catlinite lighting, and gleaming cork flooring.

Leaving the station, and turning to his right, Sonny gave his attention to the opposite wall of the first floor space.

On the south wall was an arena big enough for a small band or a single Native American Dancer. Beside the dancing area was a large can cega. Traditionally called "The Drum," it would provide music for the dancers: the heartbeat of The People, The Drum would be attended by several men who would strike a beat, and sing traditional songs in unison.

Dressed in regalia representing their tribe, and stepping to the beat of The Drum in celebration of the ways of The People, the dancer's performance, mingled with the beat of the drum, was a breath-taking spectacle, Sonny reflected.

Here, on Friday nights, Native American and local bands would play. Friendly competition involving patrons voting for their favorite group would add spice to the evening.

Saturday evenings would see Native American dancers performing. Boy Ladd would narrate as Jingle, Grass, Fancy Shawl, Traditional, Hoop, and other dancers performed their art.

Moving to the back wall of the first floor dining area, and regarding what appeared to be a Lakota tepee of buckskin, Sonny admired Lena's whimsical solution to a first floor workstation. Hidden within this authentic display was a small kitchen with two grills, two griddles, a deep fryer and one refrigerator. Indian Tacos, various soups and buffalo burgers, to name a few. would be prepared in this creative area.

Returning to the front of the building, and skirting the arena to the staircase at the western end of the southern wall, Sonny ascended the

stairs slowly, as if to savor what he knew awaited him on the second
level, the fine dining area of Cedar Woman.

Pausing at the top of the stairs, Sonny allowed himself the pleasure
of feasting his eyes upon the second story dining room.

Laughing to himself, he remembered Lena calling it "sumptuously
simple," enjoying the oxymoron once again.

She's absolutely right, he said to himself, sighing deeply and
enjoying the view before him. *She nailed it. It is simple, yet everything
is here to assure a guest's comfort.*

Inviting and warm, the room was serene and uncomplicated with its
subdued, shimmering lighting and elegant settings.

The same four top and two top cherry wood tables and chairs were
featured here – echoing catlinite light fixtures and luminous cork flooring
filled the space with glowing amber light.

Linen tablecloths in a deep shade of sienna covered each table.
Instead of daisies, bundles of fresh herbs nestled within small hand-
thrown pots in a delicate shade of ocher. For tonight, however, a small
bouquet of wildflowers would accompany the fragrant sprays.

Paintings by such talented Native American artists as Steven
Yazzie, of the Navajo, whose art "explores the beauty and chaos of the
natural world colliding with man's ideals"[105] and excellent examples of
Ledger Art,[106] lined the walls of the simple and graceful dining area.

It was a room to fill all of the senses. Soft music by Native
American musicians such as Sonorous, a Jazz band led by Matt Yazzie,
(brother to artists Steven Yazzie, and Michael Little), and Brent
Blount[107], an elementary school teacher, whose performances on the
Tenor Sax, Clarinet, Blues and Jazz Guitar, and Native American Flute,
played in the background. Beautiful art lined the walls, silky linens
covered each table, echoed in napkins and upholstery. The aromatic
scents of freshly prepared foods would soon drift through the entire
restaurant, and guests would feast on delicious meals inspired by Native
American cuisine.

Here diners would enjoy bison filets in fragrant onion gravy,
braised buffalo shanks in honey poblano sauce, and elk meatloaf served
with roasted root vegetables, as well as quail stuffed with fragrant herbs,
partnered with goat cheese risotto. Oysters and mussels in a delectable
broth, salmon served with wild rice and steamed vegetables, walleye
partnered with sautéed mushrooms in a delicate wine sauce, trout

---

[105] Steven Yazzie http://www.stevenyazzie.com
[106] Plains Indian art, drawn on paper – circa 1860 - 1900
[107] http://www.brentblount.com/

simmered in a delicious fish broth with fresh greens and scallions, sweet potato hash, and salads of mixed greens, cranberries and toasted walnuts were included on the menu as well. Sage bread, berry pudding, Lena's own Aztec Chocolate Cheesecake, and of course, the Three Sisters: corn, beans and squash, comprised the menu as well.

Although the heretofore-dry city of Westerville passed a law allowing the sale of alcohol in restaurants in 2006, Lena decided to not include alcohol on the menu, as she was too aware of the effects of alcohol on her people. However, patrons could bring one bottle of wine for every two guests, and no cork fee would be charged.

The fully equipped kitchen was large and immaculate, with its wood-fired oven and gas stoves, as well as a separate griddle and grill, complete with utensils and cookware, for the preparation of allergen-free foods.

Sonny turned to ascend to the third floor, but hesitated. No sounds had emanated from the room, but although he considered himself a courageous man, he was hesitant to climb the stairs and enter the room...alone.

Looking around nervously, his admiration for what Lena had done to the space drew his mind away from the tragedy of that fateful night in the mid 1800s.

It seemed proper that the level where two children died so many decades before, should be turned over to the education of the young.

The third floor, once the scene of a terrible fire, was allocated for the use of teachers and individuals who wished to instruct students in such areas as Native American and American Literature, pottery throwing, Music Appreciation, music lessons, and voice and dance lessons. The only specification was that the lessons be given gratis; no student would pay or be turned away.

Stacked against the spacious room's south wall were folding chairs and tables, easels, and shelves which would soon be filled with the various items the instructors would use in their classes.

Pottery wheels lined the north wall, while the east wall boasted a wall-mounted barre and mirrors for those who would be taking dance lessons.

She is such a giving soul to allow this space to be used for free. But that's Lena Young Bear. Her soul is as big as the universe, Sonny pondered, as he admired the roomy, airy space.

All seemed to be ready for the night ahead. Nodding with satisfaction, Sonny descended the stairs to the main floor. There was still a lot to do. Soon the restaurant would fill with guests celebrating this very important night.

Chapter Twenty Eight

I think over again my small adventures,
My fears, those small ones that seemed so big,
For all the vital things I had to get and reach.
And yet, there is only one great thing,
The only thing:
To live to see the great day that dawns,
And the light that fills the world.

Inuit

Slowly, slowly, Grandfather Sun began his decent. Gliding, floating, he dipped toward the horizon as amber, rose and turquoise filled the sky. The twitter of birds increased as sparrow and crow, dove and robin gathered in preparation for slumber. Wakan Tanka stretched His fingers across the sky, pushing back the day, heralding the twilight in preparation of a new dawn.

July 18, 2010
8:30 p.m.

Sonny waited for Lena's arrival beside the arena, decorated in celebration of the day. Guests milled around, admiring the restaurant, helping themselves to hors d'oeuvres of roasted potato wedges with a sun dried tomato dipping sauce, and broiled oysters on the half shell with a toasted bread crumb and Manchego cheese topping. Small rounds of fry bread dressed with tomatoes, onions, garlic and olives, salmon roe served on a bed of wild rice, diced turkey, bell peppers and a salsa aioli in lettuce cups, and small blue corn pancakes topped with sour cream and strawberries were only a sampling of the evenings fare. The aroma of delicious foods wafted in from the kitchen on the second floor, and the soft light of dusk shone in the large, polished windows.

Brent Blount sat to one side of the arena, the lilt of his flute filling the air with sweet, fluid notes.

Handsome in their traditional Buckskin Dancer regalia, Sonny and Logan stood on the opposite side. They laughed often, greeting guests as they walked by, relaxed and filled with anticipation of this happiest of days.

Julie, Mary and Peter, waited patiently as servers, dressed in ribbon shirts or ribbon dresses, passed among the crowd, offering flutes of champagne, Lena's one concession to alcohol in the restaurant.

Jingle and Traditional, Hoop and Grass Dancers, waited patiently as The Drum prepared for the evening's festivities. Later, the dancers would compete, counting Lena, Sonny, and Logan in their numbers. There was to be a series of Team competitions for this special occasion, where Jingle, and Traditional dancers, for instance, would line up, and dancing in unison, would first dance in line and then form intricate patterns, as in a marching band. The team, who performed the most complex moves, while staying in unison, and in formation with their teammates while dancing their style, would win the contest.

All was in readiness. Expectation mounted as people awaited the arrival of Lena Cedar Woman.

Lena chose to dress for the occasion in her new office on the third floor. Attaching a multi-colored parrot drop, the fan-shaped ornament vibrant in colors of green, yellow, red and blue to her hair, she turned as she heard a light tapping on her door.

"Come in," she smiled, guessing who was about to enter.

Peter walked in. The effects of his brain injury were almost completely diminished. Indeed, most observers would not be able to tell that Peter had suffered from the traumatic event of 22 years before. He hesitated, and smiled.

"Little Bird," you are so beautiful!"

Lena nodded her thank you. Turning to the floor length mirror, delivered that morning in preparation of the evening's event, she gazed at her reflection.

"Waste," she murmured. "Lila waste."

Brent was given the signal. Nodding, he placed the flute to his lips, and the light yet haunting notes of "The Birth Of Wakinyan[108]" floated through the food and herb-scented air. All turned toward the back of the room. The large, brass doors of the elevator slowly opened, and Lena and Peter stepped out.

Strikingly handsome in black slacks, a crisp, white shirt, yellow turquoise bolo tie and black, fringed buckskin jacket, Peter Catcher stepped into the hallway leading to the first floor dining area of Cedar Woman. Head held high with pride, arm linked with his daughter's, he strode into the room with all of the power and grace of his youth.

---

[108] http://www.youtube.com/watch?v=WrNYi25VS-A

An audible gasp filled the room as Lena came into view. Her long, glossy hair fell to her waist, the multi-colored parrot drop a striking contrast to its shining, ebony strands.

Her dress was of white buckskin. Medium length Kimono sleeves with fringe detail flowed into a tunic silhouette. The hemline was likewise adorned, both sleeve and skirt fringe flowing to meet below her ankles. The impression was one of ethereal movement and grace.

The bodice was fully beaded in a pattern passed down from one generation to the next. Beads in Sioux blue, sky blue, black, Sioux green, chalk white, greasy yellow and red, dipped below the curve of the boat neckline. The mountain design, sewn in a lane stitch, also depicted stylized tipis and arrows that "showed the way." Crosses, representing the Morning Star, divided the beadwork into an harmonious and elegant pattern. Her leggings and moccasins were of the same white buckskin and echoed the design as the dress.

Slowly Lena approached the arena where Julie, Sonny and Logan now stood. Taking Sonny's hand, Lena smiled up at him, her countenance full of love and trust. As their hands clasped, her hair seemed to float upon the air. Sony appeared to expand, to shimmer, a silver light enveloping the couple.

$$\square$$

Time froze. All sound, all movement ceased. Within Lena's ears was the single sound of her heart's beat, and as her hand touched Sonny's, the sound of his beating heart as well. As heartbeat fused with heartbeat, as soul merged with soul, and recognized its eternal partner, time seemed to stand still. Time no longer held any relevance; time was subjective; time held no meaning.

$$\square$$

Julie gasped. Now she understood. Those many years ago, she witnessed the nimbus surrounding Lena, and knew that it was a sign of some import. Confused at the time, she now understood. Lena had indeed met her half side, but not in the form of Michael. Sonny was meant to fulfill his destiny with Lena, but somehow, a sort of cosmic mix up had occurred. Now, it was corrected.

Before her stood Sonny and Lena, both surrounded in a glowing light. She watched as the two nimbi joined, and she could distinctly hear two hearts beating as one.

Lena turned and beheld Julie, her eyes wide with wonder. Behind Julie stood Michael in full regalia, and hovering above his left shoulder was Lena's old friend – the humming bird.

Lena turned to Sonny. *Was it possible?* Yes, Sonny saw them too, evident in the look of awe upon his handsome face. Lena turned to her son, and joy filled her already overflowing heart. Her son could see his father!

Logan looked upon the spirit and smiled. Surrounded by a glowing beam of light, Michael returned the smile and gave a slight nod. Logan sighed, and in a voice of awe whispered:

"Thank you Grandfather Great Spirit, and Spirit Nation for this good day. Thank you Grandfather Great Spirit, and Spirit Nation for the blessings in this day. We walk in a good way. It is indeed a good day. Thank you, my mother, for this father."

"Pilamiayelo Tunkasila Wakan Tanka, Wanagi Oyate kici le anpetu waste. Pilamiyayelo Tunkasila Wakan Tanka Wanagi Oyate kici le yuwakan waste anpetu. Mani mahe ikuseya waste. Iye awicakeya waste. Lila Pilamiyelo Ina, Ate kici le.[109]"

---

[109] Pee-la-mee-yah-yeh-loh tdun-kash-ee-lah wah-kahn tdahn-kah wan-ah-ghee oh-yah-tday leh ahn-peh-lduh wash-tday. Pee-lah-mee-yah-yey-loh tdun-kash-ee-lah wah-kahn-tdahn-kah wan-ah-ghee oh-yah-tday leh you-wah kahn ahn-peh-tduh wash-tday. Mah-nee mah-hay ee-kyhsay-yah wash-tday. Ee-yay ah-wee-cha-key-ah wash-tday. Lee-lah pee-lah-mee-yah-yey-loh ee-nah ah-tday kee-chee leh

157

Cedar Woman's Recipes

Rez Coffee

For a 12 cup carafe, add eight tablespoons of dark roast coffee grounds instead of the usual six.

Braised Buffalo Shanks in Honey Poblano Sauce

4 three inch thick buffalo shanks
6 tablespoons olive oil
1 large carrot small dice
1 1/2 medium Spanish onion small dice
2 ribs celery small dice
3 cloves garlic finely chopped
Sea salt, black pepper
2 cups tomato puree
2 cups buffalo or beef stock
2 T fresh thyme chopped finely
3 T fresh basil chiffonade
1 T cilantro chopped finely

For the Sauce:

4 roasted poblano peppers
1/4 cup honey
1 clove roasted garlic
1/8 cup spinach(for color)
Olive oil
Sea salt and pepper to taste

Pre-heat oven to 325 degrees f
Oil skillet (preferably cast iron), bring to med high heat. Rub shanks with oil, salt and pepper. Sear shanks until nicely browned all over. Place shanks on heated plate. Take skillet off heat and add onion, celery, carrot

and garlic. Sauté until tender. Deglaze pan with stock reduce by half. Add tomato puree. Return shanks to skillet and bring to a boil, cover, put in oven and cook for 2 hours or until very tender. Put roasted poblanos, garlic, spinach and honey into blender or processor, blend until smooth. Keep blending, slowly adding oil until emulsified. Add salt and pepper to taste. Serve shanks on roasted corn salsa top with roasted poblano sauce, and a little goat cheese.

Three Sister Soup

1 ham hock, pork neck or salted pork – approximately 8 ounces
1 medium onion with the skin
3 medium potatoes or two large, peeled and diced
1 butternut squash, peeled and cut into bite-size pieces. The bulbous part saved for baking.
8 ounces green beans
1 15.25 can of sweet corn, drained
8 cups of water.

Place pork and onion in water and boil for approximately one hour or until liquid is reduced to six cups. Remove ham hock and onion and discard. Add squash and potatoes and cook until almost tender. Add green beans and cook approximately six minutes. Add corn and serve.

Cedar Woman's Aztec Chocolate Cheesecake

12 oz. Semi Sweet Chocolate, finely chopped
1/3 cup Kaluah
1 Tablespoon water
2 teaspoons vanilla extract
2 pounds cream cheese, at room temperature
1 3/4 cups sugar
1 teaspoon Mexican cinnamon (you can substitute what it is in your pantry)
1 teaspoon cayenne
4 large eggs

Position a rack in the center of the oven and preheat to 325 F. Lightly butter an 9-inch round spring form pan that is at least 2 inches deep. In a heavy pot, melt the chocolate with the Kaluah, water and vanilla. When melted, remove from the heat and let stand until cool. In a large mixing bowl, using a handheld electric mixer at medium speed, beat cream cheese until smooth. Combine sugar with cinnamon and cayenne. Add to cream cheese. Add eggs, one at a time. Beat in the cooled chocolate. Spread the batter evenly in the prepared pan.

Bake in the preheated oven until the top edges of the cheesecake are puffed and golden brown, about 1 hour 15 minutes. Let the cake cool in the pan for 30 minutes. Run a sharp knife around the inside of the pan to release the cheesecake from the sides (if they haven't already pulled away during the cooling process). Remove the sides of the spring form, cover the cake with plastic wrap, and refrigerate for 30 minutes before serving. Bring to room temperature before serving, or eat cold. Makes 8 servings.

Wild Sage Bread

Ingredients:
1 package dry yeast
1 cup cottage cheese
1 egg
1 tablespoon melted shortening
1 tablespoon sugar
2 teaspoons crushed dried sage
1/2 teaspoon salt
1/4 teaspoon baking soda
2 1/2 cups flour

Combine sugar, sage, salt, baking soda and flour. Dissolve yeast in 1/4 cup warm water. Beat egg and cottage cheese together until smooth. Add melted shortening and yeast. Add flour mixture slowly to egg mixture, beating well after each addition until a stiff dough is formed. Cover dough with cloth and put in warm place until double in bulk (about 1 hour). Punch dough down, knead for one minute and place in well-greased pan. Cover and let rise for 40 minutes. Bake in a 350-degree oven for 50 minutes. Brush top with melted shortening and sprinkle with crushed, roasted pine nuts or coarse salt.

Elk Meatloaf

2 lbs. ground elk
1 cup bread crumbs
2 eggs
1 6 oz. can tomato paste
1 large onion chopped
4 cloves garlic, minced
1/2 tsp. ground sage
4 Tbs. flour

4 slices smoked bacon, chopped
1 jalapeño, seeds removed and finely chopped
sea salt & pepper to taste
1 Tbs water

Preheat oven to 350 degrees

In a large bowl mix all the ingredients together. After mixing the ingredients, place in a loaf pan. Bake for 1 1/4 to 1 1/2 hours or until done. Let it stand for 10 to 15 minutes.

Serves 6 to 8

Pueblo Oven Bread

In the pueblos, this bread is baked in outdoor ovens called hornos. This recipe has been adapted for indoor home ovens, and is actually easier than it sounds.

Ingredients:

1 package dry yeast
1/2 tablespoon shortening
1/4 cup honey or sugar
1/2 teaspoon salt
1 cup hot water
5 cups all-purpose flour

Dissolve yeast in 1/4 cup warm water. Mix well and set aside. Combine lard, honey and salt in large bowl. Add 1 cup hot water and stir well. When mixture cools to room temperature, mix well with yeast mixture. Add 4 cups of four, stirring well after each cup. Spread 1 cup of flour on cutting board and place dough upon it. Knead until dough is smooth and elastic (about 15 minutes). Put dough in large bowl, cover with cloth and put in warm place until dough doubles in bulk. Turn dough onto floured surface again and knead well. Divide dough into two equal parts. Shape each into loaves or rounds. Place the loaves on well-greased cookie sheet, cover with cloth and allow to double in warm place. Put into preheated 350-degree oven and bake until lightly browned (about 1 hour). Use oven's middle rack and place a shallow pan of water on the bottom of the oven.

Sweet Potato Hash

3 strips of bacon, diced
1 cup corn, if frozen, thaw. If canned, drain.
1 shallot
1 sweet potato, diced
2 tablespoons chives, chopped
Salt
Pepper

Sauté bacon until crisp. Set aside on a paper towel to drain. Add shallot and sweet potato until potato is tender. Add chives, salt and pepper.

Serves two. Great for breakfast.

Cowichan Candy

1/2 gallon water
1 cup pickling salt
2 cups dark brown sugar
1 cup real maple syrup
salmon, cleaned and cut into 1 inch strips I make larger pieces
3/4 cup honey
1/4 cup water

Mix together the water, salt, sugar and syrup. Stir until all ingredients are dissolved. Add Fish and brine for 24 hours. Remove fish and drain off excess brine by patting with paper towels. Smoke anywhere from 8 hours to 1 1/2 days, depending on your smoker. Use the 3/4 cup honey mixed with the 1/4 cup water for basting. Don't over smoke or you're going to have jerky! Apple and Cherry woods are great for this recipe.

NOTE: Works well with venison also.

Lemon Dill Aioli

3 cloves garlic, peeled
2 Tbsp fresh lemon juice
1/4 C. fresh dill sprigs
1 egg yolk
3/4 C extra virgin olive oil
salt and pepper to taste

Puree the garlic, Lemon juice, and Dill in the bowl of a Food Processor. Add the Egg yolk and pulse to mix. With the machine running, slowly add the Olive oil through the feed tube until a thick sauce if formed. Adjust the seasonings with salt and pepper. Serve with salmon cakes.

Canadian Sioux Fish Chowder

1 cup chopped white onion
4 cups cubed potatoes
1 tablespoon salt
1 tablespoon pepper
5 cups raw fish cubed
1 quart bowling water
2 cups milk
1 cup half and half
1 bunch chives chopped

Add potatoes, onions, salt and pepper to water and cook for 10 minutes, until vegetables are soft, but not completely cooked, then add fish and cook 10 minutes. Add milk and half and half, then stir well and cook 15 minutes longer. Do not boil. Serve with chives.

Blueberry Special

1 cup of fresh blueberries (or thawed)
1 cup of diced fresh heirloom tomatoes
Basil leaves
2 teaspoons Honey
Lime

Tear fresh basil into small bits to release their fragrance and add to the tomatoes and berries. Drizzle the honey, and squeeze the juice of one fresh lime onto the ingredients. Toss and enjoy.

www.coyotecooks.wordpress.com

Mom's Fritters

1 1/2 cup milk
3 eggs
pinch of salt
3 teas Baking Powder
enough flower to make batter thick enough to drop from teaspoon into hot lard.

You can add fruit too. Mom used to put cooked rice and raisins in sometimes. We sometimes we dipped them in maple syrup.

Mildred Peterson

Grandmas Fritters

1 cup flour
pinch of salt
2/3 cup milk
2 eggs
1/2 cup sugar

Drop from spoon into hot lard and brown.

Mildred Peterson

And from Spotted Eagle Horse:

Buffalo Stew

6-8 Wild Turnips
5 lbs Bison meat
1 Med onion sliced
6 cups Water

Cut bison meat into chunks, lightly brown in large stock pot. Add Wild Turnips, chopped onion, and salt and pepper to taste. Boil until meat and turnips are tender.

Raw Kidney

2 Lbs fresh beef or bison kidney
Salt to taste
Tac Bac Crackers or frybread

Make sure kidneys are as fresh as possible, preferably still body warm. Slice thin, salt to taste, and serve with Tac Bac crackers or fresh frybread.

Fried Deer Liver

1 Lb fresh deer liver (bison or beef liver will work)
Salt water
1/2 tsp salt
1 tsp basil
1/4 cup flour
Vegetable oil or lard for frying

Soak fresh liver in water for up to 2 hours, skip if using store bought livers. Drain, and pat dry. Slice into thin slices. Mix flour and spices together, dredge each slice in flour mix. Pan fry in oil over medium heat until golden brown and tender.

Wasna

Equal portions of dried un-seasoned meat and dried chokecherries
Fat or lard.

Slice meat into a thin, tongue shaped slices, and dry. To dry in the oven, bake meat at 250 for 6 hours or until meat is dry and brittle. Pound dried meat until soft and crumbly, pound chokecherries until consistency of cornmeal. Mix together, and moisten lightly with meat grease or lard.

In-A-Hurry-Hurry-Frybread

1 16oz package frozen dinner rolls, thawed
OR 1 roll refrigerated can biscuits
Lard

On a lightly floured surface, roll out each dough ball or canned refrigerator biscuit into approx a 6" circle. Cut a slit in center of dough circle. In a heavy cast iron skillet, heat lard or cooking oil. Fry pieces one or two at a time in hot oil, until golden brown on both sides. Remove from heat and drain on paper towels, or (as we do on the "rez", in a paper bag!)

Serve as NdN tacos or with wojape

Ga-Boo boo bread

3 Cups all purpose flour
2 tsp baking powder
1/4 tsp salt

1/2 cup powdered milk
2 tbsp sugar
1 cup water
1 tbsp shortening, lard, or oil

In a large bowl, mix together dry ingredients. Make a well in center of flour mix and add water. Mix to combine, but don't over work the dough. Turn dough out on to a lightly floured surface, and knead gently, approx 10 times. Pat into a round loaf, about 1 inch thick, and about the same diameter of a large cast iron skillet or frying pan. Heat shortening, lard, or oil in cast iron or skillet, over medium heat. Cook about 8 minutes on each side, if bread browns too quickly, reduce heat.

Bread should come out the color of a biscuit

"Rez Grape Drink"

1 liter grape juice
3 lemons
Sugar to taste

Squeeze lemons into grape juice, and add sugar to taste. Serve cold over ice.

Sage Tea

(Note that this recipe uses wild "white sage," and not the more traditional "cooking sage")

3 cups fresh picked white sage
4 cups water
Honey to taste

In a pan, add water and fresh picked sage. Bring to a boil, then remove from heat. Never boil herbs as it removes the medicinal qualities, and can cause them to become bitter.

Allow tea to steep for 10 minutes. Great for colds and stomach ailments.

Dictionary

1. Wakan Tanka – Wah-kah Than-kah – Mysterious Creator
2. Mitakuye Oyasin – Me-tdah-coo-yey oh-yah-seen – We are all related
3. The Good Red Road – To walk in balance. To follow the rules of Creator.
4. Wambli – Wahn-blee
5. Ina – Ee-nuh
6. Ennit – Used to request or give agreement
7. Cha – Sha – a form of interjection
8. Tanksa – big sister
9. Ohan – Oh-hanj - Yes
10. Cuwayla – Chew-way-lah, Little Sister
11. Wopila – Woe-pee-lah - Thank you
12. Lakota legend of Spider Woman and Coyote
13. Cuwitku – Chew-weed-koo – Daughter
14. Cuwihpiya okise – choo-weeh-pee-yah oh-kee-shay - one who makes you whole
15. Rez – Short for Reservation
16. Waste – Wash-tday – Good
17. Ate – Ah-tay – Father
18. Wouanihan – Woah-oo-ah-njee-hahnj (nj is a French J sound).
19. The Three Sisters – The three sisters of corn, beans and squash, were grown together by Native American farmers, who asserted that they only grow and thrive together. This belief was very sophisticated in its foundation, as each plant replaces to the soil what another one takes.
20. Wasicu – White person
21. Lila – Very or much
22. Chia – Older brother
23. Tunkasila Wakan Tanka – Tdoon-ka-she-la Wah-kah Than-kah – the Grandfathers or spirits
24. Zitka Mine – Ahee-tdkah min-eh – Also called Hokagica To – Hoh-kha – (glottal G) – ee chi-ah Td-oh – the Water Bird or Blue Heron. A healer who also symbolizes slef-reflection
25. Wanagi Canku – Wah-nah-ghee Chan-koo – the place five steps away from the edge of the world. On the fourth step a spirit steps into the spirit world.
26. Unci – Unchee – grandmother
27. Mihinga – Husband
28. Mitawin – Wife
29. Tankasilus – The Spirit Helpers
30. Taku skan skan – Soul

31. Canumpa – Pipe or sacred breath
32. NdN – Indian - preferred spelling used in written materials
33. Ina Mahto Luta – Mother Red Bear
34. Mahto Luta – Red Bear
35. Hunkapi – Adoption Ceremony or Making of Relatives Ceremony
36. Can cega – Chahn-chay-ghah - Drum
37. Pesla – Pesh-lah - The Bald Heads, the Green Berets of the Sioux
38. Oyate – Oh-yah-tay- People
39. Much of dialog contributed by Julie Spotted Eagle Horse
40. Kachina – Kuh-cheen-uh - Meaning "Life Bringer" now seen in Native American forms of art as in dolls, pottery and jewelry.
41. Dine – Deen-ay – Navajo Artists
42. Potato Dance – A potato is placed between the foreheads of two dancers. The last two dancers to keep the potato in place are the winners.
43. NdNz – Plural for NdN
44. End dialog by spotted Eagle Horse
45. Skinship – NdN term for common ancestors
46. Tiyospiya Tdee-yosh-pee-yah – Family
47. Pehan – Peh-hahn – Crane
48. Wiacca Ska – Wee-ah-kah-shkah – White Plume
49. Sni – Schnee – No
50. Dance the Drum out – Dance to the Powwow Drum until it ends for the night
51. 49'ers – Less formally structured NdN love songs which include English
52. Wakalapi – Wah-kahl-lah-pee - Coffee
53. Toksa – Doh-ka-sha – Good bye or see you later
54. Hau Kolas – Hoe Colas – Hello, friends
55. Wojape – woah-jzas-pay – Berry pudding in which fry bread is dipped
56. Hecusniyela – Hey choo schnee yeh lah – Don't do that
57. Ista Wambli-win – Eeesh-tdah wahmblee ween – Woman with the eyes of an Eagle
58. Honor Beats – Three accented beats that occur in between the choruses
59. Hahn – Hanj – an informal form of Ohan or yes
60. Ape Numpa – Two Strikes
61. Wakinyan Zitka – Wah-keen-yahn-zheet-kah – The Thunderbird
62. 'Ridger – A slang term for someone from Pine Ridge, or who has ancestors from Pine Ridge

63. Begin dialog of Julie's lightning strikes provided by Julie Spotted Eagle Horse Two Strikes Martineau
64. Arikira – Ar-ih-kih-rah – An allied nation of the Sioux
65. Heyoka – Hey-oh-Ka – Laughs on the outside and cries in the inside. Chosen not self-appointed, they are considered holy people.
66. Wicaca Wakankis – Wee-chah-sha wah-kahn – Holy men
67. Tanikawin Blo – Tdah-nee-kah-ween – Old Woman Hill or Old Woman Ridge
68. Prayer ties – Small squares of cloth, about 1" square, usually made as a group: pinches of tobacco are placed in them while praying. Different colors have different meanings, and the color used depends on what is being prayed for. Participants also tie in the Altar colors of the Water Pourer. The number that you tie depends on what the Water Pourer tells you to tie.
69. Owl feather – The owl is the messenger often used by hayokas
70. Third Door – The third of the four doors or rounds of a sweat lodge ceremony
71. End dialog by Julie Spotted Eagle Horse Martineau
72. Sicangus – Shee-kahn-gjoo – The name of the dominant group or "camp" that inhabits Rosebud. One of the Seven Camps of the Sioux Nation
73. Wambli Gleska – Wahmblee Glay-shkah – Spotted Eagle
74. Inipi – Ee-nee-pee – Sweat lodge
75. Wincincila – Ween-cheen-chee-lah – young woman or young lady, often applied as a term of endearment
76. Ina Waste Otawin – Ee-nuh Wash-tday oh-tdaween – Good Mother of Many
77. Hantewin – Hahnz-tday week – Cedar Woman
78. Lila Waste Winayn – Lee-lah Washdtay Ween-yan – Lovely young woman
79. Wiacca Sinte – Wee-ah-kah sheen-tay – Tail Feather People
80. Takoja – Ki-dah-koh-zhah – Grandchild
81. Winyan Mita – Win-yan Meeta – My Woman
82. Wicasa Mita – Wee-cha-sha Meeta – My Man
83. Tunksila – Toon-cash-eela – Grandfather
84. http://www.brentblount.com/
85. http://www.youtube.com/watch?v=17h34SywAHY
86. http://www.youtube.com/watch?v=7Ki9qeH8Oeo
87. Mokoche` Wanblaka Tuwa Ista Numpa Winyan – Mah-koh-cheay Wahn-blah-kah Tdoo-wah Eesh-tdah Noom-pay Ween-yahn – Two-Eyed Woman Who Sees in Both Worlds

88. Hau, Mikauye Oyapi, hetchetu yelo – Hoh, Mee-kah-ooh-yay oh-yah-pee heh tdchey tduu yeh loh – Ho all of my relations. I have spoken and it is so.
89. http://www.clintonville.com/parkrec/rosegarden.html
90. En-dree – Albanian meaning Light
91. Dee-tee
92. Meer-pwah – a combination of one part diced carrots, one part diced celery and two parts diced onions used as a base for many types of cuisine, especially in French dishes.
93. Besara – Baysa-ar – honor, trust, faith
94. Era – Air-uh - wind
95. Dejan – Dan – God is my judge
96. Luli – Loo-lee – flower
97. Lale – Lah-lee – Albanian – little brother
98. Sunka Ska – White dog
99. *Christopher Bullfrog Catcher,* Christopher Shiveley Welch, Saga Books, page 27
100. Cates ice hemaca – Chahn tday see chay hay mahn chah – Sorrowing I am
101. Sunka Gleska – Shoon kah glay shkah – Spotted Dog
102. Tutokanula The strong leader of the people who lived in the valley
103. Tisayac – The guardian of Yosemite
104. Miowak Legend – http://www.americanfolklore.net/folktales/ca7.html
105. Steven yazzie – http://www.stevenyazzie.com
106. Ledger art – Plains Indian art, drawn on paper – circa 1860-1900
107. Brent Blount – http://www.brentblouont.com

108. Pilamiayelo Tunkasila Wakan Tanka, Wanagi Oyate kici le anpetu waste. Pilamiyayelo Tunkasila Wakan Tanka Wanagi Oyate kici le yuwakan waste anpetu. Mani mahe ikuseya waste. Iye awicakeya waste. Lila Pilamiyelo Ina, Ate kici le.[110]

Pee-la-mee-yah-yeh-loh tdun-kash-ee-lah wah-kahn tdahn-kah wan-ah-ghee oh-yah-tday leh ahn-peh-tduh wash-tday. Pee-lah-mee-yah-yey-loh tdun-kash-ee-lah wah-kahn-tdahn-kah wan-ah-ghee oh-yah-tday leh you-wah-kahn ahn-peh-tduh wash-tday. Mah-nee mah-hay ee-kyhsay-yah wash-tday. Ee-yay ah-wee-cha-key-ah wash-tday. Lee-lah pee-lah-mee-yah-yey-loh ee-nah ah-tday kee-chee leh

Lightning Source UK Ltd.
Milton Keynes UK
UKOW06f0848290316

271079UK00022B/1006/P